"K-pop My Cherr
A Client Liaisons N
Written by Amelia Oliver and
Copyright © 2018 Amelia Oliver and Kate Hastings

K-pop My Cherry

The Client Liaisons Series : Book Three : A Client Liaisons Spinoff
K-pop My Series : Book One
Amelia Oliver & Kate Hastings

The Client Liaisons titles are interconnected standalone reads, best experienced in intended order, however can be enjoyed individually.

This is an erotic romance story.
Contents suitable for 18+.

Contents

Authors Note

We have the utmost respect and admiration for not just the K-pop industry, but also the South Korean people, culture and language. After all our interest (aka obsession) has lead to the writing of this book and the spinoff of an entire new series.

We aren't however, Korean.

So while we spent countless hours researching, and cross-checking, and tapping away furiously at translator apps, we don't claim to be experts and we hope you'll forgive us for any errors.

We unequivocally intend no disrespect.

Prologue

Previously in Overexposed

Shoving the last of my hot pocket into my mouth, ok, the last of my second hot pocket into my mouth, I roll it around on my tongue, sucking in cold air at the same time. Those little fuckers are quick and flavorsome when you get home late, but they're also like chewing lava balls. Dropping my plate to the top of the outdoor table on my postage stamp sized balcony, I walk back over to the edge. Pressing my belly firmly against the cold metal railing atop the glass below, I twist out and look up into the sky.

Damn the L.A. smog, the wind tonight ensuring it's carried a blanket to mute my normally decent sky view. Decent, but not great. Living in a one-bedroom apartment in Calabasas, if I wanted great, all I needed to do was hop my ass to the Malibu Creek State Park, something I did a few times a month at least. The views from up there were awe-inspiring, but I got home from work too late tonight and I want to be in the office early in the morning.

And when I say early, I'm talking ass crack of dawn early. Like Piper and Cassie early, and those two nut-jobs think nothing of getting up before five a.m. Respectively, one to ride the waves and the other to ride a horse or some shit, but more likely to ride their tasty men. Not that I can fault them for that, but I'm more of a night owl myself.

Unable to get my fix of mother-natures finest, the stars, like I'd hoped, I grab my empty plate and move back into my open plan living room-dining room-kitchen, leaving the sliding glass door open to let some fresh air in.

I stick my plate in the dishwasher and make myself a cup of peppermint tea. There's a buzz around me, an unexplainable energy I feel thrumming through me. Ok, maybe not unexplainable, but questionable to me in a way. I've recently become rather obsessed with something and in turn that makes me happy, down-right giddy if I'm being honest. And if the rumors are true then I feel like it's my destiny to take the client since this obsession correlated harmoniously with this possible new job. I make sure I have my tea and anything else I need before sitting down, because once I dive in I won't be coming up for air anytime soon, bladder be damned. With my urine tank emptied and tea in hand I cross the short distance and flopping onto my sofa.

Tucking my legs up next to me, I lean into the oversized arm and reach over it to fish my phone and ear buds out of my purse beside me.

Why do I need ear buds when I live alone you ask?

Because that's how I roll, and it makes what I am about to do so much better. Like, waaaay better.

I get the attraction of big screens and surround sound and subwoofers and all that shit...if you're caught up in proving how big your dick is. When I'm home, I like my viewing experience personal, as in my phone screen in my hand and the sound directly in my ears. All the better for one-handed viewing, you feel me?

Set to go, first things first, I tap through my lock screen and hit up the usual suspects, but with a single-minded focus, I'm only binging on my fave accounts on Instagram, Twitter, Tumblr, sending a few particularly clit-twitching morsels to Piper and Ryver.

By the time I get to YouTube, I've finished my tea, turned off my lamps and burrowed further into the sofa, lying sideways as I prepare to indulge on what I've been denying myself of all day.

Ignoring all my subscriptions and my inbox, I go straight to my saved playlist which contains no less than 1.1k videos. I told you I was obsessed, don't judge me, this playlist fits my specific need and is not to be denied. Selecting one of my favorite crack compilations, everything in the world ceases to exist for me but the face, and it must be said - body, of the man filling my screen.

His voice, his laughter, his smile, his pout, his intensity when he dances, his stupidly melodic voice when he sings – all of it sets me alight. I've had obsessions before; this is not new territory, but not in this way. Never in the way I feel about him.

I'm not insane, the cheese hasn't slid off my cracker, but even though I know that's how it sounds, I'll be honest...I don't really give a fuck. Clearly with new uploads daily, not only from the group and their team, but the fans called F.A.M.L.Y (Fans. Alliance. of. Music. Loving. Youth.) who constantly supply us with compilations, news, gossip, it's in my face everywhere I go, on every social media just there waiting for my greedy hands, eyes and brain to absorb. I blame them for my hunger…and him.

I hold him close to my face, close enough that were he real and not an image of exquisitely formed pixels behind glass, I'd feel his breath against my lips. The compilation switches clips, and it's a close-up of him doing warm up vocals before going on stage. He's not looking at the camera, so it feels like a private moment, as his voice builds slowly through the notes. He moves his shirt-covered arm around him as he paces, the fat, worm like veins of his forearms and the backs of his hands showing from beneath the rolled sleeves. His fingers are long and thick as they grip the handheld mic, dancing around the cylindrical object as his lips tease the ball like cap at the end. The lyrics leaving his lips fill my ears, like they are intended for me only, and I've never heard anything more beautiful in my life. I scream with my mouth closed, the feeling of 'too much' and 'overwhelming' girliness that comes over me barely containable, he's too fucking everything I can't deal.

The combined vision of all of this sends a wave of heat deep into my belly, radiating out into my body, completely sensitizing my flesh.

I close my eyes as his voice peaks, the strength of the note obvious in the softness with which he releases it, like it's a breath, and a shiver runs the length of my spine.

Not that there was any doubt, but watching as his eyes lift to the camera, lift to mine, and feeling his smile as he realizes he was being filmed, I know with certainty that what I plan to do in the morning is serendipitous, but also absolutely the right thing.

Releasing a big breath, I press pause, and with my buds still in my ears, open my Spotify playlist for sleeping, and stand, walking over to my patio to close and lock the door, but a gust of wind hits me, and I see the smog has lifted. Walking out and the edge once more, I move to my telescope, 'Come say Hello' by Superhumanoids playing in my ears as I close one eye and look up into magnified space. My insides are keyed up from my videos, my thoughts racing about all the points I want to bring up to Sawyer as I'll be begging for the account I want in the morning. I'll have to figure out what to do with apartment, have dinner with my parents before I leave, get everything settled with my clients. Nothing I can't handle, and if I get the account I'll be on cloud nine anyway.

I've never wanted something so badly, a job and well, him. The moment I saw him by randomly stumbling around YouTube, I knew I was meant to find them. I connected to the music instantly, the dancing, the beauty, and yes, him. It's so hard to explain when the feeling and what takes over when you know you're meant to meet someone takes over, because it's so unexplainable. The find the constellations one by one, stopping by to give Pluto a hello even though I can just barely see, and although it's not Pluto anymore I'll still refer to it as such. Tough break to be downgraded, so I like to give her a little love. Just as I attempt to focus more, I see something dart across my eye, a shooting star.

A sense that my decision and my plan is exactly right, and everything feels to fall in line in that moment. I will go to Sawyer tomorrow and pitch that we need to take KT7 as clients. I close my eyes and make a wish, which I'm sure you can guess. With a new sensation of rightness in my soul, I head back inside and lock the door behind me, walking toward my bedroom with a little extra bounce in my step.

The light from my phone screen hits my chest, catching my eye as it bounces off the holographic glitch font on my oversized tank. The words, 'Fit to Fuck", an inside joke from a girl's night out, emblazoned across my tits makes me smile.

It also makes me think about how the catch-phrase came about, and the advice Cassie gave as she coined the words every one of us now have on a shirt, thanks to moi making a group order. Walking into my bedroom, I think better of sleeping and decide that if I do get this job and get my way, I will need to be fit to fuck. Changing my playlist from sleepy music to something more suited to working out, I settle on 'Look Back' by Betty Who and start doing squats in the middle of the room.

Fit to Fuck? You bet your ass I will be.

Chapter One

(Hana)

During the twelve-hour flight to Seoul, South Korea, I had tons of time to brush up on my notes. My love for Asian everything, began with one of the first apartments I ever remember living in. We moved a lot when I was younger, but this two-story shithole off the Sunset Strip was the first place I really called home. Picture a run-down hotel, the kind where there's a courtyard in the middle with a pool and all the doors to the apartments look out onto it. No water in the pool, paint chipped or none existent on everything, and a bunch of characters with their own bizarre life's and quirks. I was the only kid that lived there, and in the first summer we moved in, my parents going off to their respective jobs while a nine-year-old me was left to roam the property, changed my life forever.

There was Mr. Anderson, a seventy-something shut in who paid me a dollar every day to run to the corner store for cigarettes and tins of sardines. He had the most beautiful telescope and we'd spend nights looking up at the stars, teaching me the constellations, taking me to science museums, and expanding my small brain with something bigger than ourselves. On top of that, he wrote many unpublished works on the topic, many of which I still have and look at from time to time. Fletcher Wielding in apartment 4B worked as a special effects coordinator for some of the biggest horror movies back in the day, sparked my love for the genre and anything grotesque and creepy. But Ms. Kim, who I called Unnie, was my biggest influence. She was so elegant, even though she was probably older than Mr. Anderson. There was something about her that just oozed perfection in a way. She was like my Mr. Miyagi, but instead of teaching me karate, she taught me about Hollywood.

She loved reading gossip magazines, lived for celebrity autobiographies and tell-all's, any television movie based on 'true life' events of someone famous. She would recite dialogue from Gone with the Wind and Cleopatra, quoting the lines like she was in the actual movies, and I was right there beside her, soaking it in like a sponge. I never out right was told how she ended up in the shithole, but as the years passed, I concocted a story in my head that she'd come all the way to L.A. to make it big as an actress, but never did.

Unknowingly, all these people shaped me, and I think, guided the course of my life into my profession. I wanted people like Ms. Kim to make it in this industry, people with talent and desire, that lived and breathed what they loved.

Reading over my notes, the word Unnie pops up, it's what younger females call an older female like one would an aunt, and I smile thinking of my friend long since passed. This is the part I'm dreading the most. The whole, how-to-address-everyone-in-South Korea. Instead of Mr. and Mrs. and all that shit we say in America, there's names like that for everyone there, but different for who you are and to who you're addressing. It's hierarchy. What I don't get, or maybe what's making me want to puke over it all is how do I know when someone's older or younger than me? I've decided I'll address everyone as if they're older than me, and they can correct me. Which weirdly is the more respectful of my two choices, because let's face it, assuming everyone is older than you back in the States is a sure-fire way to make people stabby. I sigh and wipe the cold sweat from my palms onto my jean-clad thighs.

My normal gig is independent clients, ones who aren't signed to major anything's and really have no desire to be. When I first joined the company, I was signed to big bands, huge clients in the arts. But I got tired of always feeling like there were so many hands in the pot, that my ideas and work were always pushed aside by a manager or someone who wanted the artists to make more money and didn't give a fuck about longevity. Yeah, ESM represented the best of the best, and we charged them accordingly. But at some point, surely that meant if we were really representing the best, we also had to include those clients who couldn't necessarily afford to pay our usual fee. So, after talking through my thoughts with Sawyer and getting the green light, I gradually stopped taking new clients along those lines, and slowly began to take on lesser knowns, artists who've created something of their own and want to keep it that way, theirs. Take Daisy Frederickson, an extremely talented indie children's book author from who-the-fuck-knows-where-it-is-but-once-you-see-the-men-who-live-there-you're-packing-a-bag-and-fucking-moving, Plantain. That girl is the shit. She's passionate, naturally creative, and smart about her audience, all of which shows in her work. But even with her

Nordic Viking clit-twitcher husband being a doctor, for Daisy, forking over our usual fee would've been like getting screwed dry. And no one wants that. Which basically means nowadays I work with a lot of painters, authors and photographers. So, working with this large of a group again has me dusting off the old 'mainstream think cap' and diving back in because I'll be working in the K-pop department.

I've been a fan of the music since I was introduced in high school, but mainly stuck to girl groups, 2NE1 being my favorite. But then, like most people do with music, I strayed away from the genre especially when I became immersed in the music of the artists I represented. However, my Spotify and destiny decided to kick me in the head when a K-pop girl favorite came on and I was reminded how good the music was. On the hunt, I kept seeing the same group pop up, the endless videos that had me watching over and over. I was drawn to them, initially for the music and details of the videos that seemed connected and to tell a story in sequence. I don't know what made me finally take notice of what they actually looked like, maybe it had been my mind protecting me from what was about to go off inside me when I did. That's when I saw him. The man who put a spell on me, casted his magic, opened pandora's box and I was a goner. His name is Jung-keun. He's the youngest in the group, younger than me but thankfully legal by American standards. I don't like to say I was obsessed because it puts a creepy weird vibe to shit. But I was obsessed, in a good way. The music, the songs, the tweets, the VLive's, the fan compilation videos, it all made me happy. I looked forward to new things from them and I knew I wasn't the only one. The scale of KT7's following is jaw dropping and overwhelming when you see the amount of social media pages, YouTube fan videos, fan art, concert attendances, and to know they weren't even being played on the radio in America is awe inspiring. There's thousands, like literally hundreds of thousands. It feels like with them there's a pulse, something thrumming beneath the surface that I know they can explode and the world of music would never be the same. I daydreamed about not only my object of affection, but the things I could do for them as clients. They're too talented and fucking good to be limited by continent or assholes in the industry or radio.

If there's one thing you should know about me, other than I swear a lot- oh, and wear a lot of black, is that I believe in destiny. I feel like things and people come into your life when they're supposed to and there's a reason for that. Maybe a friend who backstabs you in the end, a learning experience. Sometimes music comes to you at your lowest and changes your life. You get fired from a job only to find a better job that you've always wanted. This is something I often say to clients when they've hit bottom, or something has happened in their career that they think is the end of them. I always say everything happens for a reason and we might not understand that right away, but it'll make sense in the end. Whatever it is, I know this group came into my life and I threw myself into it, I didn't know it at the time, but it was because I was going to eventually work for them.

My boss, Sawyer Elliot, not only emails us weekly about the jobs that every staff member is working on at the moment, but also includes where they're currently located and the status of the job. But she also sends out the list of new client's ESM takes on. It was before dawn I think when I got the email. When I saw the name, KT7 aka K-Town 7, I thought I was dreaming. I thought I'd really gone off my rocker and was teasing myself for how fucking cray I was over them. But no. I came to awareness and stared down at the email.

NEW CLIENT, KT7. WOULD INCLUDE RELOCATION, TRANSPORTATION AND APARTMENT PROVIDED. KNOWING KOREAN NOT REQUIRED ALTHOUGH HIGHLY SUGGESTED. JOB MAY HAVE REQUIRED EXTENDED STAY. ESM GOAL IS TO GAIN OTHER SOUTH KOREAN TALENT AND CREATE NEW MARKETING OPPORTUNITIES. PLEASE EMAIL WITH INQUIRIES.

SAWYER ELLIOT.

Immediately, I replied, telling Sawyer that yes, I accept and asked when do I leave? Like the panic inducing boss she is, she replied to meet me at her office when I got in, so we could discuss, and she could weigh her options. Options? Were there other people applying? Ohh hell no. No. this job is mine, it's my destiny. What were the odds that the very night before I'd hatched a plan to convince Sawyer we needed to contact the group to offer our services, and here they are offering the job to us?

I don't think I ever got ready for work faster in my life. My heart raced, and my hands shook as I felt like time was ticking and I would be damned if someone else got this account. I was prepared to bring out the big guns to

Sawyer, even that I'd quit the agency if I didn't get it. I'm so willing to go childish for this job. I didn't even stop for coffee, ok. I was almost sick to my stomach that Sawyer was legit gonna give this job to someone else. I love the girls I work with and yes, they might be good with this account, but I was great for it and no one, NO ONE was going to do as good a job as me when it came to this.

When I got to the ESM building, the lights were off, and it was then I remembered it wasn't even seven a.m. the light traffic on the 405 should've reminded me of that. Drew, Sawyers assistant isn't even at his desk, but her door was open, and I nearly ran to it, pausing just outside to slow my pace and fix my hair.

"I'm getting this job, Sawyer. I know I'm the best for it, I know I can make this group global. They have so much desire and drive, if it's what they want I will do everything I can to make them a powerhouse."

I stop talking as Sawyer looks up at me over the top of her dark tortoise-shell framed, almond shaped glasses. Her hair is down today, though all the long blond strands have been swept across to one side of her neck, the wavy tendrils resting against the swell of her generously sized, maroon bandage dress covered, boob.

"What?" she asks.

"I'm the best person for this account, Sawyer, you *can't* give it to anyone else. I'm telling you, giving this account to anyone but me would be a mistake."

"And, if you don't mind my asking, why would that be exactly?" Sawyer questions, rising out of her chair and coming around to where I'm standing at the front of her desk. Propping a hip against it, her posture might look casual, but I know she's just given me my opening to prove myself. To convince her to give me this new client.

I pause a moment, letting my mind gather my shit before I spew it out. In that moment, I see his face, Jung-keun and I know I *have* to get to him. Taking in a deep breath, I wet my lips and let it fly.

"Established in their segment, but not yet widely known, these guys are on the cusp of something massive. Anyone of our team could manage them, but I will take them there in a way that protects what makes them intrinsically, well, them. That's what I do best; you know how I am with all my clients.

Who they are comes first to me, and while these guys can't really be considered indies, in that their online fan base is mind blowing, they actually are when you factor in that the general market place still has no clue who the hell they are. And, I'll make sure it happens in a way that they don't feel like they're selling their souls to do it. Also, this move for them needs to be about longevity. The talent these guys have is...put it this way, they don't deserve to experience the bright burn of wide-market entry only to have it followed by the 'where are they now' crash. You and I both know that the 'new talent' label starts to be slowly picked off almost the moment it's given, the industry perpetually ready to hand it to someone else. There are pitfalls all over this thing, ones I can help them navigate their way through, and do it in a way that is best for them."

Just then, Drew comes into the office, looking at me surprised probably due to my earliness or maybe I look like shit also from my earliness. He hands Sawyer a folder as he says hi to me.

"Morning, Drew," I nod. "Nice tie," I add. He smiles, and I think it's more than just the compliment that has him looking at me this way.

"Well," Sawyer sighs, looking through the paperwork in the folder and I can't tell where she's at, should I start the begging or the threatening first? "I've heard everything you've said and-"

"You're gonna make me wait? I'll have a freaking heart attack if you won't tell me right now, Sawyer. Do you want that on your conscience the rest of your life?"

She looks up and off to the side, thinking.

"Not funny," I sing-song.

She looks back at me and gives me a small smile. "You were my first and only choice for this client, Rebel. I know they're in good hands. Now, take a seat, let's talk details."

The paperwork in her hands has my name on it and I literally fall into the seat behind me with an exhausted sigh. One day my man will hear about this, hear how I not only came into work looking like a train wreck to get this account, but that I nearly also died of a heart attack for him.

We talk, but it takes me a long ass time to really hear her. I'm going to South Korea. I'm going to my destiny.

Since pushing Sawyer to give me this gig, even though it turned out she was already all about shipping me to OG K-Town anyway, I've been inundating myself with all things K-pop even more than before and maybe more than the recommended acceptable dosage. Even though I have no fucking clue what's being said ninety percent of the time, the melodies and music, mixed with the dance moves and gorgeous look of each member, is enough to make anyone a fan and I don't want to hear shit denying that fact. Sadly, when I told people where I was going and what I was going to be doing there, my excitement was dulled by a lot of negative feedback. Why would you wanna go there? Oh my God, I hate that music. They look like girls. Well, who the fuck asked you? Regardless of where and who, how can you not be sucked in by the music. But getting these reactions made me realize my job was going to be full of challenges, one I was up for.

I've signed up for a Korean language course that sends me lesson plans via email and haven't learned a darn thing. I've been watching lyric translation videos of the songs by KT7; but find myself watching the guys dancing instead. Oh, the dancing. Lord can these dudes dance. It's like watching a flock of birds or school of fish, the way these seven men move as one is phenomenal. And as for the videos of their dance rehearsals, when they're all dressed in street clothes and you can hear their feet hitting the floor over the recorded track - sweet donkey riding Mary, hold the fuck on. But when they stomp, like all of them at the same time, and I'm hit with the resounding boom of thigh power driving fourteen feet into the floor, what happens below my navel can only be described as *chogcoghan,* translation: moist.

Hey, maybe I'm picking up Korean faster than I thought.

* * *

When I exit the plane, the Korean symbols bombard me as I try to get my bearings and figure out where the hell I need to go for customs, my luggage and to meet my ride to the apartments. Taking out my phone, I pull up my translator app and cheat a little on where to go, feeling overwhelmed as the people rush by me speaking a language I don't know, while I attempt to make out the signs all around and eventually navigate to where I'm eleven percent sure the baggage claim is.

I sent the bulk of my things ahead of myself a few weeks back, and only have my purse, laptop bag and one giant suitcase with clothes now. I'm going to be residing in the same apartment building as the band, which I researched ahead of time to see that these alleged "apartments" are basically fucking mansions in multi-level buildings. Apartments in Hannam The Hill are nearly 3,000 square feet and run for a cool 7.5 million American buckaroos. Many occupants include politicians, corporate leaders, and celebrities, including our boys who all live together in one apartment. Like I said, they've been gaining a lot of popularity and make a lot of money, so why they live together, I'm not exactly sure.

Hearing the bell ring that alerts passengers the luggage is coming, I thank fuck and lift my chin as I make my way over to the belt that should be pooping out my bag any minute. And no, I didn't read the sign, I followed the dude that sat in front of me on the plane. Eventually, my leopard skin Betsy Johnson suitcase comes tumbling out and I heave it onto the ground in front of me. Adjusting my purse and laptop bag, I pull up the handle and press the wheel with the toe of my Fausto Puglisi platform sandals and begin toward the exit as I scan the names being held up on pieces of paper and bodies kept apart from travelers by rope.

"Rebecca-dongseng?"

My head turns to see a man my height holding up a paper which does indeed say my name and I smile at the man as his expression still looks at me with question.

"Hi, yes, it's Rebel though, just Rebel," I correct, and he begins bowing his head in understanding.

"Come, come," he says, waving a hand toward the end of the walkway, and I nod as he disappears into the sea of people.

The airport is packed and still overwhelming with the sheer volume of people and noise. Once I finally make it to where the roped off section ends, I see my new friend hurrying toward me to take my luggage before he begins walking ahead of me and leading us toward the exit.

"Fred," he tells me over his shoulder once we reach outside the airport, which is still chaotic and packed.

"Fred?" I repeat, more in disbelief than in question.

"Your name Rebel, my name Fred, I don't ask question."

I nod with a raise of my eye brows, since, touché.

"Car, here," he nods, and I just continue to follow since there's eight-million vehicles lined up along the road.

We stand at a crosswalk amongst a sea of people and wait for the light to change so we can continue and eventually I notice the back of a black Range Rover begin to lift and assume that's our ride, Fred is tossing my bag in, while another man is exiting the driver's side and opening the door behind him, motioning for me to enter.

"Thank you," I smile and take my bags into my hand as I slide into the luxurious ride.

"Noona," a man already sitting in the back greets with a bow of his head and I smile in return. I recognize him as one of the band members, the tall rapper, "Hello," he smiles with another bow of his head.

"Hi, you can call me Rebel."

"Noona, please," he tells me, his smile turning shy while avoiding eye contact.

I've read this about South Korean men, respectful and shy, especially when encountering a new female.

"Noona it is then," I smile, hoping that maybe once he warms up to me he'll feel comfortable calling me by my name.

"I'm-"

"Wait, I cut him off. "Let me test myself," I add.

With a spark of daring in my belly, I squint my eyes and take a stab at his pronouncing his name, "Hyunjoon-ssi?" Ssi meaning mister.

Again, he bows his head as a sweet wide smile spreads over his lips.

"Phew," I let out a rush of breath overdramatically while wiping some metaphorical sweat off my forehead and he then looks at me. "One down, six to go," I add. I know their names, of course I freaking do, how can I not with the millions of hours I've put into them. It's the pronunciation I'm trying to maneuver.

Dimples appear in both his cheeks and I feel myself getting all gooey inside. I've seen these guys on my phone, on my computer, in videos and interviews and know they're all attractive, but in real life, I'm gonna be a goner.

"You can call me, Joon," he adds.

"Got it," I nod.

"Was your flight fine?" he asks as the other two men enter the vehicle and we begin to move.

"It was, I slept for a while, worked for a while."

"Good. Are you working with your other clients while here too?"

"I won't be taking on any new other clients right now, and anything my other clients need I can do from here. You guys are my main priority until I'm told otherwise."

Giving him a smile, he quickly looks away and out the windshield as we finally leave the congestion of the airport.

"Do you need to stop for anything on the way? I want coffee," Joon says.

"Coffee is good," I nod.

He then clears his throat and says something to the driver in Korean with the word Starbucks included.

"You speak English really well," I tell him once he's finished.

"Oh, thank you."

"I think I read somewhere you learned from watching American television?" I question with a smile.

He nods, shooting me the dimples again, "I did."

"That's amazing," I credit. "The other guys been working on learning it?"

"Not really. They know more than they let on, but no," he laughs with a shake of his head.

The driver says something, and I look ahead as we pull into the drive thru.

"Americano, you?" Hyunjoon asks me.

"Same," I reply.

Once we get our coffee, Hyunjoon tells me we have about twenty minutes before we get to the apartments and we both sit drinking our coffees as I look out the window at my new home. He asks me if I've ever been to South Korea before, asks if there's anything I want to do while I'm here, then tells me about some of the places and things they all like to do when they're at home. Most of the things include eating and shopping which I can totally get on board with.

"The guys are practicing but should be back around the time we arrive. I've heard your apartment isn't ready yet, so I think you will be staying in ours until then. Did your boss tell you that?" he asks and just then, it's like my phone connects to the world and begins buzzing with notifications.

Grabbing it from my purse, my work emails, texts and messages begin to all come in at once, and sure enough, there's one from Sawyer.

I've just had word that there's no hot water in the apartment, the water heater needs to be replaced and I'm working on getting that done for you ASAP. There's an extra bed in the client's apartment that you can use until then. Let me know if this is a problem and Drew can book you a hotel. Sawyer.

"I must warn you though," he begins.

"What's that?" I ask, at the same time processing if I'm cool with sharing a space with six hot guys and my main crush. It doesn't take me long to decide, even if the words *reverse harem* crossed my mind before I shoved them out.

"The guys, they don't get much interaction with females other than fans and some staff. It's not that they won't like you, but they might be...what's the word," he says to himself.

"Skittish?" I answer.

"If that means wary or nervous, then yes. Or they might be completely welcoming. I don't know how they'll be, just so you know."

"Okay," I nod, and because I'm a go with the flow kind of girl, I mostly am. Something on my face must say otherwise though.

"We sound weird," he sighs with a smile.

"No, not at all," I smile back with a little shake of my head. "I think it's sweet as hell."

"We've lived together for seven years, just us seven, some of us, the younger ones since they were 15, 16. We don't feel comfortable with many people. Believe me, the pleasure is ours to have you as a guest, but I want you to know we're putting a lot of trust in you with this."

I nod my head once, understanding and also feeling that if I reply and tell him I know, it'll somehow undermine the meaning of what he's confided in me, so I remain silent.

The name of the apartments including 'The Hill' in the title, is no joke. The compound is on damn near a mountain and feels like we're heading toward a Mecca as we cross over a bridge toward them. Buildings arranged in a cascade as they line the side of the hill, with lush green trees cocooning them.

The man-made structure blends in yet also stands out with how well it fits in with mother nature.

"Beautiful, right?" Hyunjoon says, because clearly there's no question that this place is gorg.

"Yes," I reply, my eyes wide as we approach the massive complex.

Stopping at the gate, the driver hands over some papers as he speaks with the guard in Korean and I take in the elaborate security and can only imagine the comfort it gives high profile residents which I must say aloud since Hyunjoon answers me.

"Yes, very much. When we used to live in the city in a one-bedroom apartment, fans broke in a few times. It's a creepy feeling.

I note that in previous interviews and articles I've read, they will never call their fans weird or anything negative, so saying that they *did* something creepy as opposed to *them* being creepy is very much the groups M.O. It's also something I deeply appreciate, yes some of their fans can be extreme, but I feel like they are just appreciative to those fans as they are to the rest. But out of what he's just said something else strikes me.

"One bedroom?" I gasp, although the breaking in thing is also shocking. My eyes widening as he smiles and nods his head. I knew they shared a smallish place at first, I didn't know it was that small.

"Three bunkbeds and one single bed in a room. That's why we're so close, I mean literally, we lived on top of each other," he finishes with a goofy smile and then we both laugh.

Entering the apartments through underground parking, my door's opened, and before I can get my hand on my purse Joon's taking it with him as he gets out of the SUV. I step out to see he's also taking my suitcase from Fred and I look around like I might be missing something, but really, I'm sort of taken aback. Not that he's not sweet as hell, but that he's the celebrity, there are three staff members here, why is he taking my shit for me? The set of elevators opens before us and me and Joon get on just the two of us. The inside of the elevator is sleek with silver fixtures and marble flooring, one side glass and showing the innards of the basement as we ascend, then it's showcasing the view outside. The view is across the hill and the property and the jaw dropping beauty of the place. I can't believe I'm here. A rush of realization comes over me, I'm here. The place I've been fantasizing about coming to is finally where I am. The reason I'm here about to be before my eyes and I look away from the view and over toward Joon who's looking at me. We exchange smiles and I already have that sense with him like we've known each other before, there's none of that awkward silence shit going on.

"You have a very familiar way about you," he says to me, like he too feels what I do.

"I think the same, but it could because I'm a fan," I state.

He continues to smile, but I see he's thinking that's not the case as he regards me. The elevator slows to a stop and I see we're on the top floor, which is only 6 stories. When we exit, I'm all turned around. The layout of the building is confusing, and I chalk it up to some South Korean-art-new age-flow-architecture or something. The floor and walls are marble like the elevator, with large windows looking out into the massive landscape surrounding the building, and what looks like a stream runs parallel to the building. The greenery such a contrast to the cool of the marble and the combination is stunning. My platforms pad on the floor behind Joon as we walk down the long corridor until we reach a single door. Joon types a code into the keypad beside the frame, then looks over his shoulder at me while turning the handle.

"1-3-6-1-2."

"1-3-6-1-2," I nod in repeating the code for the lock, mentally repeating it over and over.

Entering the apartment, the lights of the entryway automatically come on and a chime echos beyond us. A long hallway greets us with what looks like closets on either side for about twenty-feet, I guess you'd need a lot of storage with seven people. Watching Joon slide his shoes off in the entryway, I mimic him, sliding my platform heels off and with my toes, line them up to the other pairs I see.

"I think we're the last to arrive," Joon comments, just as I also hear voices coming from the main part of the apartment. I also notice when Joon, whose gaze was where I'd been before, now pull a surprised face like I've disappeared, before looking down at me. "You're short," he states.

"I am," I nod with a sigh.

"Cute!" he says with a smile and the tone of his voice is high and playful. Ugh, his smiling dimpled face is so fucking adorable I just want to eat it.

"Me cute? Please. Says the dude with dimples like donut holes." I smile back at him, and he nods, conceding my point but I can tell I've made him shy by the way he looks away.

With that, he turns into the apartment. Sure enough, there are men in here, deep voices, the smell of men, the feeling of being in the presence of them, hits me instantly. One by one they all notice my arrival and conversation stops as they take me in and I stand there with my arms by my sides as I'm inspected, before I bow my head slightly in greeting.

"This is Rebecca," Joon introduces in English then in Korean.

I really need to stop thinking the words *reverse harem* as I look at these men towering over me. I always thought Asian men would be short, but not these guys, hell no, I'd say the shortest is at least almost six feet. My eyes go to theirs one by one, and then, they land on him.

Chapter Two

(Du)

Five of the six male faces look at Joon as he speaks, but not him. And that's because he hasn't stopped looking at me, and I haven't stopped looking at him. He's openly taking me in and I feel like my brain is trying to connect with my eyes that this *is* real, that *he* is real. If I thought my crush was beautiful via screen, it's not prepared me for him in reality. His eyes are dark and looking at me in a way that has my heart beating faster, my lips parting as I try to take in more oxygen in a subtle way. His lips are parted also, and I see the hint of his two front teeth, his jaw line has me drifting into my head at all the things I've dreamt of doing to it, and I feel lost in him. One of the other members laughs and I snap out of it, but instead of acting so obvious, I blink and give my crush a smile and keep eye contact with him as he continues to regard me. I realize they weren't laughing at me and gradually turn my attention to the others as they all look at me again, this time expectantly.

Ok, Reb, you've got this, quick rundown.

Jinho: Singer. The oldest of the group but still younger than me, has the fullest lips I've ever seen on a man and I admit it's the first thing I look at when it comes to him. Known for infectious laughter and terrible dad jokes. Oldest, yet silliest. Has broad shoulders and an amazing smile, also let it be noted one of the members who struggles most with dancing. My nickname for him: Broad Shoulders guy.

Youngjae: Rapper aka Shoogi. Quiet, reserved and often looks deep in thought. He's petite compared to the others but still bigger than me. He writes and produces songs for them and other artists and has a mixtape out. For as serious as he can be, he's also funny and laughs a lot. My nickname for him: IDGAF dude.

Hyunjoon: Rapper, aka Joon. Leader of the group although not the oldest, speaks Korean, English and Japanese. Has an IQ of 148 and if you don't know, that like makes him a genius. Tallest of the group. Has several mixtapes, as solo projects are called here, and writes most of the groups songs. Owns dimples. Also known for struggling with dancing and destroying anything he touches. My nickname for him: Dimple destroyer.

Seunghoon: Rapper, aka Hooni. Funny, angelic and sweet, all describe his personality and smile. But like the others, transforms when he's on stage to become a sexy and dominant fucker. Owns dimples. Dance leader. My nickname for him: Pure Sunshine.

Jaimin: Singer. Dances like his body was created for the art. His smile is infectious, and he laughs with his whole body and it causes his eyes to nearly disappear. Clumsy and often falls. Former ballet dancer. Loves to play with my crush and has me often wishing I was him in videos when I see them teasing each other. Beautiful and sweet. My nickname for him: Mochi.

Ye-Jun: Singer, aka Ye. His face legit looks like it was created by a computer, it's that flawless. His skin looks airbrushed and just as perfect in person. His hair always looks fluffy and touchable, often wearing a headband on his forehead that shouldn't look hot, but it does. Makes the best derp faces, dabbles in acting and was on a television series. Known for his rich taste in clothes and odd pairings, like wearing silk pajamas during the day like it's an actual outfit. Hates wearing shoes. Loves using the Musically app and posting on Twitter. I think he's the most misunderstood, but you can tell he has a big heart. My nickname for him: Too flawless to be real guy.

And last, but by no means least, Jung-keun: aka JK, Singer. Dancer and most importantly my crush. Has wide brown eyes and brown hair he doesn't normally change the color of like the others. Is the youngest of the group and they really baby him. He's teased for being good at everything, which he seems to be. Often compared to a bunny by fans because of his semi protruding front teeth, his round, full cheeks, and the way his nose cringles at the bridge sometimes which causes his nostrils to pull up. He's a jokester. He's said that he thinks he's a combination of all the members since he's been with them since he was fifteen and I think that's also true from what I've seen. My nickname for him: My future boyfriend.

Again, my brain is still trying to compute that these men I've been watching for hours via my phone are actually real and in front of me. I almost panic. I know their names, of course I fucking do. But part of me worries that it will look too stalkery for me to say them without them introducing themselves. But wait, they don't know I'm a fan. I'm here for work, of course it won't be weird to them if I know their names. I want to make a good impression, give them confidence that I'm here for them, and get them comfortable with me as quickly as I can. The first few minutes in building a solid client relationship are important, and more so with these guys given I'm going to be staying here. Pointing at them one by one, I say out loud the nickname I've created for each of them to help me memorize their faces, along with their real name.

"Sunshine- Seunghoon," I say with a smile of my own and he nods.

"Hooni," he tells me his stage name.

"Broad shoulders guy - Jinho."

"International handsome," he smiles, blowing me a kiss, which I know through my absorption in all things KT7 is his signature move with the fans.

"Hyunjoon, I got you, "Joon."

"Too-flawless-to-be-real-guy, Ye Jun."

"Ye," he nods with a smile.

"Mochi-Jaimin," who smiles at my nickname for him.

"IDGAF dude - Youngjae," I smile at him, and in return I get an eye crinkle and a one-sided mouth lift. Not quite a smirk, not exactly a smile and perfectly him.

"Hi, I'm Shoogi," he adds

Oh fuck, I suddenly realize I can't say JK's nickname I have for him and I stand there frozen for a minute while he looks at me expectantly.

"Jung-keun- JK," I finally spit out.

My words fade on my lips as the youngest member and I connect eyes again. Holy hell. I wasn't exaggerating when I said all these men look fake with their flawless skin and perfect, well, every-fucking-thing. But him, I can't.

"Jung-keun," he agrees, nodding his head slightly while still looking me in the eyes, something I'm realizing the others hadn't done. "And you Noona," he adds.

"Joon called me Rebecca, but everyone calls me Rebel, so whatever you feel comfortable––"

"Redbull?" One of them queries, and I force myself to look away from Jung-keun to see it's Ye.

"Re-b-el," Joon sounds out for him and he repeats, but it still sounds like Redbull and I like that just the same, so I let him know.

"Yup, that'll do," I confirm with a smile and a nod.

I can feel that Jung-keun's eyes are still on me as I step back and clear my throat for them all to look at me, not wanting to allow his gaze to set me off my target. I decide each time I look his way it might be safer to avoid his eyes and look at the thick silver hoops in his ears instead. But even they are sexy, so now I'm hit with a visual of tugging on them with my teeth and burying my face against his long neck. *Get it together, Reb.*

"While I have everyone here, I want you to know that I honor the privacy of my clients, and I understand completely your need for a separation of your public lives from your home lives. I take the trust you've shown in me seriously, and I appreciate you letting me stay with you for a few days. However, I'd like for our relationship to go beyond this. I want to know all of you on a level where you are comfortable sharing with me the goals you have not just for the group, but maybe also on a personal level. What you hope to achieve in your careers. Trust me, I've heard just about everything so nothing's too over the top I assure you. I also want you to know that I will do everything I can to make that happen, willing to go above and beyond to help you reach your goals. Your success and happiness are why I do this job."

Joon has translated some bits of my client intro speech, which I tweaked a little given what he'd shared with me on the ride here. As I've been talking, the guys have alternated looking between the both of us. Except for JK. Nope, eyes like dark cocoa magnets that one and not ten minutes in, dude is killing me. I'm hoping that the Jagger-long, double wrapped, black linen scarf around my neck is covering the cherries on my sundaes, if you catch my drift.

Speech over, they all nod before returning their attention to trying to say my name correctly.

"Jinho made lunch, well their leftovers from last night's dinner," Joon tells me, coming up to my other side. "Are you hungry or would you like to settle?"

"Oh, I'm down to eat," I reply fervently.

I notice then the other guys have moved and are all gathering around a massive low-level dining table and its then I really take in the beauty of the apartment. Clean lines full of steel and smooth raw materials. The floors and walls of the living room and dining room made of shiny cream marble, while windows line the exterior wall. The view is of the water and bridge we crossed over to enter the compound.

"Beautiful," JK says, again beside me and I hadn't even noticed he was there.

"It's breathtaking," I reply, still looking out the windows on my way to the table.

"Well, get used to it, you'll be here a while," Joon says from in front of me.

"Hopefully," someone at the table says and I smile, continuing my walk over.

Sitting down on the floor, I tuck my legs to the side as the other members sit around me at the table. There's a massive pot of something in front of me, along with several bowls of rice, sauce and condiments. Silently, they wait for Jinho to begin because I know from Unnie that it's customary for the eldest to kick start eating before everyone else. When he does, the guys all take their chopsticks and begin taking food from the bowls, bite by bite, dipping them in the sauce or piling white rice on with a finesse I find enviable. There are plates in front of everyone, yet I only see them use it to pause their chopsticks there to add something to the bite, and for a moment I feel out of sorts about it. These men are like brothers, sharing food and double dipping clearly isn't a thing for them, but me? I'm a stranger.

"Hand me your plate," Joon says, a mouthful of food bulging the side of one cheek.

Removing my chopsticks off the white plate in front of me, I lift it to Joon who is diagonal from me and he scoops some of everything onto it, while the conversation around me doesn't falter. It sounds like they're still trying to say my name right and chastising one another mixed in with some other conversation. A voice across from me, low and steady has my eyes darting forward. JK has his hand on Joon's hand that's scooping something and maybe questioning his choice. There's something about JK that has my attention on him, yes, he's speaking, but not to me. He's the youngest of the group, but he's clearly well-respected, something I know isn't common amongst the culture, and to see an older member listening to him shows how close these guys are.

"Do you like wasabi?" Joon asks.

I shrug, "It's fine."

JK then says something and Joon scrapes a bit off the portion he was giving me.

"Very hot," JK says, looking at me. There's something so endearing when I hear him speaking English. The way he prolonged *very* and ended *hot* with a hard T. I smile and nod once in thanks, reaching over as Joon hands me my plate back.

Taking my chopsticks in my left hand, I open them with ease and familiarity, thank you Unni Kim. The group around me all "Ohhh" in surprise and I almost laugh at the sudden attention. Pinching the beef and vegetables between my sticks, they "Ahhh," then wait for my reaction at the food. Shit, it's delicious. I moan slightly and nod, looking at Jinho next to me.

"Good, yeah?" he asks.

"Mhmmm," I nod again, retrieving another bite.

I listen to the conversation around me, and with every bite of food and the easiness to which I feel like the guys are around me, I begin to relax. However, a set of big brown eyes watching me the entire meal can't be ignored. JK doesn't speak much, but he laughs occasionally at what's being said and every time he does, well, my insides notice. It takes a long while for me to notice my phone going off in my purse by the door and realize it's probably Sawyer.

"Excuse me," I nod, getting up and trying not to slip on the marble floor as I charge for the phone in some sort of game to answer it before it switches to voicemail.

"Hi!" I say loudly as I swipe answer, like the volume will also stop the transfer.

"Reb, you got my message about the apartment, does that arrangement work for you?" Sawyer asks, and I begin to walk up and down the long hallway.

I assure her it's fine, that it'll be good for me to get to know the client and also might be beneficial since I'm an outsider and I need to earn their trust. That's always the case, but this setting is different than any other I've done for work and I know it's imperative that I prove myself to them. As Sawyer goes on about something to do with one of the other girls, I overhear Joon say, "I think it's someone she works with."

Looking over toward the table, the others are eating, but JK has his head turned over his shoulder. He's looking at me before saying something to Joon in a low tone that means I can't hear his words, but you bet I watch as his lips form, before he faces away from me. Joon nudges JK's elbow with a shake of his head. I swallow thickly and turn my back, trying to concentrate on Sawyer. But fuck, I can't. I can only think about the man who seems more intent on me than I've ever experienced with a client, no, with anyone. He's watching me more than how you observe someone new, but more like he's never seen anyone like me before.

I can't help but feel some kind of way about it. I know it's *my* destiny to meet him, but destiny didn't say anything about him wanting me, ok? I think it's natural and not bad for a work relationship to be attracted to the people around you. I'll chalk it up to him being interested in the mere fact that I'm new to his world. Because I seriously can't get my hopes up that he'd potentially be interested in me.

Ending my call, I return to the table and apologize quietly once more, not wanting to interrupt the conversations going on. I begin eating, totally wrapped up in my food enjoyment and mentally note that I need to snap a pic next time and send it to the food porn goddess Cassie, my friend and colleague, along with a detailed double entendre filled description of the flavors.

"Everything fine?" Joon asks, and I look up to him.

"Yes, couldn't be better," I smile, noticing JK looking at me intently, before he ever so slightly knocks his elbow into Joon's ribs.

"So, tell us about you," Joon nods.

"What do you wanna know?"

Joon speaks in Korean and it seems like everyone speaks at once and I laugh as Joon is bombarded.

"Where are you from?"

"L.A."

"We...love...L.A." Jaimin says with short pauses in between his words, that I know are because he's determined to use English correctly. These guys are something else.

"L.A. is pretty cool," I nod.

The word 'cool' begins circulating around the table and JK says something to Joon.

"Do you have a boyfriend?" Joon asks.

"Not really," I shrug.

"Not really?" Joon laughs slightly. "This means, yes?"

"No," I say with a nod, but as soon as I see a puzzled frown form on the face across from me, I realize I've sent a mixed message. "No," I clarify with a headshake this time. "No boyfriend."

I could mention I have had boyfriends before, but don't know how South Koreans feel about promiscuity or sex before marriage and a whole world of shit I'm not prepared to lead a discussion on, fumbling like a nervous eighth grade health class teacher. Oh, don't get me wrong, I could totally rock that discussion under normal circumstances, but I am after all still trying to make a good impression.

For most of the meal, I sit and listen while eating. I don't want them to feel like they need to change the way they normally are just because I'm here and I don't want Joon to feel like he needs to translate everything they say. Thankfully, they don't seem to be and he's certainly not. I like it. It's settling me, and eating is a large part of South Korean socializing, or so I read. But there is something that's also got me reeling a little. They eat so loudly. Not only that, but they put so much food in their mouth at one go. Like, think a chipmunk or a hamster's cheeks, they're fully loaded and ready to chomp. I'm not sure if this is a culture thing or a dude thing, but I find myself staring at them in wonderment as they shovel the food in. They also talk with their mouths full and make loud sounds emphasizing how good each bite is.

As I watch Ye expertly grip and maneuver an intact noodle-slab-looking thing into his waiting mouth, I speak before I can stop myself.

"Holy shit," I mumble, I thought to myself, but few of the guys laugh openly, repeating my phrase of 'Holy shit!' which only results in yet more masculine laughter.

Way to go Reb, teaching English abroad - one profanity at a time.

"It's a Korean thing," Joon says with a smile, keeping his explanation simple, and in a way, I guess it is. No one can accuse the men at this table of not being appreciative or grateful for their meal or of their time spent with each other as they eat.

Evidently looking to compete with each other and I suspect to also gain my admiration, Jaimin catches my attention before inhaling a whole bowl of noodles. While not to be outdone, Hooni rapidly scoops out the remaining the contents of the bowl closest to him, fitting the entirety of it in his mouth.

This interaction feels good. I was worried from Joon's pre-meet-speech, that the guys wouldn't even want me sitting with them or something. To see them eating normally and trying to involve me, to make me laugh, I feel like integrating into the crew might not be as hard as I thought.

Returning my attention to my food and wondering if I could fit all of it in my mouth at one go, I feel someone watching me. JK's eyes are staring at me as I look up. I can't believe my crush is within reaching distance. I can't believe I'm here. I give him a small smile while he blinks and looks down the table at Shoogi talking.

Dinner now over, everyone starts to collect dishes, so I stand to help, my change in position forcing more air into my lungs and I'm not quick enough to stifle a yawn.

"Please follow," Joon tells me, and gestures for me to shadow him out of the dining area. "We hope you don't mind sharing a room," Joon tells me as we all walk down the hallway, yes, all eight of us.

"No, not at all, I hope no one minds sharing with me," I reply. "I don't want to be putting anyone out."

"What does that mean?"

"I don't want to be troubling someone to have to sleep somewhere else, I can sleep on the couch-"

"Oh, no, no," he says, stopping me, "no, you are not."

"Ok, thanks again for letting me stay," I add.

"JK is the only one without a roommate, but you don't want to stay in his room," Joon says. "He barely has room in there for a bed and he doesn't even sleep there."

I nod, even though he's now walking in front of me, the others behind me.

"We put an extra bed in with Jaimin and Hooni, they have the largest room in the place so..." he shrugs.

I wonder if most people, or rather women would be weirded out to be sleeping with total strangers. But for me, they're my clients and what better way to get to know a client than to live with them. We enter the room I assume is where I'll be staying, and it indeed is massive. There's a bathroom on either side of the doorway, then walk in closets line the entryway and then there's the wide space of the room. Two beds on either side, set up almost like a dorm, with a large bookshelf in the middle to divide the room. There's two sets of furniture, one for each guy. However, the furniture is personalized to the occupant and I love the shelves of little anime characters and collectables on Jaimin's side while Hooni's side is more minimalistic and ultra-tidy. Beside Jaimin's bed in an out of the way space, is an actual bed, and I wonder if that's where I'll be sleeping.

"Is that all right?" Joon asks.

"Absolutely," I nod, setting my purse on top of the white comforter on the bed.

I turn to look at them all standing there, Jaimin with a smile plastered on his face which causes his eyes to nearly shut and I smile back at him, it's hard not to. The guys are laughing and talking animatedly except for one, JK. He's looking at me, the bed, Jaimin's bed, back at me, between the two beds and begins to almost anxiously stick his tongue into the side of his cheek before mumbling. No one seems to be paying him any mind, so I try not to too.

Joon says something, and the guys begin to exit while Jaimin comes over toward me. Pointing at the dresser beside me, he opens a drawer, revealing he's cleared one side of each of the drawers for me to put my things.

"You didn't have to do that, thank you," I smile, placing my hand on his arm and I hear a clicking of a tongue behind us. Sure enough, it's JK, who's just standing there watching.

He says something to Jaimin in a tone I consider angry-ish, but Jaimin just laughs.

Still laughing, Jaimin speaks to me with a nod and walks to the door, smacking JK's arm in the process as they exchange words which causes Jaimin to laugh even more. I stand there looking at JK, wondering if there's something he needs. I widen my eyes and turn to face him, but he just looks at me for a moment before turning and following Jaimin.

I don't unpack everything, but put my panties, bras and clothes for the day in the drawers, leaving my shoes and pajamas still in my luggage. I'll have to go through the stuff I sent earlier to see if there's anything I need right away, but I think I'll be set with what I have for a bit. I assume the whole fixing the apartment will take a week tops and I don't want to unpack just to repack.

When I'm done, I hit a wall. Either the time change is catching up with me or just from travel or eating, but I find myself saying I'll just lay down for a minute to check my phone and charge it, and I fall asleep.

Chapter Three

(Se)

Next thing I know, the room is darker than it was when I laid down and there's a blanket over me. I roll over and look around for a clock, finding none, I reach under me to where my phone has disappeared and see it's early evening.

I can't hear anyone talking, but music is playing in the distance and I assume the guys are still in the apartment somewhere. I sit up and stretch, rubbing my face with my hands, my mascara crumbling beneath my fingers. Ugh, I can only imagine what I look like, I hate falling asleep with make-up on. I feel greasy and gross and decide a shower is what I need before emerging back into civilization.

I grab clothes to change into afterward and my toiletries bag, deciding since I'm sharing Jaimin's side of the room that I'll use his bathroom. Entering the dark room, I search for the light switch with the flat of my hand for about ten minutes until it finally triggers the lights to come on. This place is so high tech it's not even funny, and for a moment I wonder if I'll be able to even operate the shower. The bathroom is marble and glass, there's gray towels hanging on the racks and the countertop has male grooming items, cologne, and a contact case with a saline bottle close by. Setting my stuff on the empty part by the sink, I use the toilet and still feel a bit groggy, jet lag having different ideas for me in mind.

Reaching over to lock the door, I then prepare myself for the shower. The glass shower door glides effortlessly as it reveals buttons and knobs and I growl in pre-frustration. Everything's in Korean, so I whip out my phone and look the words up, managing to at least get the water flowing. At this point I don't care about the temperature, I just want to get clean and be done. Stripping my clothes off, I test the water with my hand and thank fuck it's warm, good job me. I wash up and can't resist smelling all Jaimin's things while in there. His bodywash smells like fucking man and God it's clit twitch inducing, so I squirt a little on my palms and use it, I'm sure he won't mind but I make a note of the name and brand to buy him some more if he notices, or maybe as a thank you present for sharing his space with me.

Once I'm dry, I slap on some lotion and dress in black yoga pants and a sweatshirt that has a cat face and ears on the hood, I brush my hair and teeth, putting the hood up before exiting with my dirty clothes in my arms, bumping into someone as I walk back into the room.

"Sorry," I tell Jaimin who looks as if he was checking to see if I was still in bed.

He nods, saying sorry back in English and his cute accent. He then stops, looks at me, smiles and says something. I shake my head and he lifts my hand to smell me.

"Oh, yeah, I used your shower stuff," I reply, using my hands to further explain my words.

Then he looks at my cat hoodie with a huge grin, his eyes becoming rainbow shaped with the action.

"Kyoot," he tells me.

I give him a smile and walk past to put my dirty clothes on top of my luggage. But Jaimin stops me with his hands on my arm, turning and pointing to a laundry bin on the other side of his bed.

"They wash," he tells me.

I don't want to be rude and really, I won't have a way to wash my stuff until I get into my place, so I nod and drop my clothes on top of the half full bin.

"Hungry?" he asks.

"Yes," I tell him, and he takes my hand.

I don't feel like he's flirting with me, I think he's just like this. I saw the way he was with the others at lunch, the way he cleared out his dresser for my brief stay, that he was probably picked by the others for me to share space with. I think he's a nurturer, at least that's the vibe I get. His was is gentle and calming and I absorb that in his presence.

"You're good at English," I say as he leads me down the marble hallway that takes us to the kitchen and living space.

The doors we pass by are closed or nearly closed and I hear music, televisions, computer keys tapping, and think everyone must be doing their own thing. I know they don't get much down time so I'm sure they want to be alone when they can.

"A little," Jaimin replies, looking over his shoulder at me with a squint of his eye.

He's still holding my hand as we walk into the kitchen, not letting go until he opens the pantry door to show me the contents. I see bags and bags of ramen, cereal, other freeze-dried stuff, everything in Korean writing.

"Are you eating too?" I ask, and he nods.

I then point at the ramen, to which he smiles and retrieves three packages of the noodles. I walk to the stove and reach for a pan sitting there to fill with water, before Jaimin is shooing my hand away and grabbing it.

"I make."

I walk to the counter and lean over, resting my elbows on top of it as I open my translator app, typing out, *thank you for cooking, I can help you.*

He waits until he's filled the pan with water, turned on the burner and put the noodles in to take out his phone, mimic my position and look at my phone for the app to download. When it's done he motions for me to show him how to use it before he types out, *no, I got it.* I giggle, because he's already done with the hard part of the ramen. We begin talking via the app, laughing because he's funny and seems to think I'm silly, since he laughs a lot at what I say. His laughter makes me laugh, and suddenly, we're startled by the water boiling over. Of course, this makes us laugh as he removes the pan and turns down the heat. When he laughs, he leans into me, either putting his head on my shoulder or his hands on my arms and it makes me soft inside. This guy is so sweet, I just want to squeeze him.

A few minutes later, Jaimin sets a bowl of noodles in front of me, handing me chop sticks as he resumes his position next to me, and it's only when he puts his sticks in the bowl, do I realize he's put it all in one bowl for us to share.

We eat, laugh, mess with the app some more and eventually end up back in the bedroom, sitting on his bed and taking snapchat photos while laughing. He's found a one-piece dragon pajama thing in his closet and put it on over his clothes, wanting to match my kitty sweatshirt. Hooni came to bed a little while ago from his studio where he's working on a mixtape, from what Jaimin told me, and is crashed in his bed.

"He's hard to wake," the translator tells me after I shush Jaimin for laughing too loud.

We get on a laughing kick where everything is funny, I think mine's due to being still tired and Jaimin's because he's Jaimin. My stomach hurts with the giggles and I'm nearly startled when Ye and JK come into the room, walking over and immediately joining us on the bed. Ye next to me and JK across from me. They speak to us and Jaimin laughs, showing them our snaps which he's saved and not posted to the app. The guys laugh at the photos, commenting here and there. Next thing I know, I'm being pulled into the frame as they all want to take a photo, together. The back of my heads on JK's chest as Jaimin and Ye lean in and Jaimin puts his hand across the front of my shoulders. Christ. We all laugh as Jaimin takes the video and moves the camera past all of us, so the filter shows up over our faces. I'm second and pout my lips to make the filter move and as Jaimin begins to move up to JK, JK stops him and adjusts his arm so we're both in the shot. I look up at his face and him down at me, he's smiling so big it makes me smile just as wide.

Ye whines and then Jaimin pans to him and I sit up, since the position made my back want to split in two. Jaimin looks down at the phone as he finishes, laughing and showing something to JK who laughs and looks at me shyly.

"JK looks like a bunny, we always have to use the bunny filter for him when it's on there," Jaimin laughs as the phone speaks to me, then hands me the phone and nudges me to take the pic of JK.

JK seems slightly embarrassed as I point the phone at him, but then gives me a wide smile that fits the theme to the filter perfectly and I smile just looking at it.

"Aw, little bun-bun," I comment, after snapping the pic.

JK mumbles something as Ye turns on the flat screen on the wall beside the bed. Jaimin moves back beside me and we continue to mess with our phones as Ye and JK talk, flipping through the channels on the television. Eventually, I lay back on the pillows, feeling too tired from laughing and travel to fight it anymore. Jaimin lays down beside me, getting under the white down comforter, and urging me to lift my butt so he can pull it from beneath me, before pulling it up over both of us.

I wake up in the night to darkness, bodies on either side of me, one I know is Jaimin and the other I'm not sure. But I need to roll onto my side and bump into whoever is there, I assume Ye, I don't know why I assume that, maybe because if I know it's JK I might just sleep hump him. He groans and lifts slightly onto his side since he's facing me, and I roll, my head resting on the elbow he has it bent with his hand under his head. Sleep grips me, just as his other arm rests on my waist, cradling me as I fade back into the depths.

Chapter Four

(Sa)

The next morning, I woke up on my makeshift bed, far from Jaimin and I had a feeling someone had moved me there. But I don't think Jaimin would, he was more than comfortable with me lying beside him before I fell asleep. Regardless I was a coma patient and don't remember moving clear across the massive bed to sleep on the twin sized cot. I wake up feeling good, my clock feeling regulated after a nap and solid sleep, however it's still dawn outside, the sky in that pre-sun stage where it's still gray. Looking around the room, I notice Hooni's arms in the air through the large squares of the bookshelf separating the room, as if he's stretching and hear a beeping, that's what must've woke me.

He sits up and turns off the alarm on his phone before rubbing his eyes or face, the room still too dark to make out which. He mumbles something in a deep voice before getting up and walking over to Jaimin's bed. It's then I see two people in his bed, both covered with the hoods of their sweatshirts and the one closest to me rolls onto his back as Jaimin groans and rolls over with a stretch.

Hooni disappears into the bathroom and I grab my phone, checking the time to see it's not even 5 a.m. It's earlier than my normal morning call, but I'm excited to start my first real day of work for the group.

"Dangsin-eun Jaimincheoleom naemsaega nanda."

I blink away from my phone to meet the eyes of JK who's laying on the edge of the bed just before my cot starts. Jaimin starts laughing and so does Hooni. They all talk in raspy, sleepy voices and the timbre does that thing that happens to women when guys sound sexy as fuck.

"He says you smell like me," Jaimin's voice app announces loudly.

I laugh and remember I used Jaimin's shower shit last night, but see JK isn't laughing, he's just looking at me. No expression. No hint as to what he's thinking. Then, he gets off the bed and disappears out of the room. I get up, shaking off the feelings JK gave me by his statement and his expression, using the bathroom quickly as I hear the shower in Hooni's bathroom start and Jaimin passes by me and enters his bathroom after me. Grabbing some

37

clothes from the dresser, I think if I remember the schedule correctly, they have dance practice all day today which means I'll be more than likely sitting. So, I throw on some black leather leggings and an oversized chunky black sweater, my black combat boots, and a long necklace before flipping my head over and gathering all my hair into a messy bun. Since I don't want anyone waiting for me, I grab my tinted BB cream from my purse and head into the kitchen. I hear the showers running in every room as I pass down the hall, so I'm not surprised when I enter the living space to find it empty. I wash my face in the kitchen sink and lather on the cream, tossing it back into my bag while getting out my travel toothbrush and paste. I go two rounds with the toothpaste since I didn't brush them before bed and when I'm done I set my purse on the table, along with my laptop bag I'd left in the entryway.

I search the fridge for something to make for breakfast and wonder if they eat before they head out or not. Remembering there was cereal in the pantry, I decide on that and pour myself a bowl. I'm done by the time the first member, Jinho, appears in the entryway and blows me a kiss and I jump up and grab the air kiss in my hand and smack it to my cheek. He gives me a smile and almost shyly turns his back to me to retrieve shoes from one of the many closets. Then, one by one, the guys stream in and it's a flutter of low-toned-sleepy-male conversation and movement, all getting their things together to leave.

"Morning," Joon says to me, sunglasses on as he nods and pulls a bag over his shoulder.

"Good morning," I reply, mimicking him with putting my laptop bag on-to my shoulder as well, and mentally note my phone in my hand, my glasses in my purse and I can't help but feel like I'm missing something.

"We'll get coffee," Joon assures me and it's then I realize that's what it is.

"Perfect," I sigh.

The front door opens and I notice one of the managers waving for me to come toward him. I make my way through the group as they continue to get their shit together.

"Hello, I'm Dong-joo," he nods his head in a casual bow. "Here's today's schedule," he tells me, handing over a sheet of paper. "I also emailed the weeks schedule to you. Just let me know if you prefer one or the other, or both."

He speaks English well and I'm thankful, because day to day conversation is one thing, but when it comes to work, I don't know how I'd manage the barrier. I kick myself for not learning more Korean before coming here regardless of the short time between getting the assignment and leaving, but instead of dogging myself, I use it as motivation to fucking learn.

"Let's do it like this for now, until I get the schedule memorized. They have practice all day today, correct?" I ask while looking down at the paper and we begin to walk out of the apartment.

We lead the troops to the elevators as the manager continues to fill me in and give me a quick rundown as I read the schedule.

"I'd also like to have a meeting at some point today with all the managers, if that's doable," I tell him.

We're in the large elevator and I can't help but notice all the members, aside from Shoogi, watching us as we converse.

"I'd also like a print up of any endorsement or sponsorship contract offers up for renewal."

"Yes, of course," he says, tapping on the screen of his phone.

"Do you need anything from us?" Joon asks.

"Nope, I'll tell you when I need you," I smile as I tap open my calendar app on my phone, getting a dimply smile from him in return.

I think Joon translates the conversation between me and the manager, causing the guys to "ahhhh" and nod.

"Did you go to school for that?" Joon then asks.

"For my job? Yes, but I learned most from working with Sawyer."

Joon gives me another dimple grin, and a tip of his chin, "We like smart women."

"Good," I smile widely. "I like men who like smart women."

When we exit to the underground parking garage, there are three black SUV's, Fred holding the door open to one of them and I give him a wave. He looks at me oddly and then bows slightly, oh right, I'm supposed to do that. I head for his vehicle, not really thinking if there's some system to who goes where, and get in the backseat, putting my laptop and purse on the floor. I don't pay attention but know the seats are filling up around me and when I get my shit situated and look to my left, JK is sitting right beside me.

He has on ripped black skin-tight jeans, black combat boots like mine and a gray hoodie with the hood pulled over his head. He smells clean and like fabric softener, the kind that bear shoves into his face and huffs like it's accelerant, and I now understand how that fucker feels when it gets all giggly over it. I want to plunge my face into JK's arm and inhale until my eyes cross.

He catches me looking at him as he buckles in his seatbelt, giving me an odd look before nodding at the belt beside my opposite shoulder. I get myself safely strapped in and we're off, our SUV in the middle of the pack. The occupants with me are three managers, JK and Shoogi, who's sitting on the other side of JK. I notice both men put their headphones in and go on their phones, but I think I left my headphones back at the apartment, taking them out of my purse when I got settled last night and not thinking I'd need them after my flight. I make a note in my phone to remind me to grab them for tomorrow and then a white earbud slides into my line of sight. Looking over, I see JK offering it to me. I smile and take it, my fingers brushing his in the transfer and I note how smooth his skin feels. Sliding it into my ear, he moves his phone for me to see as he scrolls through his Spotify. He stops on a song and looks at me, I nod even though I've never heard of the song or artist before. It's in Korean, smooth and R&Bish, I like it and look out the window as we drive through the city.

During the song, JK nudges my elbow and I look to see he's giving me a thumbs-up in reference to the song, which I return with a smile. During the course of the drive, I notice something. The three of us sitting in the backseat, JK isn't touching me. The gap between our bodies is at least two inches and he's not particularly tiny. Trying not to be obvious, I glance over to Shoogi's side and see JK is sitting so close to him that they look crammed in the corner.

Were they really that skittish with me that they'd rather sit uncomfortably the whole time than for the side of his body to make contact with mine? I feel, guilty. Like I should've sat up front, or with Joon or Jaimin who seem to have no problem with me physically. But I remind myself of what Joon told me about them. They just need time to accept me. I mean, we practically shared a bed last night, he's letting me use his headphones, he can't be that afraid of me, can he? Maybe that's why I was moved onto the cot, JK didn't want to sleep by me?

Even though early, there's traffic, and we listen to two more songs before pulling up beside a building and I click into business mode. The sign above the door says Massive Smash and this is the company that the group is signed to. It's a management company, record label, K-pop powerhouse where they do everything for the group. Out of all the companies in South Korea, this one wasn't big, in fact they were in debt until KT7 made it big and it makes me happy, yet doesn't surprise me, that they would stick with the once fledgling label.

We all get out and head inside, I follow since I have no clue where I'm going. Joon looks back to make sure I'm with them because the building lobby isn't large but there's a lot of us piling in. The doors to the only elevator open and it's full before I can get on but hear someone beside me waving Joon and the others to go ahead, knowing it's Jaimin. The doors close and for a moment I think it's just us two, but he says something over my head, connecting eyes with another person and I turn to see it's JK. The two men talk, Jaimin laughing at what he says and what JK says in reply, and I can't help but smile, even though I have no fucking idea what's being said. My head begins to throb slightly and realize we didn't stop for coffee, fuck. I'm firmly dependent on at least one cup a morning just to avoid that caffeine withdraw headache I get and know my day will be fucked if I have to deal with that. Without thinking, I bring my fingers to my temple as I check my emails and moments later, the robotic tone of the translator is asking me what's wrong.

"Need coffee," my phone replies, and Jaimin puts his hand on my shoulder.

"Don't worry," he says, causing me to look at him as he points up just as the elevator dings and slides open.

We get on and JK hits the button and the doors close, both men look at me like they're worried and I give a reassuring smile that I'm fine, but that doesn't stop Jaimin from nearly escorting me out of the elevator like I'm about to faint or something. He guides us over to a table in the huge white room where at least thirty Starbucks to-go cups are sitting. There's cold coffee and hot coffee and there's nothing more that I love than sipping on a nice hot cup of joe, but I need caffeine STAT. Grabbing one of the cold brews, Jaimin is there stuffing a straw in the lid for me and with his hand over mine, bringing it to my lips. This guy. What a genuine caring dude.

"Jaimin," JK says loudly from the other side of the room, since Jaimin has stayed in front of me watching my every move as I down the coffee.

"Good, you?" he asks with a thumb up.

"Jaimin, you're a lifesaver!" I nod, practically breathless from drinking and put my hand over his in thanks.

I'm all about the body contact, especially when it comes to returning a gesture that's so sweet, I want him to know I don't mind his way of being physical. I think Jaimin will be how I earn these guys respect, because even though it seems to be his nature, it still surprises me just how nurturing he is to me who's still practically a stranger. He gives me a smile before finally leaving me and joining the guys at the other end of the room.

All the managers are here, most of which I still need to meet and learn the names of, and more people who I assume are staff are doing various tasks. I waste no time setting my laptop up at one of the many white tables that take up a section of the space. I soon find out the reason for the tables are for people to sit, obviously, but when the guys are here all day, they eat here, work here, nap here. Everyone's so dedicated it feels like a family, a collective effort, and I love the vibe.

At first, I sat with my back to the guys practicing, listening to the song that played over head on repeat as I typed out my ideas for them. when I look up during several emails to find the right words to type, I notice staff enjoying the music, even if it's the fiftieth time it's played today, God knows how many times before this day they've heard it. But that says something about the music. I have no idea more than half the lyrics and I'm loving it too. This is what is going to sell them in America. The music. Forget not knowing the language, forget where these guys come from, the music is what connects people to them, and it's fucking good.

"Anyong haseyo," a chipper voice says, as the chair becomes occupied beside me.

"Hi," I smile over at the young woman.

She's beautiful, with warm brown eyes, a small face with high cheekbones, full lips and long, thick, wavy black hair.

"I'm Hannah," she introduces herself in English.

"Rebel, nice to meet you," I reply, extending a hand. "You're American?" I question.

"Yup," she nods, opening a can of Cola-Cola. "I was born in D.C., been back here for about six years now," she informs me.

"Cool," I reply, leaning back in my chair and giving my brain and hands a break from work. "What do you do?"

"I'm on the glamor squad."

"Ohhh, nice," I smile with a raise of an eyebrow.

"It's cool, they by far are my favorites to work with," she says, tipping her head toward the guys and I turn sideways in my chair to face her, but also to see the guys practicing.

They're bathed in sweat, damp clothes sticking to their slick skin. Each one has a look of determination on their faces as their bodies move in precision. Strong and fierce, fucking sexy. To see it, to witness it with my own eyes in the flesh, not on the small screen of my phone, it's transfixing. I feel hypnotized, unable to look away, I can't will my eyes off JK. It takes me a long moment to realize he's looking back at me. Why does seeing him slick, breathing heavy with an intense drive in his eyes make me think about fucking?

"Good, right?" Hannah asks, knocking me out of my ogling.

"Uh, yeah, that's an understatement," I blink away from the contact, looking over at Hannah.

"Want a tour? You'll be here a lot if you're going to be tagging along with them."

"I'd love one," I smile, standing almost immediately in the sudden urge to stretch my legs and get my senses back in line.

I feel like the only way to do that is to get some distance from the guys and I don't know why exactly. I can handle hotness, they aren't my first clients to have that magnetic superstar quality about them, no, this is something else. That deeper feeling I had for them before I came here.

We leave the den of sin and venture into the hallway. Hannah points at each room as we pass by doors, which most in this hallway are all training rooms for performance practices and what not. She shows me the bathrooms, the lounge, the cafeteria, and the hallway where each member of the group have a room where they can make music or do whatever they want. I know they spend a lot of time here, so I assume they're like little private spaces for them. The building is simple and looks like it's recently undergone some updating, or at least is in the process. It's by no means flashy or in your face, it's

modest and humble in a way that reminds me of the seven amazing performers working their asses off in this moment.

Hannah and I of course begin talking beauty and style amongst other
things. I tell her that I've changed my hair color eleven times last year, but my
record is twenty-two and that I might change it while I'm here. Six months
ago, I went back to my near natural color to give it a rest and an extended stay
at a deep conditioner treatment center. But dirty blonde is boring for me, I
don't feel like Rebel 100% with it, and I wish I could've come to South Korea with some dope color. We talk about her *go-to* make-up choices and some
skin care stuff she insists I need to try while I'm here and we decide that on
the next off day we're going to go shopping together. She also gives me some
tips for a South Korean new comer. Like, be wary of any guy who refers to
you as a 'white pony,' don't go alone with a guy to a place called a DVD bong,
and that I'll probably also need some essentials from home flown in.

I like her and I'm happy to have found someone I don't need to deal with
on a professional level. I'm one of those people who need female friends and
even though I've only been here one day, I'm seriously missing my girls back
home.

"And we're back," Hannah announces as we turn the corner and have returned to where we started.

"Oh okay," I nod confidently, thinking I have the layout pretty figured
out.

"So, where are you staying?" she asks as we stand just outside the practice
room.

"The same apartment building as the guys."

"Ohhh, fancy," she smiles.

"Right, the place is like a fucking palace," I comment.

"Well, I've never been, just seen online, it was big news when it was built
a few years back."

"When I get settled, come over, we can have a girl's night," I suggest.

"Really? Oh my God that'd be awesome!"

Just then, her phone begins to beep, and she retrieves it from her pocket.
"I have a meeting, I'll come check on you later," she tells me, beginning down
the hall again.

"Thanks for showing me around," I wave and watch as she disappears.

I linger in the hallway, the music filtering out and I lean against the wall. I did it. I'm here. This is what I wanted, and I got it. I feel like dreams, attainable dreams can and do come true if you are determined and work hard. I wanted this job and to come to South Korea and here I am.

Chapter Five

(Da seos)

The song is still playing when I come back in to work, the sound of rubber from sneakers squeak on the floor, the sound of synchronized feet landing has me looking over at the dancing still going on. I don't know how they do it. I love a lot of things, but I couldn't do it over and over for hours on end. Especially something physical. The drive they have is enviable. There's no overbearing manager standing there cracking a whip and telling them to move or keep going. It's them and this is their work ethic. So many 'performers' in the states could learn a thing or two from them, and the thought reminds me partly as to why I quit taking on larger acts a few years ago. Talentless 'stars' who wouldn't know hard work if it hit them in the balls, celebrities who got there because they knew the right people or had a pretty face, fake as fuck and I'm sick of it. These seven men in front of me, who started as boys, worked their asses off, improved, never gave up, who are now practicing one dance to one song over and over all day, are finally making a name for themselves and fuck if it doesn't make me feel inspired. I want to do everything I can for them, move mountains if I have to to get them opportunities they wouldn't get otherwise, and I know their talent and dedication will help me.

I send out the mass email and text to the members of staff I need to consult about the changes I want to make, asking to meet before everyone leaves for the night from the practice space. I'm not 100% sure of some of the technicalities of the contracts and my Korean translation, although Asha from legal back in the States at our headquarters assures me if my translations are correct I should have no problem resubmitting those points for renegotiations. But since I'm not sure, I want to discuss those points with the team first before just going ahead and changing them. I also want to touch base with the guys, since we've yet to have a sit down and talk business.

"Joon?" I say, coming up behind the tall man as the guys take a break from dancing.

"Hmm?" he asks, turning around as he towels off.

"I'd like to meet with you guys before the end of the night, preferably before the meeting I have scheduled with your staff."

"We're sitting down to eat, let's do it now," he nods.

"Oh, no eat, you guys need a break," I reply, waving my hand.

Either my voice or my action has the rest of the guys looking at me, all stopping what they're doing.

Joon smiles, shaking his head like what I've just said is funny. "Reb, we don't ever get a break, it's fine, we won't have time if we don't do it now."

He called me Reb. I smile; but I feel bad they don't have any downtime, but I also understand. You don't make it big and take over the world if you don't work for it. I nod, and then Joon tells the guys, who head off for their containers of food and come sit around me at the table I've been occupying for hours. I've already cued the translator program on my laptop with the presentation I have for them. A container is set down beside me before my shoulder's nudged and I look up to see Shoogi nod down at the offered food and then back at me. Did he just bring me food? I blink at him, more in surprise than anything else, before saying thank you, then quickly correcting myself and bowing my head in thanks. The sound of the folding chairs around me glide across the smooth white flooring as the guys come to the table one by one and sit around and across from me.

They must be tired and hungry since this is the quietest I think I've ever heard them. I'm typing and not really paying attention to who is who, but unconsciously count the number of chairs I hear. When there's been seven, I look up, happy that no one's staring at me but rather all are shoving food into their mouths. The lid to the food set down for me is removed and I glance over to see Shoogi is the one doing it, who also slides it closer to me in the process. But I don't want to eat until the presentation is over. I give them a few minutes to mow down and it's when they all seem to stop and drink the water bottles in front of them that I press the start button.

I propose my ideas for new ventures with the companies they already have contracts with, to expand and create new product. I also add that each contract has a cut to the label they're signed to, who I assume in turn takes a cut and divvy's it between the members how they see fit. As soon as the money talk begins, I look around at them, understanding that most artists, I mean the ones who do what they do for the love of it, cringe and instantly spike up when anything to do with payment comes up. But I don't see a reaction, which honestly surprises me. I'm stuck on it, assuming that these guys surely have a say in some of the things I'm mentioning. It prickles me, actually, it makes me sort of mad. If my suspicions are true, my hunch, then it down right fucking pisses me off.

My head turns as I search for one of the guys managers and when one makes eye contact with me and I wave him over, I look at Joon.

"Can you tell him to clear the room, please?" I ask, but really, it's a statement.

I don't wait for him to answer me but begin furiously making notes on a new document on my laptop, not giving a shit if the rest of the presentation gets talked about. Joon tells the manager and they go back and forth for a moment before the manager sighs and speaks loudly, the guys looking around and at me in confusion. The room slowly but surely empties, and I wait until the door is closed, and the eight of us are alone in the massive room.

Closing my laptop, I rest my arms on the table and look between the members. "I want your opinions."

"Hmm?" Joon and a few others question.

"I want to know your opinions on what I've said, the ideas I've proposed. What you should be paid. This is your show. You all work hard and devote everything you have to what you do. I want to know what you think that's worth. I want to know what things you guys want to promote, what you guys want things to be like, what you want your name on. I want to know what you guys want."

"We don't-" Joon begins.

"Don't tell me some formulated response that your label has branded into your brain. I want to know what you want."

It's silent after Joon translates. I feel the tension. I know I feel some kind of fired up inside myself and I hope they do too. They need to see this is their time to capitalize on what they work for and do. I've had this battle with nearly all my clients, but I feel like with these guys, it's going to be more like a war. It's not them who will fight me, but the company, however, I know if I have the guys behind me, it will strengthen my argument. When no one says anything, I sigh and take a deep breath.

"I know you feel indebted to the label, and I'm not saying you shouldn't. But I've seen the numbers, the money you bring in and you are not being paid what you should be. On top of that, I want you guys to be a part of projects and produce things you want outside of music. I don't think you understand that it's you that has the say, not your label. I hate to slam them, but you need to realize this is a business and that's what they're doing, making money off you, which is the point. But they also know they're nothing without you. No other group on this label or any other label in South Korea as a matter of fact makes what you guys do. You need to think about your future. Things are going to the moon right now for you, but in reality, it won't always. Think about ten years from now, when you buy a house, when you get married, when you have a family and you need to support them. Money is the side of things I know you don't want to think about or be concerned with. But you need to be."

They all look around at one another, not saying anything but communicating in a silent dialogue that only family and people who are extremely close can manage. I sigh and look down at the keys of my laptop, trying to think of another way to break through, when Shoogi begins to speak. It's low and slow as he looks at me and I turn my head to look at him.

His lips pout out in a way I notice that they all talk, but it's hypnotizing and sexy, even if we're talking about serious shit here. Shoogi talks with his hands moving gently to the rhythm of his words and at one point he brings them to his lips and runs one long digit beneath his bottom lip, then stops and looks at Joon, so I look at Joon to translate.

"We've had an idea to create...cartoon characters. A whole line of alter egos with merchandise and whatever else. We started talking about it a while ago as a supplement income, since we didn't think we could renegotiate contracts. But the idea grew, and we really want to do it."

Nods go around the table.

"We don't want to step on anyone's toes by going back on something we signed. We're grateful for every opportunity we've had and to those who took a chance on us in the beginning. But we do want to look further into new ventures with larger sponsors, worldwide sponsors. We think that will help us gain traction in other countries," Joon ends with a nod and a closed mouth, dimpled smile.

The words of two senior members opens a dialogue which Joon translates to me. Ideas of lowering prices on CD's, but adding more swag to each physical copy, including secret tracks. More talk about the cartoon characters which I can see having butt loads of potential and something the guys can get a massive percentage of the profits from. We talk for another twenty minutes or so until one of their managers comes in and announces break time is over. I give the guys all a smile and a bow as I thank them for their time and contribution. I feel that buzz I get only from my work charge me up, as they get back to practicing and I get back to typing. I have a lot to work on tonight before my meeting with management. I email a friend back in California who does graphic design to see if she can steer me in the direction of a group or business who could help me with the characters. While I wait for a response since it's only early morning in Cali, I get the information to contact the distributors for Massive Smash and request a meeting with them A.S.A.P. I need to find out if we can press the CD's for cheaper while still keeping the quality of the product intact. I've never had to handle CD production before so I'm unfamiliar and need to do some homework on the matter.

While I wait for replies, I also contact Cola-Cola, the largest soda distributor in the world. I send an email with an idea of making the guys brand ambassadors, how this would represent the world in which the company represents. I also attach a group bio, list of awards they've won, other accolades and achievements, along with attaching a few music videos of the guys. After doing some digging, I also find out that the guys are active in UNICEF and decide to attach the good deeds they and F.A.M.L.Y have contributed towards clean water distribution.

I'm lost in my work, not being distracted what so ever by the seven dancing, sweating, gorgeous men mere feet away from me. Nope, not once...well, maybe once. Or twice. Excuse me, my names not Saint Rebel...but it fucking should be. It's like as soon as I save the document, my alarm is alerting me that I have fifteen minutes until the meeting I have with staff and I'm tapped on the shoulder.

"We'll be meeting in the conference room. Min-ssi is here."

Min-ssi or Mr. Min in English, the President of Massive Smash and the man who, up until now, has been 'too busy' to have set up a meeting with me. I wonder if someone overheard my meeting with the guys and now his schedule has magically cleared up. Grabbing my laptop, I stand and stretch, making sure I have all my notes for the meeting.

"Fighting, Reb!" Joon says behind me and I turn to give the guys a wave as they cheer me on.

Strutting my way down the hall, I follow as I see staff entering a room and assume that's the place to be. Upon my arrival, I'm greeted by one of the managers who speaks fluent English and he ushers me toward the big boss, who's already taken his seat at the head of the table.

"Hi, I'm Kai, I'll be translating through the meeting," another one of the guys managers tells me as we reach the boss and I bow, yet I'm only responded to with a slight nod of his head.

He's a short pudgy man, dressed in casual attire and instead of acknowledging me, he looks through papers on his desk without a word. Everyone in the room finds a seat, while I see an empty seat at the opposite end of the table. Then, all eyes turn to me expectantly. With the Rebel nerves of steel, I survive on, I unleash my ideas. What I want to do with the group and what the group wants to do. The translator is somewhat distracting, but I don't let it trip up my flow as I rip through my presentation with gusto and passion, the way I always do, and when I'm done, I sit down.

Everyone is looking at me, then at Min-ssi. He barely made eye contact with me, but rather looked at the papers. It's something I can't stand, being made to feel ignored during a presentation, but oh well, we're carrying on with the things the guys wanted, whether this dude approves are not.

Eventually, Min-ssi says something before standing and leaving me there as everyone else gets up and leaves.

"What?" I blurt at Kai, who's the only one left with me in the room.

"He said you have six months," he tells me.

"What?" I repeat.

"I don't know."

With a near growl, I stand and begin stomping down the hallway, through the people who were once occupying the room and are now in my way.

"Excuse me!" I state, waving my hand in the air for Min-ssi to stop walking away to his office.

It's then I look back to see Kai like a mile behind me and I reach out, grab his shirt and pull him toward me.

"Ask him what six months means," I state.

Kai looks at me and then him and then back at me before speaking Korean. Min-ssi looks stunned by my behavior, but fuck this guy, how rude. He finally replies to the translator before again heading away from me.

"He said you have six months to do anything you want with them, if it fails, you go home."

Chapter Six

Six months, I can do a lot in six months. I've done more in less time, no problemo. So much about being here has been a dream come true. Living in Seoul. Working with a K-pop band. And not just any K-pop band, *the* K-pop band. It's been one week since I arrived and I feel like I'm making decent headway. I've looked into how CD manufacturing works and am all set for my meeting in the morning with the distributor. Although still trying to find a graphic design studio for the guys cartoon idea, I feel like I've also gotten familiar with the process via my friend in California, who I just might fly her ass out here to do it for us. Nothing in this business happens instantly, so I'm used to waiting. However, I make it a point to send a group message out to the members of KT7 daily in regards to the status of what I'm working on. We live together sure, but I always prefer things in writing and I think it also makes it easier for them to translate themselves.

Suddenly living with seven guys who happen to be clients has been interesting, however not necessarily all it's cracked up to be, even if it is only short term.

Don't get me wrong, as I've said before, all the guys have been welcoming and have gone out of their way to make me comfortable. But I'm sure it's strange as fuck for them to be abruptly sharing their private space with a clueless non-Korean speaking chick. Regardless of how freaking awesome I am. Particularly when you consider so much of their professional life is public fodder.

Thinking on it, I'm sure there's a Snow White and the seven dudes joke in this situation somewhere. Seven hot dudes, that is. All of who seem to have spectacular lips or incredible dimples. A few of the guys have both. FML. It's like having them was a prerequisite to join the band. I can see the talent scouts at Massive Smash now.

Sing? Yup.

Dance? You betcha.

Don't have pouty lips and dimples? Bzzz! Take your talent and go dude, we're only looking for kitty crushers here.

Speaking of which, you don't think living here with seven men hasn't been wreaking havoc on my cat. Good thing it's got nine lives. I'm fairly certain the wide-awake feline between my thighs is going to need all of them to survive this contract.

Several times I've had to quickly get my shit together mentally. Awareness slowly tickling along the back of my neck finally alerting me to the fact that I've zoned out watching their flawlessness as they interact with one another. Language barrier be fucked. I could wax poetic for freaking days on the incredible balance both masculine and feminine elements seem to have struck when creating each of them.

I'm sure they've all noticed my sly stare fests but they're so polite and respectful they must be letting it slide. That or they're having a field day hanging shit on me knowing I don't understand the language. Conversationally, along with the apps, we've all been relying heavily on intonation and facial expressions when Joon isn't around to interpret for us. Obviously, hand signals have been useful too. So, given I've not seen any of them throw the bird at me, or twisted their index finger near their temple while simultaneously pointing at me with the other hand I indicating that I'm crazy, I think we're ok. So far at least.

Which is why today, a down day for me, I'm taking my greedy eyeballs out and providing something else for them to look at.

The guys are on a day off too, but the reality is that they never truly are. For example, right now all but two guys are in the living space, furniture pushed out of the way, and they're working through the timing of a new dance routine. Like when has precision ever been an issue with these guys? Um, never! As for Jaimin and JK, from what I can gather, Jaimin seems to be of the opinion his vocals aren't strong enough. JK is with him in one of the other rooms doing runs, riffs, licks and other voice shit. Just the echoing of JK's voice, and hell, even Jaimin's through the breaks in the song playing on repeat in the living room have me flustered.

Regardless, the relentless work they put into everything is mind blowing. I knew going into this contract that these dudes were perfectionists, however since actually being here I've realized that there is no such thing as perfect for them.

They're always striving to be better.

To do better.

To give a more to their fans.

It's a work ethic like nothing I've ever seen.

It's inspiring and if I'm honest, it's a little worrying. That however is too big of an issue for me to be digging into at this early stage in our working relationship.

Banging outfit – black racer-back crop top, fishnets pulled up to cover my torso, black frayed jean shorts and combat boots, I'm ready to head down to the garage. Throwing my Alexander McQueen handbag over my shoulder while pushing my circle, black sunglasses that say CROSS MY HEART HOPE TO DIE STICK A NEEDLE IN MY EYE on the front of the thick black rims up onto my head, I make my way to the apartment door. I'm looking forward to my day out exploring the city I'm now living in, but I also think it's good that I'm giving the guys the day to be themselves. Without catching me gawking at them. I wish Hannah had the day off because not only could I use an estrogen fix, I could also use some girl talk and a drink. But sadly, she doesn't and I'm gonna trek the city alone.

"Redbull!"

I hear one of the guys call my name, so I turn back but leave my hand on the handle of the apartment door.

"Yo?" I reply.

Jinho is coming towards me and despite him speaking, it's the expression on his face along with his raised open palms that tells me he wants to know where I'm going. Approaching me, I take in his wideness, shoulders really. He's tall like Joon but has massive shoulders I would like to take a ride on sometime, that are also magnified by the long cardigan sweaters he wears often. They should look terrible on him, like something my mom would wear, but guess what? OF COURSE IT LOOKS SEXY AF ON HIM.

"Where go?"

"Out," I say and point to the door but Jinho doesn't react, so I try another approach. "Shop." Pointing to myself I then mimic carrying bags.

Jinho nods then aiming his voice behind him, loudly calls out in rapid-fire Korean and the only word I catch is my name.

One thing you have to get over when you don't speak a language, is assuming everyone is talking about you, because hello, you're so important.

But whatever Jinho is saying right now however most certainly *is* about me. Maybe he's just letting everyone know I'm leaving and that look on his face is more of recognition than anything else.

A chorus of voices seem to reply to what Jinho said and with his further reply rocketing right back at them, I'm getting the impression it's become somewhat of a lively fucking discussion and clearly my thoughts of this being something inconsequential is wrong.

"What's the problem?" I ask, letting go of my grip on the door and taking a step closer to him.

"You no go," he states, and while it has to be said it's polite, it's also an order.

One that gets my hackles up.

"Yes, I go. I'm having a day out. I've been working my ass off and I need a mental day off."

I shove a hand into my bag and pull out my phone. Messing with the touch screen, I spin it around and show him the search results I've found for local shopping areas.

The voices at the end of the hall are quieter which is how I hear the gently clomp of trainers coming our way.

Joon speaks with Jinho and Jinho replies.

Pushing my own voice back into this animated conversation I request, "Joon, please kindly tell Jinho I am a twenty-seven-year-old woman with a smart phone and an even smarter mouth. I can find my way around your beautiful city for one day. I made it all the way here without losing a kidney to the underground organ market, I can handle a trip around town."

Joon asks, "You're twenty-seven?" his face and tone a disbelieving one. But instead of me replying, I give him a pointed look. "Of course. That is not, um, problem," he tells me and before I can ask what the problem actually is, Jinho yells out a name I know only too well and then walks away from the bullshit he started.

Watching Jinho hastily leave, I continue to explain myself to Joon.

"Look I get you guys are super polite and might feel responsible for me or whatever and to tell you the truth there's a large population of dipshit American dudes who could stand to learn a thing or two, but this, is crazy right now. You guys enjoy your day off, and I'll go shop, find fashion that is extra, eat shit I can't pronounce but looks tasty as hell and I'll be back before it's dark."

Joon nods, a cheeky smile teasing his lips. "I understand all that, and I get you. But the thing is, in our culture, people usually don't just go out on their own," he stops, then looks at my attire.

"That's ridiculous-" I begin, a whole list of circumstances to which people would need to go out alone, but he cuts me off.

"And also, not dressed...as such," he adds.

Putting my hands on my hips, I look at him opened mouthed.

"Bare arms and showing too much skin is something our culture-"

"I'm not South Korean, I don't have a modesty/pride thing, I'm wearing what I'm wearing-"

Next thing I know, JK is charging towards us, the long lines of his body strung tight. His arms and legs moving purposefully with no wasted or unnecessary action. They're clearly the limbs of a man who commands attention when he moves. One who is deadly when he dances. His rich chocolate eyes are wide and trained on me and are the only reason I can think as to why I seem to be rooted to the spot.

He's talking to Joon, and like Jinho, his Korean is rapid and expressive, however JK's tone is much lower. Not softer, just lower. I'm certainly feeling it lower.

Shifting my bag from one arm to the other I use the movement to also press my thighs tighter together, casually crossing one booted foot over the other, leaning onto the open door. I'm not at all surprised to feel the heat level between them is on the rise.

I sneak a glance at Joon hoping to get a clue as to what the hell this new objection is about. All I find though is a full on, deeply dimpled smirk so I'm still none the wiser. My eyes decide for me to snap back to JK's and it's as though they're offended I'd turned them anywhere else.

Joon is explaining something to JK when a shock of candy-floss pink catches my eye. The noise level down the hall has increased again and I look around JK's tall frame to see Jaimin coming towards us, the cap he's pulled from his currently pink hair is being held out to JK.

I notice then that all the other guys are huddled together a few feet back, whispering and giggling like naughty school children.

What the fuck is going on?

I bring my focus back to the trio in front of me and see Jaimin has also been the bearer of a black hoodie and a wallet. Both items are now in JK's possession

"Fred's already lined up to drive me, I'm not going alone, so you dudes really need to chill..."

The look I get from JK stops any further words from leaving my lips. Him walking towards me and making motions with his hands for me to do the same stops my heart. The heat level in kitty territory has reached tropical and I wonder if I could get my hands to stop trembling long enough to DM my girls the moist gif. Probably not.

"Have fun!" Joon calls as the door behind us closes and I hear a cacophony of raucous laugher erupt the moment it catches into place.

Because it looks like I have a chaperone.

A very sexy, very recognizable so he will probably get mauled instantly, chaperone.

Oh, fuck it.

Who said you couldn't take in the sights of Seoul from the back of a luxury vehicle.

Not this chick that's for damn sure.

Chapter Seven

(Ilgob)

Sitting in the back of the SUV, it's quiet. I mean, quiet aside from JK softly humming beside me, a song I can't make out, but fuck. This guy could literally fart on my lap and I'd be swoony.

I don't know if I should even say something, if I should be pissed or grateful. This is his day off too and I'm 100% sure he doesn't want to spend it like this, but then again, he did volunteer himself. JK says something to Fred and I make out the district I mentioned wanting to go to, then again with the silence. JK's still holding the black hoodie that Jaimin gave him and I don't know why he has it, he's already wearing a black hoodie, the hood pulled up over the black hat with two silver hoops hanging on one side of the brim, he's also in his standard jeans and Timberland boots. The workman look works for him, and so does just about everything else the motherfucker wears.

I train my eyes out the window, taking in the beautiful sights of Seoul as the humming resumes. JK is quiet to begin with, well most of the time, other than when he's trying to make the guys laugh or is just being funny. The way he talks is low, not deep necessarily, but fucking pillow-talky. The way he sings is like that too, breathy and- fuck, just fuck. I cross my legs in the spacious back seat and note the sound of JK's humming shift direction, like he looked at me as I situated myself and I don't move my eyes from the window to look.

Moments later, something's tossed onto my lap and I look down to see it's the sweatshirt. Looking over, JK is putting one of those black surgical masks on over his lower face and nodding down at the sweatshirt.

"I'm not wearing this," I tell him.

Since all I can see are his eyes, I know the look he gives me is one of annoyance and the words he says seem to be one of exasperation as he snatches the hoodie from off my lap. Fred parks and I get out of my side, while he's opened the door for JK. I know I'm expected to go out the same side as JK, but whatever. I look up at what seems to be a mall-ish type building, one I recognize from online in my search and wait for JK to come up beside me. His elbow nudges mine for me to lead the way and so I do, as I also notice the increasing stares directed at me. At first, I thought it was that people knew who JK was, but you can only see 5% of his face with that mask, so no, it's me. I don't want to feel self-conscious, most people in South Korea I notice stare, that's what they do, but this is different. Or maybe it's different because Joon was right and I'm being a dick. Like he knows my thoughts, JK nudges my elbow again with the sweatshirt, and begrudgingly I take it, stopping as I begin to set my purse on the ground, but JK takes it, holding it for me as I slip the zip up over my shoulders. As much as I can tell he doesn't want to look at my exposed shoulders, he sneaks one more side-eyed glance before they're covered by the thick material. Even though it really doesn't suit my outfit, I feel more comfortable in it and almost like me covering myself also made JK relieved. Handing me back my purse, we begin to walk, and I take in the stores signs which all seem to be neon or flashing in some sort of way to draw customers in.

JK remains one step behind me at all times. I don't know if this is because I'm older and he doesn't feel equal to me, do I need to ask him to walk beside me? I don't know. But he follows me silently, in and out of stores. I like it. It felt weird at first, but I realized after the second store, that I think it's his way, observant. I start to hold up things I like and show him, seeing his reaction and eventually he begins to give me a nod or a shake of his head in-regards-to the item. When I purchase something, he takes my bag before I can even get my wallet back into my purse and replies in Korean when the cashier speaks to me. When we hit up H&M, he makes a noise and I look to see him nodding toward the men's section and I nod for him to go ahead. As much as I wanted to do this alone and for as much not talking as were doing, I find myself looking for him as I pass through the store.

I shouldn't like that he's babysitting me, but I do. I shouldn't like that he wanted me to cover up, but I do. Because even though I think it was more to stop people from gawking at me and me feeling uncomfortable, I think part of it too was for him too. In my head, I think he couldn't control his eyes looking at me in the SUV, that the sheer sight of my bare arm made him excited. There's something so sensual in knowing that hidden flesh is meant for a lover, that even the skin of my shoulder is desirable. I think about him humming, his lips right there where my shoulder meets my neck, low inaudible Korean being mumbled against my skin about how good I smell and taste as he glides his tongue along my pulse point. The low moan he'd exude as I lapped my tongue along his dick.

"Redbull."

My head jerks to JK standing beside me and then down as I realize I've clenched the hanging clothes in front of me with both hands as I drifted off into la-la land. Letting them go, I wince at the clear distress I've now imprinted on the materials and move down the aisle like nothing just happened. Shit, my pussy feels like a fucking jacuzzi and I don't even want to think about the state of my nipples right now. I'm more appreciative of the sweatshirt now, one that mind you smells like Jaimin's shower gel, since I assume one this small has to be his. It smells good, but having sat beside JK two times now, his smell is more enticing. So much so, I'm literally telling my brain to shut the fuck down and go offline before I do something stupid.

"Food," JK says from behind me once we've left the store and I nod.

This time, he takes a bit of a lead, knowing where he wants to go but also never losing sight of me. I'm surprised no one has recognized him, but again, covered face and most people here also have their faces covered so it's not like he sticks out because of it. Like a man on a mission, he leads us to the food court where I'm bombarded with some tried and true American standards in the culinary department. All of which have the food we all know and love with a little Korean twist, whether it be a shrimp burger instead of a fish sandwich, or bulgogi meat instead of beef, along with corn and sweet potatoes on pizza, they do shit different here, okay. But it's those little things I enjoy about the culture, taking something and making it their own.

We settle on Burger King where I tell JK to order for me whatever he's getting for himself and I go find a spot to sit. The area is busy as most mall food courts are and I find two high top stools along a bar that looks out into the street. Retrieving my phone, I open my emails and get caught up on some work shit that really has nothing to do with me. Sawyer's weekly brief email has my name and beside it simply states: South Korea and see below that Cassie is in Montana. Her name reminds me I need to take a pic of my lunch to send her and also remind her how loud South Koreans like to eat and what a turn on it is to eat with a table full of men. That thought has my brain catapulting into the future and JK reacting to his burger. Offline brain please! Opening the translator app, I type in what I want to say and have it all set for when my lunch partner sets the tray down between us. He's saying something, I think about the food and I make out that he's so hungry, and so am I. Sure enough, there's two of everything on the tray aside from one heaping dessert thing in a cup. We both unwrap our burgers as JK pushes his mask below his chin and we begin to eat. Once my stomach feels adequately sustained enough to set my food down, I press the button on my phone and bring it closer for JK to hear.

"Thank you for coming with me," comes out in Korean and JK nods, cheek bulging from food.

For some reason it doesn't feel like enough, again, it's his day off and what guy likes to go shopping with a girl. Taking my phone back into my hands, I type out my next translation.

"What did you have planned for today?"

After shoving more food in his mouth in a way that should be disgusting, he pulls out his phone. I admire the amount of food not only he, but all the guys in the group can fit into their mouths in one go. The way South Koreans eat breaks all rules we follow in America. They are loud eaters, slurping noodles, moaning with every bite, it's their way of enjoying food and complimenting the cook I've found out via Hannah. At first, I was internally cringing when someone would talk with food in their mouth, but now, I like it for some reason. It's rebellious in a sense to all I've grown up knowing, and who am I to dislike anything rebellious.

"I have photos I want to edit."

I've noticed he's always carrying a Nikon, other than now, snapping pics and seeing something through the lens that we don't.

"I would like to see the photos you take some time, if you're willing." I express via my phone.

Art being one of the clientele I represent, I've really come to spot the talent and intricate details artists create, even if it's a photo of a fire hydrant or some inanimate object.

"Would you?" he asks, setting his phone down, looking over at me with a small smile that doesn't show his teeth, and returns to his burger. I nod and begin eating again.

We're silent for a bit, eating and looking out the windows before us. I don't finish my burger but down my drink as he crumples up the wrapper for his devoured burger, pulling the cup of dessert toward him. Opening his chopsticks, he breaks them apart and secures them between his fingers as he digs into the patbingsu. He shovels in the top layer of red beans and fruit, then piles a smaller bit on the tips as he drives it towards my mouth and I open for him, accepting the sweet tasting goodness. Ask me how I feel about a guy feeding me back home as opposed to now. I know it's again something they like to do, and I've often see the guys feeding each other as well as sharing their food. It makes me feel, accepted. Like I've joined the inner circle or something. When in Rome, right?

We finish our meal and again, JK takes my bags without hesitation. I wonder if he wants to keep shopping because I want to go out to the street and walk around, so before putting my phone away I suggest it. He nods, putting his mask back over his mouth and I lead the way toward what I think is the exit.

Once we emerge from the building, I pause and look around, not having any clue where to go. JK walks past me with a slight bump of his hand against mine and I follow as he heads toward the SUV and Fred leaning against the side and reading the paper. JK speaks to him as he opens the backseat and tosses our purchases in, then he's walking toward me holding out something and I see it's a black face mask like his.

"What?" I ask in confusion, unsure why I'd need one of these, I'm not someone to recognize.

"For the fine dust pollution," Fred says loudly from his post.

"No sick," JK adds, moving closer with the mask.

The tone of his voice has me reaching for the mask with no hesitation, fuck ruining my make-up, my lipstick's already gone from eating, so I take it and put it on. I know he's being courteous and treating me like the other guys in the group have, but there's something clearly different since I like him in a different way. It's a special feeling, like being doted on and my wellbeing is so cherished that he would be concerned with my health on top of it. God, I was gaga over the man before I met him, but now, knowing him and the way he is, I can't ward off his witchcraft. But I need to keep my cool. I can't look too much into anything. He's just being him, being the guy he was raised to be, and I'm 100% sure he's like this with every woman.

We walk the streets and I knew South Korea would be beautiful, but pictures don't do justice to a place like this. No detail is missed on the newer architecture, looking flawless and so perfect it's crazy to believe it's manmade. We turn down a street with colorful store front signs luring you in, there are a lot of people shopping mixed in with those just passing through to carry on with their day. We pop in and out of shops, not buying but browsing and we eventually stop at a vender for some street food. It smells delicious however I have no idea what it is but go with whatever JK gets for me. I offer to pay but he ignores me, doing some research on the plane I read that men never go Dutch with paying, that they will pay no matter the situation with a female. It still doesn't stop me from offering, offending him or not.

Food in hand, he points over down the street and I begin heading that way, and for the first time, he makes the move to walk ahead of me and lead the way, checking back at me every thirty seconds of course. Nearing the end of the street, I see a black railing and trees lining something, but can't tell what until we get closer. Down a small hill just beyond the railing is a stream. There's greenery on both sides, along with cement walk ways on either side, little cement stones to cross periodically, and colorful paper lanterns crisscrossing back and forth over the water. It's fucking gorgeous, and I smile at the sight before me. Still leading, I follow JK as he starts down the hill to sit and begin eating. It's amazing how something in the middle of a city can be so peaceful, and even though people walk by, I feel like we're the only two around for miles. I keep taking photos and JK keeps nudging my arm and urging me to eat. I take a few bites of the delicious meat stick thing before resuming my photo taking.

This is when we start taking photos of each other, me for the sole purpose to send to my girls but using the excuse of it being for the food and Cassie. In reality, I haven't been able to take many photos of the guys themselves to send to my girls in our chat, so I seize the opportunity and snap away. I don't have to give JK much direction, once he sees my phone raised for a shot, he poses in some funny/fucking sexy way that comes so naturally I can only imagine how many photoshoots they've actually done for this to be so natural. I also feel like he's relaxing with me, showing me the funny side of him he tends to show the fans and his bandmates. I relish in the time, feeling like some fangirl giggling over everything he does, and I get the sense he's doing things intentionally to get that reaction out of me and by God he can fucking take it.

We start walking again and this time, we move side by side. Our hands occasionally graze or our bodies bump, and every time a zing of sensation shoots through my whole body. At one point the sidewalk narrows and gets crowded, so I grip the back of his sweatshirt as he tugs on the sleeve of the same arm. It's awkward, so instinctually I grab his hand and hold it as we stay together through the commotion. I can't help but smile over this, feeling his big warm hand covering mine, but the moment is gone a minute later when we're back to some more space and he lets go.

I feel like we've walked miles since the stream, which is fine, the sun is still high in the sky and if I had my way, I'd walk these streets with JK forever. I see signs for something coming ahead and again the walkways become thicker with people. He doesn't take my hand this time, but ushers me ahead of him and motions for me to walk. Beautiful, full bloom flowers come into view and huge leafy trees as a massive Buddha statue enters my line of site. I don't know what religion JK is, and I don't think it's about that, I think he wants to show me some of the amazing places to see in the country he lives in. We wander around the grounds, statues and temples married in with nature so well in a way South Korea has mastered the art of.

We spend a long time there, taking photos, of each other and me of the flowers. There are rose of Sharon plants all over and I take pictures when I see them because each one I see looks more stunning than the last.

"Mugunghwa...South Korean flower," JK tells me after I comment on how beautiful they are. He then types on his phone to show me, the Hibiscus Syriacus is the national flower and it makes sense why they're all over.

At one point we sit outside one of the temples to just take a moment to be silent and at peace. There's something about being with JK that gives me an inner peace too. We are comfortably silent most the time and I think he feels fine being this way with me also. I never get the feeling at any point today that he's bored or wants nothing more than to ditch me, go home, and do his own shit. I know I already said thanks at lunch, but as we leave the temple and stand in line at another food vender, I use my translator again to tell him thank you. He nods one time in return and I can't help but smile at how one simple gesture from him lights me up inside.

We eat and walk this time, I think heading back to the street of shopping we were at before the stream. When we arrive there, I give myself a mental high five for my sense of direction. Once done eating, we enter a small boutique and I'm instantly assaulted by my brain triggering and firing off that every item my eyes land on, I love. I almost don't know what to do with myself, where to go or in what direction, what garment to grab first. With a nudge to my back with his elbow, JK forces me out of the entryway and into action. I'm in fashion heaven and as I hold dresses, pants, shoes and purses up in front of me to get a closer look, I realize everything is from one designer and one I've never heard of, but guessing by the price tag I'm behind in the game. To own one's own store and have it filled with only your creations means this designer is a big deal and I want it all, unfortunately, I also need to eat and live for the next few months, so I can't blow a years-worth of salary in one go, but it doesn't stop me from trying on everything I want just to satiate the sadist in me.

I leave JK in the shop as I disappear into the changing area and for a moment I want to ask him how things look, but know better and instead, I snap pics of myself in the mirror to also send to my girls for second, third and fourth opinions. I decide to splurge on a pair of black pants that are torn up at the knees and fit my ass perfectly, along with a pair of mile high platforms that have a cool neon floral pattern that will match the pants. When I emerge and head toward the counter to buy, JK's already standing there and conversing with the cashier. The woman who'd accompanied me back to the changing area and spoke a little English, starts putting back the clothes I've decided not to buy and begins speaking Korean loudly. The cashier looks up at me and I smile, but I slowly begin to realize it's due to whatever the other woman's saying, and I decide to not take it personally, assuming maybe they think I'm poor or something. However, I can't ignore JK standing straight and looking over at me out of the corner of my eye.

Handing the woman my card, I look over at him, confusion on my face as he just looks down at me. I can't tell if he's smiling or displeased behind the mask and wonder if maybe he doesn't like what I've decided to buy. He takes the bag before I can and thanks the women, saying something more to the cashier who replies with a small bow.

"I think I'm all shopped out," my phone tells him, and he nods, turning toward the mall and we begin to head back. My feet are sore, and I feel like I've done adequate damage to my VISA.

Fred opens the back door and I slide in, noticing the tension from the store still on JK as he sits down beside me.

"What's wrong? Was it something at the store?" my phone questions.

JK looks at me, then takes his phone out. He begins vigorously typing on his phone, pausing and letting out a sound of thought and maybe frustration. This time, he doesn't let it speak to me, just hands me his phone and I look down to read.

"They were talking about your underwear."

My brows furrow, and he takes the phone back to type more. I was wearing a thong, what's wrong with that? At least I was wearing something. Again, he hands me the phone.

"No wear that here. Sex store sell."

And it clicks, they were shocked I was wearing something that's considered only for the bedroom. I swallow, feeling a blush creep over me. Was JK shocked too, offended that I was wearing that? I assume he was uncomfortable by the ladies talking about such a thing and maybe badly of me. Fuck, why do I care? So, what if he thinks I'm a slut or something. But no, of course I fucking care. Who wants a guy they like thinking badly of them? Not that being a slut is a bad thing, but you know what I mean. A million thoughts explode in my mind of what I can reply to that with. Like 'oh no my doctor told me to wear these, I need them for medical reasons.' Ugh. As I attempt to scramble a lie, JK's taken back his phone and is typing more, probably a stern warning that if I want all of South Korea to not know I'm a skank that I should wear proper underwear to try on clothes.

"You always sex underwear?"

I blink down at the phone, what the what? Is this bait? If I say yes, then he could possibly to lay into me about the slut shaming I'm opening myself up to via clothing store clerks. Or, was he genuinely interested in what covered my delicates on the daily? I think about earlier, when he could barely look at my naked shoulder. I type on my phone, feeling a rush of excitement pulse through me. This could be the moment I know for sure, based on his reaction, if he's into me. That he's not just treating me special because it's the way he knows, or because I'm different and new to his world, but that he's interested in what I'm laying down. Rereading my words for the third time, I hesitantly, with the mask of confidence, hand him my cell.

"Sometimes...sometimes I wear nothing."

Chapter Eight

(Yeodeolb)

It's been two days since my day trip with JK and I still feel buzzed from the experience. How did JK respond with my commando panty message? His eyes narrowed, he pulled the phone closer for a reread, then proceeded to fumble with the phone and it fell to the floor of the SUV, mumbling "Joesonghamnida" which means I'm sorry, over and over as he attempted to retrieve it and hand it back to me. I got the boy flustered and for the first time with him, I felt like we were broaching territory I was comfortable with, flirting. Mild flirting, but all the same. I felt like now when he looked at me, it was unlike before, like he was admiring me with different eyes and seeing me not just as some weird American chick that crashed into his life. I wanted time with him, just us, but knew that a trip alone would probably not happen again anytime soon. I often fantasized about scenarios where we ended up alone and no matter what, my mind didn't go to sexual, just having fun and laughing.

God, he has me fucked up and not knowing myself these days. Ever since I started being attracted to guys, everything was a rush to kissing, touching, sex, there was never just couples stuff, partly due to my parents being gone all the time and having an empty apartment. I never thought anything in the past was wrong or bad, but now I see that nothing was ever meaningful or a relationship even. I want that with him, and I know I will. But something about this, I was behaving differently than I normally would when I've been interested in a guy before. Why am I not lusting after him like a pig in heat? I find him sexier than all get out, and admire his looks and body, but his personality has me twisted. The way he seems to look after me, to care about my well-being. Jaimin does the same, and all the guys do for me in their own way for the most part, but something tells me that with JK I need to be smart about how I go after him or something.

While my head tries to make heads or tails of the situation, all hell breaks loose in Cali. I wake to Jaimin smacking my butt and then I recognize the ringing of my cell, I feel like I just fell asleep and don't even open my eyes as I answer.

"Reb, we have a situation," Sawyer says through the phone.

"Yeah?" I question groggily, as I sit up and try to navigate out of the room through the dark and half shut eyes.

It must be late if Jaimin's asleep already, either that or he was bored and crashed. The light on in the hallway has me getting my bearings just as Sawyer says, "Chapman Reeves is threatening suicide."

"Again?" I groan as I walk down the hall toward my laptop charging in the kitchen.

I know my reaction seems cold, but the guy's a painter, he threatens suicide at least four times a year. I usually freak over it, panic and damn near go into cardiac arrest. But then once he's calm he laughs and tells me it helps him get his creative juices flowing, makes me want to kill the bastard myself.

"Did he call you?" she asks.

"Nope-" I inform her, pausing as the other line begins to click, "That's him now."

"What do you need?" Yes, Sawyer's my boss, but she's also a part of the team.

"Can you head over to his apartment?"

"On my way."

"Chapman," I answer the other line.

The lights are on in the main living area and kitchen, but I don't see anyone and decide to go sit out in the darkness of the courtyard.

"I can't do this anymore, Reb," Chapman moans.

"Where are you?"

"On the roof of my building, I have pills too-"

"Sawyer's on her way over, you'll let her in?"

My tone is soft and calm, but inside I am nervous, fearing one day he might actually do it. Another reason for my annoyed reaction to Sawyer's call is a shield, a defense to protect me from shit I can't control, and not being in California to go and talk to him myself makes my stomach knot.

I sit on the grass at first, looking around the baron space that's enclosed by some bushes while a few separate seating areas have been hap-hazardly placed about. So obvious guys live here, I think to myself. I let Chapman do all of the talking, about how he hates his work, his career, hates his life and nothing's worth anything anymore. I try to not let his words affect me, because again I know in the end it's more like he uses this time to vent it all and conjure emotions but hearing him talk so lowly of himself is making me sad and again I wish I was there to hug him and sit with him. At some point Sawyer shows up and he begins talking to her and not me, setting the phone down but I can still hear him reciting to her all he's said to me. I'm relieved someone's with him, and even more relieved when Sawyer picks up his phone to tell me she's got it under control and will call me later.

Once we hang up, I feel the tears begin to pool in my eyes and I tilt my head back to look up at the sky. Since we're on a rooftop at the highest point of the city, I can see the stars unaffected by light pollution and smog. The stars shine bright and instantly, they call to me. The night sky reminds me of so many things, memories and comforts. I think about looking into the telescope with Mr. Anderson when I was a kid, thinking how infinite and grand it all was to me then and still is to me now. It puts into perspective that I'm one person, one little thing on this big earth in this massive galaxy and enormous beyond.

"Reb," JK's voice calls out behind me, I didn't know he was there, but it doesn't startle me. "Sad?" he then asks.

"A little," I confess, my eyes remaining on the stars.

JK steps closer, looking up for a moment before he looks down at me and then sits. He's close, so close I feel the heat from his body, although we're not making physical contact. I'm just in my sleep shirt and shorts, while he's in black track pants along with his black hoodie and I feel exposed in this moment, but with him, I don't mind. He mimics my position and looks up too and we're both silent for a while.

"Do you believe in destiny?" I finally ask although I think he won't probably understand anything I'm about to say. But the need inside me to talk, to confess and just let shit out makes it not even matter, maybe even makes it easier.

He makes a noise and nods his head slightly.

"You know some cultures think their destiny and the cosmic forces are linked? If they have decisions to make, they look at the stars. They look to the moon to decide when to plant crops. They won't get married during the new moon," I trail off, looking down as I bring my knees up to my chest and wrap my arms around them. "I felt like I was supposed to know you...one night I looked in my telescope and saw a shooting star. A few hours later I got the email that KT7 was a new client and everything made sense to me. I wished on that star that I'd meet you. I *knew* I was supposed to meet you...not just the guys, I mean more specifically *you*, Jung-keun. I thought it was just attraction, physical attraction, drawn to you because it was a sign I'd work with you. But when we met, there was something pulling me to you, undeniable attraction I knew went beyond what I thought. The longer I'm here the more I feel like destiny had it planned for *our* lives to meet at this time, at this place."

I look at him, as he drops his gaze and blinks over at me, confused naturally. I smile at him even as the tears hit me again, releasing the ball in my chest from listening to Chapman and JK's eyes take on such tenderness and almost helplessness as he watches me almost laugh as I try to collect myself.

"I'll also have you know I almost suffered from a heart attack trying to get you as clients," I state, thinking back to Sawyer's office.

"Pardon?" JK questions and I begin to laugh until once again it turns to tears.

I close my eyes and when I open them, he's holding up his arm, offering me his sleeve to wipe my face. When I don't move to take it, he lifts it toward me and runs the thick cotton down both my cheeks to clear them. When he drops his arm, we're leaning toward one another and I want to hug him, or for him to show me comfort through a touch or something. I don't know if in this culture I'm supposed to verbally allow him to be physical with me and that it's ok.

"You can kiss me," I whisper.

His eyes drop to my lips, then back up to my eyes and I part my lips in expectation.

"Chuwo," Jaimin says from somewhere behind us, and JK pulls away.

Looking down at his hands, he and Jaimin exchange words and I look over my shoulder at Jaimin, smiling in apology since my phone call clearly woke him up. Moments later, JK stands and looks down at me, saying something before I understand, "Come."

I get up and follow him over to Jaimin who's looking at us smiling, that smile that makes his eyes vanish and JK smiles back but smacks a hand on his chest as he allows me to enter the apartment ahead of him. The two go back and forth and I guess I should go back to sleep, but I know my mind will be racing over the Chapman thing and just the feelings of having JK hear my confession, even if he didn't understand.

"Reb, game?" Jaimin says from behind me and I turn to see them in the living room by the flat screen, both looking at me.

I can see in JK's eyes he wants me to play, I can't explain it, but like he doesn't want me to go away. Maybe it's in my head and it's what's comforting me, but I like where my head is at.

I nod and walk back over as they both grab controllers and turn on a game console in a bureau. The television flicks on and then the main menu to the game screen, at the same moment a strap connected to the controller is slipped onto my wrist and then pushed into my palm for me to grab. Jaimin is controlling the selection and JK is barking out orders in that way they talk to each other and I smile as they bicker over which game to play. Then they pause and look at me before pleading their cases to me about the game I should pick. I don't know what they're saying but I know what game I want to play, and I point at tennis. JK groans as Jaimin cheers and raises his hand for a high five, which I comply. We stand apart from each other and after the two do more bickering, I watch JK motion his hand between us as to let me know we're on a team together.

We play this game for almost two hours, then a driving game neither me or Jaimin are good at so we complain and crash purposely over and over until JK finally wants to quit. We play a dance game, well, they play a dance game. I like watching them obviously, but eventually after a few rounds they catch on to my non-involvement and urge me for a turn. I let Jaimin pick something for me, "Wake Me up Before You Go-Go" by WHAM and I bounce and Carlton my way through the routine, and much to their surprise, I get nearly a perfect score. I admit the games and these two are keeping me entertained, but I also can't help but feel a little guilty over the Chapman incident earlier. Even after Sawyer texts me sometime later and gives me the all clear, Chapman himself sends me a message saying he loves me and hopes I forgive him. So maybe it's not that that's making me feel so vulnerable tonight. I told JK something significant to me about the shooting star, that feeling of confessing to someone something private and almost slightly embarrassing is tough enough, but to reveal it to the person it was about and they probably didn't understand the heaviness, well that's a whole other feeling.

I'm happy with having met him at all, I'm happy with the relationship we've established thus far, I think in me telling him a sliver of my obsession before I got here was because I do want things between us to move along, clearly, I told the boy he could kiss me. Now, I wonder if that was the right thing to do. I've never worried about coming on too strong, normally that's not even a blip on my radar, but I think I may have crossed the line with this one. Looking at him as he dances and plays the game, his mouth open, his eyes zeroed in on the moves on the screen, his body moving like a well-oiled sexy machine, it hits me. Crossed a line? What the fuck is wrong with me? It's the mess with Chapman and feeling sorry for myself that JK didn't hear what I said and tackle me immediately that has me doubting myself. I need to snap out of it, I won't let Chapman and his selfish ass ruin my time here and this time right now.

We play until the sun is beginning to rise and it's then we all realize we've been up all night and in some silent decision, all head toward the bedrooms to try and get some sleep. Heading into the bedroom before Jaimin, I decide fuck it and not re-wash my face or change my pajamas for clean ones, since I already got ready for bed hours ago. I flop down practically face first, not re-alizing until my body's melted into the mattress that I'm still in Jaimin's bed and nowhere near my own. Fuck it, his bed's big enough for us both. My eyes close and I feel Jaimin get in the bed behind me, sleep coming over me when I feel Jaimin get in the bed behind me, wait what? A hand curls around my back and side, a hand resting under my hip. Turning my head and opening one eye, I see JK there, cuddled up beside me as he takes a long breath and closes his eyes. Jaimin says something on the other side of him but I give up the battle and fall asleep with JK's face the last thing I see.

* * *

I can't explain the flutter of excitement that went through me when I woke up that morning and JK was still right there. He was still sleeping, his face soft and perfect. I just looked at him, the room a muted light from the sheers in the windows. I knew Jaimin was still asleep and I didn't give two shits if he woke up and witnessed my ogling. I'd never been able to just *look* at JK. He's more perfect in real life than I ever could have imagined. No, he's *not* actually perfect. His skin has some marks and a scar on the bone of his cheek, but it's perfect to me. Stubble is coming in on his cheeks and upper lip, his mouth open in a way that only he can make look attractive. I just look at every part of him that's visible to me, including his hand which is currently resting on my stomach. Fighting the urge to touch his face, I can't resist the hand, taking it into mine and pausing at that moment I make contact. This small interaction makes me feel some kind of way. I lift it off me and reenact the first human seeing another human or some shit. I touch his fingers and compare the size to mine as I press my palm to his. Jaimin sighs and the bed shifts, clearly knocking into JK's back because his body's jostled, and I take a glance at his face to make sure he's still asleep, but he's not.

"Annyeong," I whisper as his sleepy dark eyes blink heavily.

He mumbles the same back before closing his eyes, then removes his hand from mine and effectively pushes me to my side and pulls my back up against his body.

Chapter Nine

We've been sleeping together ever since. I figured the first night was because he thought I was still upset from my phone call, I think that because the next morning Jaimin asked if I was better as JK stood there waiting for my answer. It's been several days since then and every night it's sort of become a thing for the two of us and Jaimin to stay up late, either eating or playing some games, usually both. Jaimin by no means is a third wheel, he's fun and I like how him and JK interact. I'm not sure how JK feels about him always being there since I can only understand a little of what's being said and by the tone, but I think maybe part of that is my brain living in a dream land where JK wants to make out with me for hours. Instead of that though, Jaimin remains, and eventually we head to sleep and all tuck into Jaimin's massive bed that could fit everyone in the house.

This morning however, was different. I woke up in the middle of the bed, remembering I'd gotten up to use the bathroom and stumbled my way back in the dark, using my hands to find the bed and plopping my ass in a free spot. I knew once I opened my eyes that Jaimin wasn't in the room, and neither was Hooni. For the first time, JK was awake before me and I instantly felt a flutter of anticipation in my belly. He was looking at me in that way, the way I'd translate as simple horniness. We were both in hooded sweatshirts and sweatpants, my face clear of makeup obviously and hello, looking like I just woke up, but his eyes saw so much more, again maybe wishful thinking, but let's pretend.

"Reb," he whispers, his voice deep and gravely and I inhale deeply at how it hits all my g-spots.

We're far away from each other, like three people could fit in the space between us and when I don't reply, he reaches his hand out for me across the empty mattress, curling his fingers in a 'come here' gesture. With no hesitation I put my hand on his and he's sliding my body to him, turning me over and scooting his body against my back as he settles in for more sleep. His breath dances along my cheek, and I wish my hood wasn't on, so I could feel it on more of me. I can barely feel his body with the layers between us, but I imagine he's hard and my mind wanders as my insides feel flustered with excitement and sexual pent-upness.

When the day came that my apartment was ready and inhabitable, I was afraid that the move would change the dynamic between us. I wanted to tell him he could come over and stay the night whenever but had yet to find a good time to say something to him privately. I could text him, but I sexily wanted to whisper it in his ear like in the movies or some shit.

The Jaimin and Jinho helped me move the two suitcases I had with me in, but really it was more to check out the place and see if they could somehow take over some of my space for their own. I'd already told them they were welcome anytime and even gave them the keycode for the front door. As much as I enjoyed my stay with the guys, I was ready to be by myself, but most importantly, I was happier with the fact that I'd not have to wear a bra nearly 24/7.

Joon called the apartment manager to deliver my previously received boxes from storage and as they began to arrive, the rest of the guys did too. Their chatting voices oohing and aahing as they entered every room. I of course had not picked any of the interior of this apartment but to say it was decadent would be an understatement. Where the bands apartment is elegant yet manly, this is straight-up modern and minimal, chrome and marble were the theme I was noticing most. White, like, everything, from the decor to the walls, white, white, white. Of course, as a chick, I immediately looked at the towels and knew those would be ruined, between make up, hair color, and periods, yeah, they were goners.

JK was the last to enter, straggling in minutes later and nearly startling me as I practically turned into him. He smiles sweetly at me, before looking down at my chest and slowly his brows began to furrow. Instantly I begin to feel a little worried over his reaction to me, oh shit, do I have a bra on? Yes, yes, I do. Well, then what the fuck?

"Hurt?" he asks, looking up at me.

"Huh?" I question.

He nods toward my shirt, and I look down, remembering the writing on the front.

Anything you can do, I can do bleeding

"Oh, no-it means-"

"Geunyeoui sidaee gwanhangeoya." Joon says, as he walks passed us to set a box on the kitchen table behind me.

JK's face becomes even more confused looking but I know Joon told him what the shirt meant.

"Noonaneun sangdanghi mueongaibnida," JK says with a lift of his chin.

"She sure is," Joon replies, throwing an arm over my shoulders as JK walks off in search of his brothers.

I could've hired a moving crew, but noooooo, I was legit scoffed at when I suggested such a thing by the guys, so when they start hemming and hawing about the boxes weight and amount of shit I have I just shake my head and shrug. But I decide to make some dinner for us as a thank you and get to unpacking the kitchen shit in the process. Really, it was all provided with the place, but I brought a few of my favorite must haves, like my Frankenstein and Dracula salt and pepper shakers. I decide on spaghetti since that's what's in the cabinets along with some other American staples Sawyer must have made sure were here for me.

It doesn't take me long since it's prepackaged noodles and jars of sauce, like I do at home which makes me feel like a loser since everyone here cooks like everything from scratch. But oh well, and for a moment I feel like I should pitch it and go get real food to make. Just then however, Jaimin and Jinho enter the kitchen, sweaty from working and sniffing loudly as they banter and move toward me over the pots. It's then I feel like this is fine and know they'll eat damn near anything. With a wave of my hand, I ask them to set the table as I drain the noodles and add the sauce, mixing it all as the guys come to the kitchen and get drinks before sitting at the table. I'm about to carry over the massive pot when a muscular torso pushes against my back briefly before thick veined, long fingered hands move over mine and replace them on the hot pads covering the handles.

JK gives me a side grin and I sigh as his biceps bulge while he removes the pot from the stovetop. Following behind, the guys cheer as the food's set in the middle of the table and Shoogi stands to begin scooping the pasta out to the awaiting raised plates around him. I laugh to myself that they're eating like we do in America, I guess since maybe this is my place or something. I walk around the table to see a seat left conveniently free beside JK and then realize I didn't get a drink.

"I got," JK says, and I look to see two glasses of ice water next to him.

Sitting down I look around as everyone gets their food and begins to eat, noticing JK is also holding up my plate along with his and when the first plate is full he sets it down in front of me. Who said chivalry was dead? We wait for Jinho to begin before we all follow, and the food is met with exuberant and at times overly animated sounds with how good it is. Not that they're mocking me or humoring me, but more like they are goofballs 97% of the day.

After dinner, the guys clear the table and do the dishes as I move to my bedroom and begin unpacking, mainly bedding. Joon shouts down the hall that they're leaving and thanks for dinner and I shout back thanks for helping me at the same time I turn to see JK standing in the doorway.

"Oh," I startle, before chucking the pillows in both hands onto the bed.

"You ok, sleep alone, here?" he asks.

Was he concerned or was this opening the offer for him to come over tonight? He moves closer as I say, "You can keep me company-"

"Jung-keun-" Jinho says from the end of the hallway and immediately we're pulling away.

We both stand there, just a step away. I want to rush over and kiss him, but my feet stay rooted. JK steps forward, reaching a hand out for me before he stops at his eldest brother calling his name again, this time closer and we both look to see as he enters the doorway.

"Annyeonghi gaseyo," Jinho waves, blowing me a kiss to which I reach out and grab to smack onto my cheek, his smile is accompanied by a small bow and I stay focused on him as JK mimics the same words and movement, before walking passed Jinho.

"Bye," I say softly and doubt either one heard me.

I like this chemistry between me and JK, but damn, he's doing serious damage to my libido. Quickly, my unpacking turns to hunting for my vibrator.

* * *

I feel almost as flustered right now watching the guys during dance practice, holy water sweat dripping off them and making their porcelain white skin glisten.

JK and I keep locking eyes, but as usual when I watch them dance I feel like they're snake charmers and I'm the snake, unable to look away or control my reactions. So, when he catches me, I don't look away, too dumbstruck and amazed to react. It makes him smile. But he quickly looks away and gets back to concentrating on working. I can't ignore the feeling it gives me though, when we connect, it makes me think stupid things about tackling him in front of everyone and getting a sample of the Korean beef.

"You're hungry?" Joon asks, and I blink up at him, realizing the music's stopped, the dancing done, and the guys are toweling off and I must've said that last bit out loud.

"Hmm?"

"You want to go for barbeque?" he questions with raised eyebrows.

"Oh, sure...I could go for some meat," I smile to myself while also praying there's no wet spot on the back of my pants while I stand.

Looking around I see JK not with the others, but rather talking to the choreographer and searching through something on his phone, before music begins again over the speakers.

"What kind of meat do you like?" Joon asks innocently.

"Short ribs, but I will take a sausage every now and again," I reply teasingly, even though my sexually charged comments go unnoticed by this lot, I still can't let a good opportunity go to waste.

Joon nods but doesn't react, as expected. The others grab their stuff, but not JK, he's now showing some moves to the choreographer. The others grab their shit and we head for the doors, while I attempt not to look like a lost puppy or something, but apparently it isn't successful.

"You can bring him the food back," Joon tells me, throwing an arm over my shoulder. Even though they've just danced their asses off for hours and should smell like a dead pig rotting in the sun for days, they of course don't. One shopping trip when I was in need of some deodorant and couldn't find any, Hannah explained to me that Koreans don't produce bacteria that causes body odor, which means they never smell like gym socks. Lucky jerks.

We go to a place not too far from the rehearsal space, gathering into an eating room where Shoogi orders the food and we sit around the long table, Jinho turning on the cooker built into the center of the table. The two cook the food to perfection and we all wait for Jinho to begin eating before the rest of us. Shoogi seated beside me is quiet as usual, eating and listening, like me. I understand a lot more than I used to, but fuck if I can contribute to a conversation. Hooni and Jaimin laugh a lot and get Jinho going about something, and even I laugh at his reactions. Shoogi tries some soup and in a move that has me shook, slides the bowl to me after a few bites while saying something in his low baritone of a voice, and I look at him unsure.

"He wants you to eat, says you're too skinny since you come here," Joon tells me, not looking away from his food.

I nod and help myself to some of the soup before sliding it back to him to finish. I nod again, thankful that he's concerned about me and happy I've once again stepped closer to being accepted by them. It is true, I think I've lost a few pounds with no cookie dough ice cream or trips to IN-N-OUT burger several times a week, but I didn't think anyone would notice. Maybe I should market the South Korean diet, I should copyright that shit.

We sit and eat for over an hour, the guys talking and eventually they all take turns trying to teach me some of their language. Some of the words I straight up butcher, and most of them are able to control their laughing, aside from Jaimin that is. Finally, Shoogi cooks a last plate and when done, puts it in a container for me to take to JK. I didn't think Joon was serious when he said that, but shit I guess I am.

Jinho says something and Joon asks me if I want someone to walk me up to the rehearsal space as we pass by the building, but I tell him no and thank him as they leave me to head inside. My insides are a ball of cracked out butterflies as I take the elevator up, and even more so when I hear the music echoing down the hallway. It's the same song he's been practicing since I came here and one I guess he's doing just for fun. Tapping on the door first, I then realize he won't be able to hear me, so I open the door. The lights are now dim in the all-white space, as he dances in front of the wall of mirrors. If I thought he was sweaty before, Christ, he's drenched, so much so his white dress shirt is sticking to his skin. The holy water is dampening his hair and drips down his nose and I just stand there. Watching. Fucking wanting. He looks at me in the mirror and slows to a stop; but doesn't turn around. Something, maybe my libido, has me setting the bag of take out on one of the tables beside me and walking to him, throwing my hair into a ponytail in the process.

"Show me," I tell him.

"Eh?"

"I want you to teach me this dance," I clarify.

He's still looking at me in question and I reach back to take my phone from my pocket to translate, but he moves to me, putting his hand on my wrist and taking the phone.

"Ok...you need, stretch," he tells me, walking my phone over to the table where the food is and setting it down.

I stretch as he begins to eat, still standing and still bathed in that sweat of his. I make a show of stretching of course, his eyes never leaving me as I see in the mirror. When I've finished, he approaches, wiping his mouth with his hand as he brushes past me to restart the song. Standing beside me he begins to move slowly; two steps then stops, and I mimic. This is how we do it, he demonstrates a few moves at a time then watches as I do the same, repeating it if I didn't do it quite right. Through the whole thing, I can't tell if he thinks I'm an ok dancer, but I don't care. The way he's looking at me in the mirror, the way his body moves, the way he smiles and lets out little laughs here and there has me ready to do just about anything.

After a thousand run throughs, my muscles are yelling at me to stop, but I'd rather eat shit than let him know he's worn me out. So just before the song starts over, I rush over to his phone and take it, searching for something else. The Yeah Yeah Yeah's- Date with the Night. It's rock and fast, something totally different then what we'd been listening to. The music comes on and I watch as JK's expression changes from question to a small smile, becoming a full-blown smile as he says something. I come toward him but move away as I thrash around and bounce on my feet, but halfway through the song I notice he's not moving. He's standing there watching me and we lock eyes. I give him a playful smile and look down as I raise my hands in the air to really go crazy.

Before I know what's hit me, hands grasp my head as JK pulls me into him and his lips slam onto mine. It's famished, I'm not sure it's even a kiss what we're doing because his lips are there but it's more his hands touching my hair and face before he's wrapping his arm around me and pressing me as close to him as possible. Kiss or not, I like it. I like it so much that I gasp, more to get my heartbeat to regulate and not burst from my chest with adrenaline. He's touching me, intimately, and it feels so surreal yet I've never felt so aware of a moment in my entire life. I'm focused on him so intently, I'm honed-in and I feel like my skin is his, like the touch is so familiar yet not, I want to explode. I gasp again and pull back, taking his face in my hands as he lets out punchy breaths, his eyes trained on my lips just before I re-secure them to his.

His fingertips dig into my shoulder while the others grip the back of my shirt by my butt into his fist. I want to lift my leg, to grind against him, anything to have more of this. Instead, I lap my tongue along his lips, changing the angle of my head in hopes he'll open his mouth and we can play some tonsil hockey. A good make out sesh beats a dry hump anytime for me and besides, I really like this. A few laps of my tongue and he slowly parts his lips, allowing my tongue to slide just barely inside his mouth. He mumbles something, gripping harder, almost too hard, but again, I like it. The definite steel rod of his erection is pressed against my abdomen and I want to reach for it but know that's way too fast. Not too fast for me, but I think for him. I like *this* just fine. He has me pulled so tightly to him I don't think I could squeeze a hand between us regardless.

"I'm so wet," I moan out, lost in everything and JK moans deeply, mumbling more words as he begins to back me up toward the mirrors.

My back doesn't even hit them as his arm still around my shoulders bears the impact before both his hands move to my chest, cupping me over my shirt. The once tentative kisses have become hot lashes of tongue and slick lips, his hands shaking as he fondles me. My fingers slide into his still sweat soaked hair and I grip it in my fists, firmly pressing our lips together.

"Joesonghamnida," I hear to my right just as Jaimin covers his face from the doorway of the rehearsal studio.

Immediately JK pulls away from me, running a hand through his hair to fix it as he stands in front of me. Jaimin begins to laugh and tell JK something as JK replies annoyedly, waving his hand in a gesture I translate as go away. I can't help but smile, putting my hands on JK's waist as I press my lips against his shirt and leave him with one small kiss before walking toward Jaimin.

Chapter Ten

(Sib)

We headed home with Jaimin that night from the studio; I sat in the seat ahead of them in the SUV as the two men conversed behind me. Jaimin's laugh filled the vehicle periodically as I can only imagine he teased JK. I however was glad for the solitude as I felt the phantom of JK's lips, his hands, his energy. His kiss was something I can't describe; it left me needy and charged up, fiending for more. It literally had been minutes and my brain was shooting off ideas of how I could get him alone once we arrived back at the apartments. But then again, I didn't want to rush things. I took out my phone, my fingers hovering over the keyboard, wanting to message him and invite him over. That's too eager. There's that part of me, again, that wants to do things differently with him than I have in the past.

I can say I never wanted more with anyone before this. Doubts come to me that should dampen my thoughts and libido, like he's younger, he lives half a world away, he's an up and coming mega-celebrity who probably won't even have time for a relationship anytime soon, but I remind myself why I'm here and what brought me here.

Putting my phone away, I run a hand over my face, feeling the heat of my cheeks as the guys continue to talk. JK's tone is quiet and controlled with an edge of unease and I wonder if it's more that he's embarrassed, but it can't be because of Jaimin walking in, he shared a room with the guy for years I doubt there's anything that could embarrass them at this point. Maybe they're making fun of me. No, stop, you didn't do anything wrong. He made the first move. But you tempted him, Rebel.

I was silent as we entered the apartment building, riding the elevator and I gave a quick goodbye as they stopped outside my door and waited for me to get in. I think they both said goodbye in return and I also think that JK remained there, maybe wanting me to invite him in as I closed the door. From the moment I was alone, showered, getting ready for bed, I found myself sighing. My head, heart and freaking hormones were fighting, and none were being rational. Destiny or not, he had me feeling some kind of way and a way I needed to get a grip on.

Pulling back my overstuffed down comforter and white silk sheet, I prop my pillows like I like and turn off the lights, grabbing my phone as I lay down. Opening my social media apps in no particular order, I end up on twitter and see a post from JK. It's in Korean so I have to copy and paste the freaking thing on Google translator to read:

I wanted to sing this to you as you fell asleep...

Followed by the link for a song.

What? Is this directed at me or F.A.M.L.Y? The song is Crime by Grey. I've never heard this before, so I click on the link and as I do, my messenger app alerts me to a new convo. Opening it before YouTube comes on, I see it's from JK who I've aptly renamed in my contacts as The Holy Water Supplier, THWS for short.

THWS: Twitter. Rest well.

Fuck. My eyes widen, the song *is* to me! and I immediately jump back to the other app, shaking like a chihuahua and let the song begin. I sit up before the end of the first line.

Tipping toeing down your spine when everyone's around
Kiss me hard forget them judging eyes
Who cares about what is to come no I don't fear the night
Let's show 'em what it is to be alive
If nothing is for keeps, can I keep you just for a minute?
I don't know what's real but I really wanna feel you now
Get a little too close can I stop your heart for a moment?

Was he...fucking with me? Like flirt fucking with me? Are our stars aligning? I bite the corner of my lip and copy the link for the song I want to respond with. Posting Touch by Little Mix on my Twitter, message: 'Have you ever been kissed so good you don't know what's what anymore?' Switching back to messenger, I shoot JK a text.

Me: Twitter back to you. Sleep tight. Xx

Feeling satisfied and of course that rush of anticipation that comes with a good flirt, I'm not shocked when my phone vibrates. However, I'm a little deflated when I look down and see the notification is from Cassie, one of my ride-or-dies.

Giving it a few minutes in case JK responds to my song tweet, I come to realize that talking to Cass might be a better way to go. Not only am I a little worked up and eager to share the details of that bone melting kiss, but I think JK and me ending our day by sending each other a song is sorta perfect.

The downside to having waited a few minutes is that other girls have since weighed in to the group chat, and in my absence are spinning theories faster than a F.A.M.L.Y vlogger on YouTube after a music video release.

Reading the notification highlights on my lock screen so I'm prepped to join the fracas, I can't help but giggle.

Cassie: Hooker, didn't take you long to eat Korean beef? Deets. Now.

Piper: Korean beef. LOL. Got her sending out sexy-ass songs, too.

Ryver: My money is on Dimples. I think she said he speaks English.

Allyson: Wait, do you ALL think it's one from the group?

Cassie: Fuck yes!

Piper: Yup.

Ryver: Yep.

Allyson: No...really? Aren't they all pretty young?

Cassie: Girl, please. Age is nothing.

Piper: And it's not like Reb is the Crypt Keeper or anything.

Ryver: No, but she does secretly listen to NPR. #Grandma

Cassie: Bahahaha. I forgot about that.

Allyson: What's wrong with listening to NPR?

Piper: Nothing, Ally. Fill you in later.

Clemmie: Saw the Tweet; catch me up – who's the clit twitcher????

It's early morning on the west coast so the girls being awake doesn't surprise me, but that they've all jumped on so quickly after Cassie's message reminds me what a bunch of gossip clams they are. Fuck, I miss them.

Thumb print to unlock and tapping to open the app and then the thread, I decide to jump right in.

Ryver: NFI. Ghosting?

Cassie: Masturbating!

Clemmie: Flicking it!

Those last two arrive at almost the same time, and all the girls fire off laughing face reactions. Bitches.

Rebel: I'm not ghosting. Not flicking it either.

Though fact was before I went to sleep, I likely would. I could still feel that kiss, *and* the song he sent, *and* the song I sent back.

As I'd expect, my joining the conversation had all the girls firing off messages at once, swooping in to pick at the details of my tweet like starving vultures who've discovered their next meal. This was a change for me, because if I was honest, I'm usually the one doing the snooping on the deets of *their* love lives, not the reverse.

If you ask most people, I'm an over-sharer. I have few boundaries and have no qualms telling it like it is. But this pull I have towards JK, it feels so different. And I mean different in a way that I really like. Like if I tried to convince myself it wasn't meant to be, *this* feeling would be a constant reminder that it's more than just an attraction. As I think about where to weigh in with the girls, I'm finding myself feeling protective of it. And that is a strange feeling too. Again, strange in a good way.

Fuck. One kiss and THWS has taken my crush and known destiny to another level. Must be sorcery, plain and simple.

Chapter Eleven

(Yeolhan)

The next day, I felt like I'd had the best coffee infused by IV, but really, I was still jacked from the kiss. The kiss JK laid on me, like dancing, was the second-best thing he was good at, the first being singing of course. I can say I've never been kissed like that, and it's true, but I've never felt this way about someone before, that also is bound to change feelings and reactions to things, such as getting my mouth fucked by the lips of a God.

He was looking at me differently today. Like he was keeping a secret and I couldn't help but also feel the same. Our looks were more frequent, longer, and always caused both of us to smile. I worked as he did group stuff and then...I get my period. Fuck. I grab my purse and quickly rifle through it for something, but all I have is a pantie liner way at the bottom. Leaving my laptop, I grab my purse and head to the bathroom to line my underwear with toilet paper and think of where the closest mart is.

I head out to the street and begin walking until I find a drugstore at the end of the street. Popping in I scan every isle since I can't read the signs, but in the back find some packs of pads, but no tampons. I grab the pads because I need something thicker than this toilet paper-boosted liner like stat.

Putting my pack on the counter I ask the woman in the best way I can if they have tampons, which involves pointing at the pads, then using my hands to mimic a tampon being inserted into a vagina. However, she must not major in mime and looks at me like I'm a crazy woman, so I give up and when I exit the store, I open Google on my phone but it's taking forever to load. While I wait I shoot a text in my group text with my girls and also one to Hannah.

Me: Tampons in South Korea, find some, aaaaaand go!

Just then my internet decides not to be a dick and loads, typing in the search, I'm met with less than comforting results. I read that tampons are hard as fuck to find.

Cassie: Oh fuck, friend.

Ryver: You shouldn't use tampons anyway. A natural flow is best for your body.

Me: There has to be something, I looked to buy them online and they have to be flown in.

Ryver: I'll send you a diva cup, that's much healthier.

Me: Fuck being healthy Stevie Nicks, I want to shove something artificial inside me to soak up this freaking reenactment from The Shining.

I take a breath and chill, I got pads, I'll be fine, but I should definitely run home since I've destroyed my underwear. Thankfully, I wore a jacket today so when I approach Fred sitting inside one of the SUV's parked outside the Massive Smash building, I'm able to covertly place the jacket on the seat before I sit down. We get to the apartments quickly and I tell Fred I'll be back shortly and ask if he needs anything. He nods and tells me he'd like to grab a bottle of water, so together we head up to my apartment, my jacket securely tied around my waist.

Hannah: Sorry, I'm just seeing this. I have a box you can have, I'll bring it to work tomorrow.

With my mind on the goal of getting to my room as soon as we enter the apartment, I'm stopped in my tracks when I see boxes and endless racks of clothing greet me.

"What?" I say aloud, mouth falling open as I step toward one rack that has a slip of paper dangling off the hanger. It's a receipt from the store of the designer I went to with JK, the one who's entire collection I wanted, at the bottom of the order is JK's signature. He bought me the whole store! I think I start to hyperventilate because I don't know what's going on, my mind's spinning as Fred gives me an odd look.

"He bought me all this!" I state.

With raised brows and a shrug, he moves into the kitchen for the water. I don't know how I managed to get into the bathroom and clean myself up, but when I go out to grab a new pair of black stretch pants, Fred is moving all the clothes into my closet.

"You can't have all this sitting in the living room," he shakes his head, and I nod like yes that's rational in this moment.

We head back to the Massive Smash building and I b-line it to Hannah, who's just walking back into the practice space. Taking her arm, I sidle up beside her.

"Sorry I forgot to tell you all about the tampon thing-"

"Never mind that," I cut her off with a wave of my hand. "I need some advice."

"Yes?" Hannah asks.

"You mentioned before about Korean guys like to take care of girls they might be interested in," I whisper since there's filming going on and I don't really want everyone knowing my business, English understood or not.

"Yes," she nods.

"But is it like normal for a guy who might like you," heavily pronouncing the might, "to buy out like a whole store for you and have it delivered to your apartment with no note or word from him?" I rush out.

Hannah's face lights up, looking how I imagined I did when I walked in on the very situation I've described.

"Oh my God, who did that for you?"

"Is it weird?" I repeat.

"No, not at all...I mean, extravagant yes, but no not weird."

"Really? Cuuuuz' I feel weird about it," I nod and shake my hands in front of me, which Hannah takes and squeezes.

"Why is it weird?"

"Because," I lower my voice, "we haven't even slept together, we're not even dating," I state. "It's just...too much."

"Maybe for you. Korean dudes love to take care of the ones they're into. They would spend massive amounts of money on friends if they knew there was something they wanted, or thought would make them happy. That's just the way it is."

Her words still don't stop the anxious feeling I have about my gift. I feel undeserving, unworthy almost and I don't know why. I don't for one moment feel like he's done this in order for me to feel the need to pay him back with something like spending time or sleeping with him. Agh, I just can't accept all of it.

"Are you gonna tell me who?" she further asks.

Hannah is well put together, like all the time. She's wearing a fitted black dress shirt and camel colored pants that seem to be tailored just for her, her long hair pulled back in a bouncy pony with long bangs framing either side of her face.

"Why do you always look so nice?"

"What do you mean?" she giggles.

"You're always so...done," I shrug.

"Oh, I well, I vlog clothing and makeup, like I get them and try them and then review. I have a bit of a following so I'm always getting fabulous clothes," she smiles.

"Shit, cool," I smile. "Oh, and as far as telling you...I'm not sure I can," I state, looking down as I think.

"I've signed an NDA, I'm not allowed to say anything that goes on here or with the group. Not like I would, even if I haven't signed one."

"Jung-keun," I blurt out, covering my mouth after with how loud and liberated I just disclosed the name of my suiter.

"I knew it, I see the way he looks at you, he's definitely smitten," she gushes in a whisper and takes my hands. "I want all the details."

"Let's sneak out for lunch and I'll tell you everything."

A few hours later we're cleared for lunchtime and Hannah and I practically skip out of the building like two teenage girls with a secret. Instead of eating, we snag cold drinks from Starbucks and hit up a cosmetic store she likes. I fill her in on everything with JK up until this point as she fills my basket with all the skincare go-to's she says I need to have, along with some basic cosmetics she claims will change my life. Noticing Jaimin's shower gel and the whole line of the brand for men, I snag a bottle in thanks for letting me use it along with some little extras to make as a gift. I don't think JK wears cologne, but I sniff some different kinds because maybe I should give him something as a thank you for the clothes. Hannah said guys are into getting gifts here just as much as chicks are, so why not?

We chat as I get the stuff for Jaimin wrapped and JK's cologne, and Hannah finally dishes to me that she too has a crush but doesn't tell me who. It seems like she's more into him than he is into her, but she says he's very cool on the outside, but she knows he's into her too. Neither has had the guts to ask the other out and she swears she's happy with the way things are, being that they're both really busy. I believe none of it of course, but ok girl.

Arriving back at the label building, I see the guys are just finishing up watching a video of them practicing as we walk back in. Shoogi heads toward the bathroom as Jinho and Joon walk over for water so I know they're having a little break. JK is re-watching the video with Ye on one side with Jaimin and

Hooni on the other, and I don't think he sees me. Jaimin smiles and turns to me as he notices me approaching and his eyebrows raise as I extend the gift toward him.

"It's a thank you gift," I nod, "For sharing your room and shower with me," I add.

"A-thank you!" he says sweetly, his smile larger, his eyes becoming slits and he hugs me.

The other guys notice what's going on and come over to check out what I've given, and they walk off so Jaimin can set it on a table to open. I remain standing there because JK is still there and looking at me, then toward the others as Jaimin seems like I've given him a puppy or something. Am I nervous? Before I can lose my cool, I outstretch my hand with the wrapped cologne. He looks now between me and the package and I wave my hand a little for him to take it.

"I got you this."

The smallest smile takes his lips before a full-blown grin, and it's then I really see why they tease him about looking like a bunny. It's not only his teeth, but the way his nostrils curve his nose up and the bridge crinkles. Did I just sigh? He takes the gift and for some unknown reason, I turn and walk out of the room and into the ladies' bathroom in the hall.

I've never felt like this; a guy has never made me nervous or feel like I was barely grasping the reigns of keeping my cool. But shit, I'd never met Jungkeun before.

I manage to get my shit together long enough to sit at my laptop and pretend to be working when all I can think of is what he thought about the gift. Then I think about the clothes he sent to my apartment. I hope he doesn't think my gift is bullshit after giving me something so extravagant. But my period is killing me in all fairness and the fact that tampons here are harder to find than a virgin the day after prom is still blowing my mind.

I avoid eye contact and sit away from him in the SUV, but I feel his eyes lasering on the back of my head the whole time. But more importantly, I haven't said shit or thanked him for the more than generous gift he gave me. The guys are tired and don't say much as we enter the apartment floor and I divert at my door. Punching the code into the lock, I quickly get the door open and close it, feeling disgusting from wearing pads all afternoon.

Heading to the kitchen, I search the cabinets for something to eat, but a shower is all I can think about. So, I take some Motrin I'd brought with me for the cramps and head to my room. However, I pause in my closet when I see all the gorgeous fucking clothes that are now mine. God, I should've bought something better than cologne for him. The beauty of the clothes reminds me how nasty I feel and head for the showers. Fucking white everything. After avoiding ruining the bathroom, I pack my panties up like a damn diaper, wrap myself in some plaid pajama pants, a KT7 sweatshirt and head for the kitchen. A knock at my door has me pausing, spinning around and heading back to the door.

I don't know who I expected, but I'm a little shocked to see JK standing there.

"Hi," I smile, and he looks at me with his hood up, his eyes inspecting my face.

"Sick?" he states.

"Eh, no, but I don't feel great," I shrug.

"Eat?" he asks, holding up a pizza box.

The smell hits me and my stomach growls, I give him a wider smile and open the door for him to fit through. Without waiting for me, he walks to the kitchen and sets the box down. Bypassing plates, he grabs some napkins I have in a little holder beside the fridge and puts two out as he opens the box and grabs two slices.

Moving beside him, I take the slice and begin eating. By the time I've finished my one piece, he's on his third. The pizza is good, and I know he's ordered it as American as he can, with pepperoni, ham and peppers. The gesture makes me feel so cared for, on top of all the other shit he's done for me.

"Thank you...for-" he stops his words and mimics spraying cologne on himself.

"Of course, I mean it's no closet worth of clothes," I shrug as my words fade on my tongue and there goes that damn feeling of losing my oomph with this guy. "I've never received a gift like what you did for me. I'm sorry if I don't really know how to thank you, the cologne is stupid, but I didn't know what you'd like-" I ramble.

"I like, very much," he cuts me off and I'm paused with my mouth parted, just looking at him.

Before I know it, he's moved closer to me, like right up to me and stands there looking at me expectantly. It's then I realize he's wearing the cologne and I don't know why it hadn't dawned on me before, but I could smell it on him when we ate. Leaning in, because hello his force field sucks me in and I gravitate to him, inhaling deeply as I look up at him, our eyes engaging one another's. The scent I chose is deep and warm, yet it's not heavy or over-powering. It accents his own scent and makes my pussy immediately flutter in reaction to the burst of sexy tang. I've purposefully leaned in closer than necessary, locked eyes and the way I'm gazing upward all mimics a closeness I want to more than hint at. When I begin to stand up straight, I adjust my feet, so the rest of my body is close to his, so close my chest nearly grazes the black shirt covering his torso. Breaking eye contact, I blink down at his lips, his perfect pink lips, the bottom fuller than the top and looking in need of being sucked.

The idea causes me to swallow before my lips part and I'm breathing heavier, without having any mind at the moment, I lift a hand. My fingertips tentatively reaching to brush over his lips and the moment they do, a rush of air bursts across my skin. The same moment, my ovaries have other ideas and cramps take the lead. His brows furrow and I turn my head.

"Sorry...I'm on my period, these cramps are killing me," I sigh, annoyed at being a girl as I often do during this time of the month.

"Oh," he says, clearly understanding my words just fine. "You come," he adds and takes my hand.

We leave the pizza and the kitchen as we walk to my bedroom. He turns down the bed, tossing the 300 pillows I have onto the floor, leaving only three, one for our heads and one he knows I like to have between my knees. I crawl in as he says something in Korean and holds up one finger. I lay down and hear the front door open and close, shutting my eyes as I put a hand on my lower stomach and press on the affected area. Not too long later, the door opens and closes once more, before JK is entering the room, holding up a white flat object. I can't tell what it is, but he peels off the backing and I see it's shaped like a large kidney bean.

"You put...where hurt," he nods, handing it to me and when I take it, he heads into the bathroom.

I feel the white thing heating under my fingers and it must be something the guys use on sore muscles or something. I quickly put it over where my cramps hurt the most and get it settled by the time he comes back into the bedroom, turning off the overhead light in the process. Grabbing the remote with a level of comfortability that has me smiling to myself, he turns on the television across the room as he lays down and opens his arm for me to nestle into his side. He begins humming softly and I close my eyes as he covers us with the duvet. I inhale his new cologne, him, and the certainty that this is all meant to be.

Chapter Twelve

(Yeoldu)

A few days later, period ended and a nice spring in my step, I head into the guys apartment, my laptop against my chest with one arm while a coffee mug and cell occupied my other hand. With some maneuvering I made it through the door and am greeted by silence. The place is big anyway that unless anyone's in the main living space or kitchen, you hear nothing from the other parts. I know everyone's home regardless since we have a meeting in ten minutes and these guys never miss appointments. Setting my stuff down on the table and firing up my laptop, I walk into the kitchen to raid the fridge. Grabbing a container, I briefly open the lid to glance at the contents which is noodles and some other shit, I hear voices coming from the hallway and am greeted by the guys as we meet at the table.

"Redbull!" Ye and Hooni exclaim loudly, still enjoying not being able to pronounce my name.

Taking my seat, I'm able to sneak a few bites of food as the guys sit down and get settled.

"You really come here just to eat, be honest," Joon says beside me and I smile as I take another bite.

Looking across the table, I stop chewing momentarily as my eyes land on JK, who's sitting across from me and seems irritated I'm talking to Joon. I give him a little wink and put the food down, clearing my throat as we begin the meeting. This isn't about anything major, just the things I've been working on and trying to book for them in America. They all look at me confused for a bit, even as my laptop translates my pre-typed notes out to them.

I look down at the screen as the line that's speaking robotically is highlighted as it goes. Then it happens, the news I received only thirty minutes before is finally announced to them.

"What?" Shoogi questions as they all glance around at one another, looking shook and confused, and I can't hide my smile anymore.

"The line of animated characters has been arranged. You guys have an appointment to meet with the graphic designers this Thursday to design your own characters and get started on the line you wanted."

The guys are elated, and I can see they already have in mind the things they want for this. Not only what they want the characters to look like, but also the kinds of merch. The idea of this line being successful, then the next possible step is opening stores and I make a note to begin looking into that.

* * *

After the meeting, I'm washing the noodle container out in the sink when I feel someone standing behind me.

"I want to show you photos," JK's translator app says to me.

Looking over my shoulder, he's standing so close I have to tilt my head up to meet his eyes. For a moment, I'm overtaken by his presence, remembering how he took me in that kiss the other day. Yes, he did take me, took me, owned me, controlled me, mouth fucked me, and it's all I've been able to think about.

Yes, we shared a bed, but we've now taken the next step, we kissed and I feel like we finally broke some invisible boundary. Lying in bed together was contact, completely clothed contact. Whereas the kiss was skin on skin. To me, a kiss can be so much more intimate than sex sometimes, you're so close, so personal. I wondered since, if he felt how right we were through the connection of our kiss. His lips were everything and all I wanted was to feel them again. I was desperate for them, for him.

We've made eyes a lot since then, and those moments never fail to get me hot and bothered. We've been posting song links on twitter, and one he sent to me directly on messenger last night. Echos- Say it. The lyrics had me thinking a million things. Was he trying to tell me something and I wasn't understanding? Or was he just wanting me as badly as I wanted him?

My limbs are weak from trying to reach you, oh
My body moves in languages only you can speak in
My heart aches for your touch when I'm sleeping, oh
I feel you move in distances worth keeping

I think I've broken some sort of world record for amount of times one person has listened to a song, because when he sends them that's all I listen to. Music is our language and it's the one thing we can 100% communicate with, other than the use of our phone translator. But there's definitely something sexier about music than a robot talking to you.

He plays the translators message again since I haven't answered, and I blurt out a yes, shaking my head to clear it. He stands there waiting for me as I finish washing out the container and put it in the drying rack. Once I'm done, he turns and begins walking as I follow, my black six-inch high heels clapping on the marble floor down the hall, my high wasted mini-skirt ruffles with the movement as I happily follow the strapping young man ahead of me. I'm oblivious to the others in their rooms as we pass by, and they don't seem to take much notice of us anyway. My outfit might seem overdone for the occasion of the meeting, but there's one thing I've learned here, that South Korean people don't often dress down, especially females. No throwing on sweats and UGG's for a trip to the market, oh no, that would cause everyone to look at you like you had two heads. I've realized that fashion and esthetic are key in South Korea and I'm up for the challenge.

JK's dressed in all black today, even his shoeless feet are covered in black socks, the hood of his sweatshirt pulled up over his head and long enough that it covers his muscle clad ass. Still, even though he's covered head to toe in fabric, I still ogle him as he strides ahead of me. There's something that has changed about my fashion sense while I've been here, and that is I do tend to cover up more. It wasn't conscious, I just found myself one day realizing that I tended to go for long sleeved shirts, high necked, or long cardigans. If I wore skirts, I wore thigh-high stockings or tights. I could tell that it put JK and some of the other members at ease when I wasn't showing off my skin like a buffet and I felt like they deserved that level of respect from me.

JK reaches his room, opening the door and walking in, holding it open for me as I walk past. I've never been in his room and I pause as soon as I take in what's around me. His room looks more like a digital media office space in New York, with computers, equipment, camera lenses and heavy-duty utility boxes that I assume hold more of the same within them. A massive computer desk takes up a lot of one wall, with two computer screens, a camera sitting beside one while the other has a microphone and some sort of recording equipment it looks like.

He retrieves another desk chair from somewhere and rolls it past me and beside the other leather one in front of the computer screen with the camera. He sits and so do I, rolling the seat closer to the desk and closer to him, although the arm rests of both chairs compete with me. I cross my legs and place my hands on the top of my black thigh-highs, waiting patiently and trying not to inhale his cologne, the cologne I gifted him by the way, or scent of his room, when I notice a reed diffuser between the two monitors that smells woodsy and warm. Then there's some Polaroids scattered just beside, and I know they're from Jaimin who's notorious for taking them. There's one of JK alone on top and then just beneath I think I see the side of my head, the blonde hair most certainly mine. I wonder if Jaimin gave it to him, or if JK wanted it, maybe asked for it even. Those crack smoking butterflies begin to spark up at the thought.

JK mumbles something and I look over as he seems to be talking to the computer and a moment later the screen is filled with a photo. It's black and white with a large waterfall.

"Bergen," he says.

"Oh, the fjords in Norway?" I ask, looking back at the screen.

I see him nod out of the corner of my eye and put the setting to slideshow before he sits back in his seat and we watch the endless photos of scenery go by. There are a lot of the guys too, and himself with some stunning landscapes as a backdrop.

"We...travel...before...just-us, for...fun" he tells me.

"I love that," I reply, *really* fucking loving that even in off time, these guys would rather spend time together than with anyone else.

I'm lost in the photos to be honest, leaning on the desk with my chin resting on my hand. He's really good and these are beautiful, and I tell him so.

"You could be a professional, but I imagine that might take the fun out of it," I comment.

But he doesn't reply and that's ok, it was more a statement than a question. I'm so absorbed by the computer that it takes me a long second to realize that JK's hand has slid over onto my knee.

My eyes scan his profile, my leg being scalded by his hand like it's on fire and I realize, he's nervous. Or maybe, again, unsure? But how? He already knows I'm into him and obviously him asking me to look at the pictures was a ruse to get me in his room, which by the way, where the fuck is his bed?

Looking around the room again, I see a tiny ass bed raised up like a loft, no wonder he liked sleeping in Jaimin's bed.

"Hawaii," he adds, his other hand back on the mouse as he hastily clicks now at the photos to move them along.

How can he be nervous when he knows I'm clearly down for kissing, I've allowed him to cuddle, and I certainly didn't push him away at the studio. I practically humped him, was he not understanding that I was down for anything he wanted to do with me? Uncrossing my legs, I put my hand over his, watching his Adam's apple bob as he swallows before licking his lips. With my hand over his, I slowly move them up my stocking, pausing when we meet bare skin. The index finger of his other hand clicks the mouse faster and I adjust myself on the seat, moving forward to open my legs a little wider. And then, our hands disappear beneath my skirt. I inhale deeply as I feel his pinky, then ring finger, then middle finger brush across my lips. Yup, no undies for me today. He must realize it at that moment as his head turns so fast to look at me I think he might've popped something. Our eyes lock as my hand moves over his and guide him to cup me.

"Jeon-e han mal-eul malhaejwo," he whispers.

But my eyes grow heavy as just his fucking hand there makes me feel like I'm about to bust.

"Jeon-e han mal-eul malhaejwo," he repeats.

"I-I don't know what you're saying," I whisper back, my chest rising as I inhale, pushing my hips toward his palm.

He moves to grab his phone to translate, but I shake my head and press him closer between my legs. The idea of the computer voice telling me anything right now, would ruin the moment. He makes a sound, like a grunt and moves his face toward mine. The computer chair armrests hindering us from getting too close, his eyes watch my face as his fingers remain still.

"Wet?" he asks, and that word from his mouth, fuck. Me telling him I was wet when we kissed, he must've liked that.

"Give me your finger," I request, moving my hand to his wrist as he extends his middle finger toward my body and inadvertently against the opening of my pussy.

A sigh escapes me as he also makes a noise as the chairs creak from being pushed together so tightly. One finger, just one, is resting there, hell, all of his fingers are just there and still and it's making me crazy with need. I don't know why he's hesitating, if he's teasing me with some sort of orgasm denial bullshit, but I need that finger and I need him to stop playing. A moment passes when we're just looking at each other and that current of sensation that happens just when we lock eyes has me nearly rocking in my seat. His eyes seem wider than usual, his breathing noticeably faster and it's clear I have an effect on him. But, he's still not doing anything, and I get the sense it's not deliberate, but I don't know what it is.

I feel like I need to be the one to move this along and I think he wants that too. I stand, sending the chair I was on rolling back a bit and JK looks surprised at my abruptness. His hands fall to his lap and I pivot to push the keyboard further back on the table before standing in front of him and taking his hand in mine as I push my skirt down with the other and let it fall to the floor. I stand there in my top, thigh highs and high heels. JK's eyes drop down and he blinks quickly two times as his mouth pops open, his breathing grows loud and he leans closer on his chair. It takes everything in me not to guide his face between my legs, but instead, I place a palm on his cheek as I look down at him and his eyes trail up my body to meet mine. Biting my lip, I sit up on the edge of the desk, lifting my feet to place them on either side of his knees on the chair and guide his hand toward me. We both watch as I hold his wrist again, using his fingers to brush over my bare lips, his middle fingers slipping between and stroking my clit. I moan and tilt my head to the side, my hair falling over my shoulder as I close my eyes and use his hand.

"Wet?" he repeats, and I bite my lower lip, looking at him as I open my knees wider.

I draw his hand closer, causing the tip of his finger to enter my sopping wetness. JK makes an almost surprised sound, I know I'm wet, shit I'm always drenched around him, but regardless this shouldn't be a shock to him. Again, he mumbles things, things I can't understand but I don't care, I like his tone and know he's obviously enjoying the barely penetrating sensation on his finger. Lord knows I am. I keep him there, thinking this will spur him into action, but he just stays there, frozen, so I begin to manipulate his hand, causing his finger to rim my entrance. With that, I'm lost. Sensation takes over and that primal urge we all have to get off. My gaze blurs as my eyes drop to his lips, his parted lips and ends of his two front teeth. I begin to grind on his digit, inhaling the scent of the room and our heavy breathing assaults my ears. I groan and reach for his other hand, turning it sideways so he can strum my clit.

"Oh...oh my-Jung-keun," I moan.

His finger shines with my juices, the sound of being penetrated, pornographic with how wet I am. It's then, something shifts, changes and it's like he realizes he's in this moment or that this is happening, because he shakes off my hands and inserts another finger while pressing harder on my clit. My head falls back as he begins to drive into me, faster than I was and definitely harder.

"Yes," I pant.

My tits bounce beneath my shirt with his efforts and I wish I could sit up on the desk to play with them, but I need my hands to support me. There's so much I want in this moment, for him to put his mouth all over me, for me to taste him, for us to fuck, but no, I don't want that. This is what I want, just him, just this feeling, we can do all that other stuff later.

His fingers curl up inside me and my back arches, my knees drawing in as I feel my orgasm hurtling towards impact. I keep chanting 'yes' and 'more' and he obeys, my eyes opening to see he's watching my face, lips parted as he breathes just as hard and fast as me and then I come. I fall forward into him, my arms wrapping around his head as I pull him into my chest. He looks up at me, kissing my cheeks and then my lips. My limbs feel sedated and lethargic like I've just been shot up with the best smack this side of the border.

A sharp knock against the door has me jumping and pulling away, but JK's fingers remain inside me, my walls still trembling around them. I don't hear the question but know it's Jaimin. My hips begin to move away as to get off the table, but his fingers won't leave, and he moves deeper inside me as he stands and looks down at me, his free hand cupping the side of my face. Blinking up at him in confusion, because surely, he knows Jaimin won't stop until we open the door, his eyes pin with me the softest look it nearly takes my breath away. I swallow thickly and close my eyes as his forehead meets mine, the need for words not existing, and my chest tightens with the feelings I have for him. The banging on the door grows louder and more insistent, but I know there's no emergency. JK begins to grumble and attempts to get me on his lap and back on the chair, but I don't want to be caught with my pants down.

"He won't leave," I whisper.

JK shouts over his shoulder and Jaimin replies, but JK doesn't and then the talking and door banging ends. With that, JK successfully slides me onto his lap and begins to move his stiff digits once more inside me.

Chapter Thirteen

(Yeolses)

Even though I was fully fine living in my apartment, I kept going to the guys apartment, like all the time. Yes, I live alone in the states, but for some reason I just didn't like being alone in this massive apartment. Orrrrr maybe it was the eye goodies I was addicted to in the next unit.

I think they became accustomed to me being there all the time anyway, because no one seems to really give a shit when they see me rooting around the fridge or laying with Jaimin on his bed as we play with our phones.

I also noticed a perk to constantly planting myself there was all the free shit they gave me. When new merch came in, the guys always received boxes full of swag with their names on it or posters and what not. They'd all sit on the floor and couches in the living room and open the boxes like it was Christmas morning. Originally it started because they received little backpacks with a galaxy background with their names on them, JK took one look and tossed his on my lap. Did he know I liked stars from the time on the patio, like he *really* understood what I told him that night? Or just thought I'd like it in general? What he did popped off each guy seeing who could toss me their swag fastest when something new was retrieved from a box.

It's funny, but really, they give me awesome shit and I don't care whose name is on it, I'll wear it. When I turn up with a sweatshirt with SHOOGI on the back, or a shirt with V's birthyear on it, all the guys tease and love seeing who the lucky guy is that day. I think it's more to get a rise or annoy JK, yes, he smiles, but then I see him pushing his tongue into his cheek and I know now that that's a move he does when he's irritated, or shall we dare say, jealous? Sometimes he bickers back and forth with the guys and I assume it's over me, so I just smile to myself and watch those pouty lips.

I also feel like in this time, I've connected to the guys in our own ways. All the guys love to shop and hello, so do I, so we do that when we can. Ye, Jaimin, and I love to use apps on our phones with each other, Shoogi loves to nap and I appreciate that, Joon loves to discuss books and music with me, particularly some of the artists I've worked with in the past. Hooni and I find the same things funny and often laugh at one another laughing at whatever we found funny. Jinho's been trying to teach me to cook Korean cuisine, and I think I've made progress so far. But for some reason, I don't think he agrees.

"What...is this?" he asks, looking down at the bowl in front of him nestled in my hands. I have to say Jinho's English is probably second best compared to Joon's, being that he tries to create sentences.

"Bibimbap," I nod.

His brows pull down, "You need lay the-"

"Don't look at the plating," I stop him with a hand in front of his mouth. "Just eat it," I tell him before putting a bite in his mouth with chopsticks.

He chews, his eyes remaining on mine, not giving me any signs of it being good or not. Finally, he swallows and turns back to finish the kimchi he's working on, leaving me with raised brows and anticipation.

"Well?" I question with annoyance.

"It is...okay," he shrugs.

"Okay?"

He shrugs again.

"No, really, tell me honestly. If I want to get better, I need-"

"Terrible," he says, looking at me.

I pull a face, more from disbelief because I thought it was pretty good. But I'm also shocked by his boldness and comfortability with telling me such a truth. I feel like it's a breakthrough of sorts, like I've been initiated and welcomed to the group.

"Well," I sigh, putting the bowl down on the counter beside us. "Don't hold back what you really think," I say loudly.

"I won't," he smiles, looking back at his task.

With a smile on my face, I sink my hand into the bowl and take a fistful of the rice I made and bring it up to his face, smearing it down. His shocked expression has me laughing, and he says something in Korean before a handful of Kimchi is pressed against my cheek and rubbed across to my other cheek. My mouth falls open before I burst out laughing, and then it's on. We both reach for the bowls of ingredients and other things on the counter, not throwing, but deliberately walking up and rubbing them on each other's faces and hair. We're both laughing and speaking nonsense as we make a mess, eventually leading to me slipping on the floor and dropping to my knees,

Jinho following, as we then scoop up mess from the floor and continue our fight.

"What are you doing?" Joon's voice booms through the kitchen and I rub my hand down my eyes to clear them, Jinho and I both freezing as we look up at him.

"Jinho's teaching me to cook," I get out before a laugh.

Jinho says something before starting that infectious giggle of his that has me laughing until my stomach hurts. Turning to look at him, seeing his state and him taking in mine, we fall over one another laughing even harder.

I hear the other guys entering, being alerted to something going on in the kitchen, asking I assume what's going on, before they're silent, also assuming the silence is due to seeing us.

"I'm gonna throw up," I gasp, trying to stop laughing.

Looking up, my eyes land on JK, who's giving me a disapproving look and doing that thing with his tongue against his cheek.

"Neoneun eongmang-ida," he says, reaching a hand down for me.

"Thank you, Jung-keun," I state, trying to regain some sort of professionalism while savoring the sensation his hand caused my whole soul, not to mention the strength he used to lift me up.

"Oppa," he corrects.

I groan playfully, "You wish!" I guess guys wanting to be called *Daddy* crossed all continents.

His eyes smile, and I realize then probably what the fuck I look like and then his teeth show, and I, for the first time, truly feel like he's teasing me. Just then, the alarm on my phone begins to chime and I remember I have GNO with Hannah tonight.

"As much as I loved to stay and clean up, I have to get going," I slyly say as I stand without slipping, and dart out of the kitchen and to the front door as Jinho shouts after me.

Chapter Fourteen

(Sibsa)

Have you ever noticed how it doesn't matter where you go in the world, all bars smell the same?

Stale beer, fried snacks, and depending on the health code, lingering cigarette smoke. Even in the bars that have not allowed smoking for years, the smell has permeated into to the bones of the space as though it's part of its DNA, and nothing short of major renovation is getting it out.

The Bulldog Pub in Gangnam is one of those gastro-pub joints, The Bulldog is British themed and by the looks of the crowd I'm making my way through, it's a popular spot amongst tourists and locals alike.

A particularly rowdy table full of guys in suits are speaking both Korean and English, well, an intoxicated version of it at least.

The exterior of the bar is so fucking small, if you didn't know where it was, you'd blink and miss it. Pretty much just a narrow brownish door stoop with three steps, jammed between two other business, the only thing that clued me in I'd reached my destination was the pink and white neon sign that hung above the door's alcove.

The interior however, as I said before, was just like any other bar. Wood floors, neon signage, glass shelves behind a long, polished bar, and a combination of chairs and tables and hi-tops with stools throughout the space. I can also make out electronic dartboards on a few walls, a couple of pool tables towards the back, and a small area for a band. The music was ok; with no band tonight, it was playing through several speakers in the ceiling, and based on the two songs I'd heard since I'd walked in, I'm guessing will be popular top forty.

We weren't here for the music though. With a particularly busy schedule the past few days, we were here for the cocktails. Plural.

"Reb, over here!" Hannah calls out, and I stop my gawking around and make my way over to where she's mid-ass lift, about to perch herself on a stool near one end of the bar.

She's looking classy as always in a beautiful hounds tooth jacket and jeans, along with some killer strappy black heels and her hair in a wavy ponytail. Taking the stool next to her, I give her props for the location choice.

"This place is the shit. Not at all what I imagined when you said cocktails at a bar. I saw upscale glass and chrome minimalism, but this place is so more my speed." Smiling at her, it turns to a chuckle when she replies.

"You've met me, right? This is more my speed too. Unless I'm in the mood to dance, that is a different girls night out all together. And we wouldn't leave to go out until after midnight, at the earliest."

"Jesus. Count me in. But I'm warning you now, I can't pull that shit off like I used to in my late teens, early twenties. One time I could party all night, only going home in time to shower and change, and then head straight into work. You pick a Saturday night, so I have all day Sunday to recover, and I'm there."

Laughing, Hannah replies. "Done. And I feel you with the recovery thing, that and I feel bad the next day if I'm dragging my ass when the guys work so hard at every single thing they do."

"Right! I know exactly what you mean, I've seen career driven and passionate, but they're something else entirely."

So much so that after only the short time I've been here, it already worried me a little, but I didn't say that to Hannah. Instead, I shared my other thought. "I really wish the guys could come out like that, with us I mean. God, can you imagine the epic level of dancing? On second thought, I don't think unleashing their freestyle skills on an unsuspecting public would be in anyone's best interest. Jaimin alone would cause every set of ovaries in the place to explode!"

I mime a booming explosion with my hands in front of my abdomen, but Hannah goes one better.

"Not to mention a heap of testicles, too," she adds, her explosion mime is her fists dangling between her legs, making us both laugh.

She's not wrong; the guys fan base included both genders. A large percentage of who went to sleep at night fantasizing about getting their bias naked and creating all level of dream-state fuckery.

This naturally leads me to thinking about my own very-real bias, my very sexy, warm and hard-bodied bias, and what he might be doing right now. I actually know he's at home tonight, likely still working on something band related, so I resist the urge to text him.

I won't become that chick.

Luckily, I'm pulled from this lie I'm telling myself by a question.

"What can I get you beauties to drink?" A friendly looking guy asks in Korean accented English.

"Trust me?" Hannah asks, and even though I do, she doesn't give me time to answer anyway. I knew she was my kind of chick. "Two coronarita's, please," she orders, and with a nod, the barman walks away to prepare our drinks.

Whatever the hell they are.

Turns out what they are, is delicious as fuck, and kinda dangerous too, because while they might go down like fruit juice, they pack one hell of a punch.

And there is a very good reason for that.

Served in a large cocktail glass, actually a small fruit bowl on a stem is probably more accurate; it's a mixture of crushed ice, tequila, triple sec, and lime sour syrup with an open bottle of Corona hanging upside down in the refreshing liquid. With a salty rim, and mint leaf on the side, I'd slurped my first one through its straw so fast you'd be forgiven for thinking I'd just come in from a month in the desert. My second I sipped, well, at least I thought I did, until the straw made a sucking sound against the ice and I looked down to find it too, was empty.

So now I'm on coronarita number four, this one I'm determined to sip because I can't really feel my lips, while Hannah is still nursing drink two.

We've talked and laughed through all the usual girl's night topics, played a few games of darts – Hannah kicked my ass – and a few games of pool. Hannah did not kick my ass at that, I'd served her hers on a plate.

Both of us have been hit on a few times, but in keeping with the vibe of the place, it's been low-key and easy to deflect, not like the sleazy cheese you to have to scrape off you in a nightclub.

I was right earlier, the music was current, and as the night has gone on, a small crowd has made an impromptu dance floor. Hannah and I have chosen to shake it right where we are, Hannah because her shoes were killer but no way meant for dancing, and me because I'm completely fascinated with a couple sitting across the room, in my direct line of sight.

They'd arrived about an hour after we had, and the dude was killing it. He'd pulled out her chair, ordered her drink, had given her his jacket when she must have said she was cold. She was the recipient of his entire focus and there was something very familiar about it. About the way he was with her, and the way he looked at her.

My belly fluttered each time I looked their way, but even though they were who I was seeing, the nice looking Korean couple was not who I was thinking about.

The place was jumping; the gender split heavily leaning towards men, meaning the women that were in the bar stood out. Romantic dude did not look at a single one of us. We could've all stripped off and offered body shots and I knew that man would not bat a lash. Nothing existed for him but her.

And right then he gets down on one knee.

"Oh my god, Hannah, look, look!" I slap my hand against her arm to get her attention quickly, having to try a few times to make the connection because her arm keeps moving out of my reach. Of course, that could be the coronarita's affecting my aim, but I don't want her to miss his proposal.

I knew that dude was up to something! Like, who is that attentive? No one, that's who.

Jung-keun is, my brain whispers, and the crack butterflies take flight in my belly.

Dude must have been psyching himself up all night to do this, no wonder he didn't take his eyes off of her. So much of it makes sense now!

"What?" Hannah asks, a worried look on her face and tone to her voice.

Seeing where I'm looking and covertly trying to point, Hannah turns her ass on her stool. "Ah, should've known, the date night couple you've been watching all night. What has you so fascinated with them anyway?" she sighs.

"Not a date Hannah, it's THE date, he's proposing, look!"

I'm already swooning, and the guy has barely made it to his knee. Well, he's on both knees, but why the fuck not I say, it's his proposal.

"Ok, girl, you need to put down the alcoholic beverage. He's not proposing." Hannah states in a way that tells me she's sure and moves to turn back towards me.

"Yes, he is, he's been all about her, all night, and now he's down on his knees," I respond, just as sure.

"Reb, what's that in his hands?" she asks, and my brain answers before my eyes.

"A ring!" I shout, and given a few heads turn, it might have been a little louder than I intended.

"In a box that size? You think?"

What Hannah doesn't say is the duh, but it's implied in her tone.

Using more concentration that it should require, I focus on the box in the man's hands. A box that's about the size of a shoebox. No, it *is* a shoebox. What the fuck?

"He's proposing...with shoes?" I ask, my confusion trying to push past what I could've sworn was happening.

"Reb, he's giving her a gift. See, he's putting her shoes on, and by the look on her face, I'd say they were a pair she's wanted for a while."

"But he's been so attentive, and romantic, and, and, and..."

"Korean?" Hannah finishes for me.

"Huh?"

"Reb that couple is Korean, meaning that man *is* Korean, and Korean men are like that, remember? Everything you've seen him do tonight is normal in a Korean relationship. He is all about her, because that's how Korean men roll."

Again, Hannah's tone is matter of fact, like shit just is. Way of life.

Fuck me. Really?

My brain tries to process this, and as it wades through far too much tequila and beer, and did I mention tequila...I know what she's telling me is true.

Because the fact is...Jung-keun *is* like that.

With me.

"Says the girl who had an entire designer inventory bought for her. Why are you in denial about him?" Hannah says, her lightly made up eyes looking right at me as her amazing red lips form the words, and I realize I've shared my thought out loud.

"Ugh," I groan and look at my hands. "Because it's too good to be true, *he's* too good to be true! I came here, knew South Korea was the right fit for me, I never felt the way I do in L.A. like I do here. I tried to pretend it was the group, my job…but it was him all along. I realized that as soon as we met that I couldn't ignore the true reason for me coming here. Part of me thinks that this is just a fun thing for him, to have a ride on the- what the fuck do they say again?" I pause and question.

"White pony," she nods.

"I'm twenty-seven, Hannah, I've never felt like this with a man before. He's so young and I think he doesn't have a lot of experience with women. I know he's *the* one, but it scares me to talk to him about it and then get rejected or something. It'll crush everything I think about destiny."

"Um…I know I don't know you *that* well, but being scared, which is what you seem to be, doesn't exactly shout normal Rebel to me," she says.

"I am scared," I sigh and frown dramatically.

Hannah smiles, takes my hands and levels with me.

"I was being sort of general when I said that Korean men love to take care of the people around them, which is true. But a guy buying you what Jung-keun bought you, isn't normal. That's like a move a husband does for a wife. Shoe guy over there is more the speed of a boyfriend here, not an entire new wardrobe, whether they can afford it or not."

I sigh but her words rattle around in my head, it was quite an extravagant gift with the clothes.

"And I thought you said you haven't had sex with him," Hannah says.

"We haven't."

"Theeeeen if he was just wanting a bang buddy, wouldn't that have been something you did right away?" she questions with narrowed eyes.

"Oh, shit," I say, and try as I might, I can't stop smiling like a motherfucking lunatic.

No kidding, if we were side by side right now, Harley Quinn would've had nothing on me.

Jung-keun isn't just into me, that sexy holy water maker is *in to me.*

* * *

I've tried three times to enter my code into the keypad, but the damn lock keeps moving. It's like that whack-a-mole sideshow, just when I move to strike; the fucker dodges to the left.

Hannah thinks it's hilarious, but that's because Hannah thinks everything I've done since we left the bar is hilarious. She's also way more buzzed than she was, but still not quite as far down the boozetube as me.

When she'd given me what I'm now calling my 101 tutorials in the dating behavior of South Korean men, I started to realize my fears about JK were all in my head. I needed to stop being afraid, proclaim my love for him and finally hear that he felt the same...soon.

"Seriously Reb, what's the code," she says for about the tenth time, but I am a woman on a mission. I won't be beaten.

"Nope, I got this," and proceed to bang my hand on the handle somehow.

"Ow," I laugh and we both dissolve into a fit of the giggles, one of us actually snorting while drawing in lungful's of precious air. When I tell the story later, the snorter is so going to be Hannah.

"Fuck, I can't take it!" Dropping all my shit on to the floor, I rest my ass against the door, grabbing my aching side from laughing so much.

I think because we were laughing like a pair of hyenas on nitrous, we miss the door opening and closing at the other end of the hallway. And the thumping steps of long, muscle packed legs until they're almost to my door.

I should have known though, because I knew that sound intimately, the thumping of his Timberlands suddenly matching the thumping in my chest. Seeing the toes of the camel colored boots enter my vision confirms what my body already knows, JK is here.

And based on the look on his face, his tongue bulging his cheek, when I haul my uncoordinated ass upright, he's annoyed?

What is that about? He knew I was going out and I warned him I'd be getting hammered, so he can't say he wasn't warned. He even made sure to have Fred drive me and make sure I got home fine, so come on, I know JK has more sense than that to be mad.

"Hey, you're here," I observe happily, like the rocket scientist I currently am.

Dark cocoa orbs pin me in place, and the floor beneath me feels like it just dropped four feet. As the whoosh of it hits my belly; my body is rocked with a wave of lust so deep that I bite my lip to prevent a moan. Or plastering myself to his every surface like Grandma's cabbage rose wallpaper.

So fucking intense, he's too much.

It dawns on me he's talking to Hannah, their Korean quiet yet so damn fast, but his eyes haven't left me. The whole of their conversation he's been giving me a full visual body check that I can feel.

In *all* my favorite places.

Reaching out I put my hand on his arm, his body my ballast as I bend to pick up my handbag.

"Oh shit, I'm going down!" I announce, and I do just that. My knees folding underneath me as I tilt to one side and crumple to the floor, my head coming to rest against JK's legs.

Two faces look down at me; one holding a manicured hand over her face, trying not to laugh and the other is holding his chin in a way that from my current angle, the cut of his jaw is bullshit.

"Your jaw is bullshit," I tell him. When I get no response other than an escaped giggle from Hannah, I clarify further, waving my hand around my own jaw, "No one looks like that, all perfect and sculptured and shit. Except you. You do. Just you."

"I'm gonna go now Reb, Jung-keun dongseng is arranging me a ride home," Hannah says, and when I look to her she tips her head his way, so my eyes go back to him and I find he's texting.

Poor Fred, he works shitty, shitty hours. I'll have to get him a muffin basket or travel mug or something.

The next few minutes go by in a kind of blur.

Me trying to get up to say goodbye to Hannah; me failing at trying to get up to say goodbye to Hannah.

Hannah laughing at both.

JK scowling at us.

Hannah and I laughing our asses off at JK scowling, which leads to him shaking his head and pressing his tongue into his cheek.

But none of that matters, because now having scooped me off the floor like a sack of potatoes, Hannah is gone and I'm in JK's arms.

My arm is across his broad shoulders, the softness of his well-loved black hoodie a caress against my bare skin. My other hand is high on his chest, my fingertips resting at the base of his neck. My purse is in my lap because JK has one thick arm under my knees, his other across my back. I can feel the heat of his palm through my top and know exactly where each pad of his fingers and thumb rest against my ribs.

If I weren't so smashed, I'd try to explain to him that he had me in a threshold hold, and how it was some kind of sign because I'd seen a proposal tonight. Well sort of. So, because I am blitzkrieg'd, I go with my other thought.

"You're so damn strong," I tell him looking into his face, the awe in my voice clear. "And hard. You're strong and hard, but your skin is so fucking soft. It makes *me* soft, do you know that?"

My fingers sweep up the column of his neck and down again, brushing along the front of his throat, greedily slipping just inside the V from the few inches of his hoodie unzipped. I continue talking into his chest, watching my fingers explore as he uses the hand under my knees to punch in the code to keypad and finally opening the door. "It's like velvet. Do you know velvet? Well, trust me your body is like velvet-covered steel. Although steel is cold and you're not cold. You're hot. Very hot. The hottest."

The bang of the door closing behind me alerts me to the fact that we are now in my apartment, so I take my hand out of his sweater and shove my purse off my lap, letting it hit the floor.

JK's eyes flare when I start to move, not out of his hold of course - I'm not insane, but just into a different position.

Treating him as my own personal scratching post, I hear his feet shift against the floor, widening his stance as I wrap my legs high on his hips, both of my arms going around his neck.

"Reb," he growls, and I feel the vibration from his chest in my own.

"Yeah?"

"Drunk."

"Shit-faced. But I'd rather talk about *your* face. Or sit on it." I run a finger across the apple of his cheek, down the length of his nose, and across his lips and they part under my touch, which causes me to groan.

"And these fucking lips. Who has lips like this?"

Then *it* catches my eye and reaching out to touch, I don't just groan, I moan over one of the many things about this man that makes me so fucking crazy I can't keep it locked down anymore.

"Do you have any fucking idea what this freckle does to me? Do you, Jung-keun? I don't think you do. I only have to look at it and I get wet. Think about it and I get wet. Freckles equals wet. Do you know how ridiculous that is?"

Unable to stop myself, I lick the perfectly formed, chocolate milk colored droplet that sits below his full bottom lip.

"That's mine, that's my spot," I tell him against his mouth, and as I look into his eyes, what stares back at me is a look I'm coming to know very well.

Possessive. Adored. Cherished.

"You're into me, I know that now. Well, I knew it before, but I get now that it's not just in a 'let's fuck around for while' kinda way. The way you watch me eat, feed me food you think I'd like, buy me killer fucking clothes I'd never consider buying for myself, you're 'Korean dude' into me. And I haven't even mentioned the songs you send me, or the way you always position yourself to be close to me. And you do that on purpose. I know you do that. And I want it. I want all of it. And even though it scares the shit out of me, the intensity of these feelings, the thing is, I'm into you, so fucking hard. Like, if I were a Korean and had a penis, I'd be 'Korean dude' into you too. That's how much I'm into you."

Placing a kiss against his lips, JK's hands tighten against my ass, pressing my lower body closer to his own as he walks me to my bedroom. I drop my forehead into the crook of his neck, breathing him in, the alcohol suddenly hitting me, and I feel tired.

"Uggh, are you getting any of this? Because there is a good chance this discussion is proudly sponsored by coronarita's, and I'm not fully versed on the staying power of a chicks memory after a night on those fuckers, you feel me?"

"Ah," he rasps into my ear and I groan, because I'm not sure he does, but he sure as shit knows what the word *feel* means.

He places me on the end of my bed and drops into a squat by my feet, his long fingers moving deftly to remove my complicated shoes. Thank fuck he showed up, and not just to get my drunk ass inside, but with the number of buckles on these things, I would've had to sleep in them.

"Up" he says, and I lift my foot to help him get to the catches at the back of my calf, while at the same time, I rip my jacket off. The action has my back falling to the bed, which makes me giggle.

"This now," he says, sparking another thought I need to share immediately before I forget.

"And that's another thing, do you have any clue what happens to me when you speak English? One word or six, JK, no kidding, that does shit to me. Deep shit." Propping myself up on my elbows, I look down the length of my body, watching as he holds up my bare foot and kisses my ankle.

"Oh fuck, don't do that, my damn ovaries will explode," I tell him, but JK only stands, his body coming over mine, his fingers pulling at then lowering the hidden zip at the side of my pants.

"Everything about you, you're more potent that watching Jaimin dance. And you're the shit when you dance, the best, but that little fucker can move."

A frown passes over his face as I wiggle my way out of my too tight to get on and a motherfucker to get off, but they make my ass look incredible, pants.

"Jaimin?" he growls, face serious, his lips pursed and pouty, causing twitches that have my legs shifting restlessly in a way that has nothing to do with me trying to get out of my pants.

"You don't need to be worried, or jealous...I've been obsessed with you even before we met," I smile at him, and the fucker grips the fabric of my pants at my ankles and rips them off me.

Like skinning a banana, whoosh, they're gone.

So now I'm lying on my bed in only my cap-sleeved shirt and a tiny magenta colored, satin and lace thong.

JK looks at my attire and steps back, running his palm across the back of his neck, gripping tightly, his lips parted.

His breathing heavy.

His eyes hooded.

His jaw sharp and his chin tipped up.

He's too fucking much, so too much in fact that the restlessness in my legs spreads to my hips, and all of it levels up to a full wiggle.

In a move that has my mouth popping open with excitement, I watch as he unzips the hoodie and takes it off, leaving him in a tight, white V-necked tee and his old, ripped and faded jeans, throwing the hoodie onto the floor. The shirt's been jostled with the hoodie removal, and I'm rewarded with a glimpse of the waistband of his Hugo Boss underwear, hugging his taut abdomen, peaking at me above the waist of his low-slung jeans.

Everything about him right now says predator, hungry, amped, and not going to be denied.

Other than being petite, you'd never use the words delicate or dainty to describe me, but here in my bedroom, my back on the bed, my bent knees dangling over the end as JK stands there devouring me with his eyes, that's exactly how he's making me feel.

"You wanted me?" he rasps, planting a knee in the bed, his hands moving into my armpits to haul me further up the bed as he settles his lower body over mine in a touch that is barely there, and I know he's holding most of his weight in his knees and hands.

I lick my lips, swallowing thickly before I remark, "So fucking bad."

That gets me a nose crinkle. A fucking nose crinkle followed by the smallest smirk, one that engages only one side of his mouth.

Of their own volition, my hands find their way to his jaw, my fingers brushing his skin as they trace the angled bone that could've been carved by Michelangelo himself.

His eyes haven't left my lips, so I lick them again, then bring my thumb up over his chin, and sweep it just under his bottom lip, over his freckle.

I lift my head off the bed, closing the distance between us, but not all the way. "Please kiss me," I whisper, "I'm about to die if you don't."

His face doesn't change but his head does move, and I feel my eyes flutter closed in anticipation of his mouth on mine. I groan as his lips brush my cheek, slightly confused when they settle against my ear instead.

"Smell you," he says, his English limited but so very concise, further removing any doubt as to what he means when he lets his lower body rest against mine, his hips pressing me into the bed.

"Oh shit." My eyes close while my hips rise and grind into his, before I add, "Told you, I'm always wet around you. Now, please kiss me before I die."

"Ok," is all he says and even as foggy with lust and alcohol as I am, I don't miss the glint in his eye.

Oh fuck.

I've loved the slow discovery of our sexual selves. Something I don't think I've ever done, or been bothered to take the time to do, with a lover. Until him. And not only is it perfect, it's just another reason why I know that what I have with Jung-keun is something that's bigger than the both of us.

But I swear, if he does what I think that glint is alluding to, I will die, because what we haven't done yet is oral. The thought of his mouth on my pussy frys my brain, and when I think of his freckle, my freckle, running over me from slit to clit, I whimper.

Somewhat misreading my neediness, he presses his mouth to me, our kiss starting slowly, but my greed for him is obvious and I don't really give a shit about technique, I just want his tongue tangled with mine.

Groaning, he drops to his elbows, so I've got most of his weight now, and it's delicious. He's so big, and hard, and I don't just mean what I can feel against my belly, although that too definitely seems big and hard.

My fingers on his jaw, his lips on mine, he takes over the kiss, and I let my mind wander to picturing his dick. I just know it's a work of art; everything else is about him is, so why wouldn't his cock be golden too? Lately I've been wondering about whether or not most South Korean men are circumcised, because no shit, I can't grasp JK in a turtle necked tee or sweater without combusting, so if his golden cock has extra skin...fucking boom!

His hands shift into my hair, sweeping it off my face as his lips leave mine to suckle against my throat, and I take in gasps of air, letting my own hands wander over the back of his head, neck and shoulders.

I can't tell you how intensely I feel what this man does to me, but I know what makes him different from anyone else is that I don't just desire JK with my body, I desire him with my mind and soul too.

His weight shifts to one side, and his long fingers run down the edge of my body, leaving the fabric of my shirt to touch skin at my hip, the curve of my ass and top of my thigh. With a hand under my knee he shifts one leg over, opening me to him and settling himself between my thighs, his lower half against the bed. I have to assume my state has him feeling daring since it seems like for the first time with me, he's following his instincts and not hesitating.

His lips have made their way down my neck and across my clavicles, lazily licking and sucking the skin over each of them into his hot mouth, and I never knew they were an erogenous zone, but based on how tight my nipples are and how much they're chafing against the lace of my bra, I damn well do now.

"You're killing me, even I can smell how wet I am. I need your fingers in my pussy, please?"

I grab one of his hands from my breast and try to bring it between us, happy to sacrifice my tit if I get friction where I want it the most.

I can't say if this is a Korean man thing, but it sure is my Korean man, and that is to say, he won't be rushed, and he won't be taken somewhere he doesn't want to go. So, while I successfully get his hand off my tit, I don't get it where I want it, but when he speaks I find I also don't fucking care.

"I want eat," he says, and the little growl in his voice along with the determined look on his face makes me gasp, and I find myself nodding, which is stupid because JK was not asking for my permission.

As careful as he is with me, showing me tenderness in his affection, it's balanced by an underlying aggressiveness, like now, for example. Having he's declared he wants to eat me, without any further fucking around, his fingers hook into my panties, and whoosh, they've gone the way of my pants.

I've barely have time to think the hotness of this maneuver through when I feel his massive hands push my thighs apart, lodge themselves under my ass and lift my pussy up to his mouth.

But then I see hesitation as I stare down at him and he looks up at me, "How you like?"

Placing my hands on his cheeks and pant, "I'll come in two seconds, just put your mouth on me, that's what I like," I nod.

I urge his face toward me, his long tongue coming out to make contact with my clit before his lips begin to suck my skin into his mouth.

"Oh, my fucking God!" I shout with a smile on my face, there's an elation of shock and it has to be said, intense happiness that this moment is happening.

Swamped with sensation, my hips grind against his conquering mouth, his tongue, lips, chin and nose all up in my business. He's everywhere, licking, flicking, sucking and nibbling, and in less than a minute I'm flooding his mouth with my cum. Any thought of holding off my orgasm, to appreciate the first time his mouth is on me, to make his time between my legs with his gorgeous face devouring my cunt last as long as I can, doesn't even enter my mind. Not once.

Not that I could have held it back mind you, no way, he took that orgasm from me because he wanted it, and because he wanted it, I was happy to have given it to him.

Mouth still working against my hot and swollen sex, I lift up onto my elbows and try to shift away, the intensity of my first orgasm not really having time to die before he's building me up again, his unforgiving onslaught.

I look down my body and find him staring at me, his shiny face and open mouth working against my intimate flesh, I'm reminded how tenacious he is in succeeding at all he does, and it would seem eating pussy is no different.

Planting my feet into the bed, I give him more access, knowing I'd give him anything he wants as long as he doesn't stop. Legs open wide, I feel my lower lips spread as his hard tongue thrusts inside me, and the sight as well as the sensation has me shoving one hand inside my bra to roughly tweak my nipple, the other reaching down to brush his long bangs out of his eyes.

The pressure in my womb and heat in my lower limbs suggests I'm about to come again, and as the muscles in my thighs tighten and my toes grip down into to the bed, I know this one is going to be much bigger than the first.

Oh fuck.

Still working my nipple, I drop the hand I have on his forehead down to his jaw, feeling it move and shift under my fingers and palm as he drives me higher.

So beautiful, so strong, this man is everything.

My index finger leaves his jaw to find his tongue, touching it as it flicks against my clit, both of us groaning when I hit my target. Together we work the slick little nub, a pre-orgasmic tremor already moving through my body when I feel JK shove two thick fingers inside me, working my hole and rubbing my walls in exactly the way I'd shown him I liked. Scratch that, with him, in the way I fucking loved.

"I'm coming, I can't not...oh, fuck!"

Pulse after pulse of thunderous, unrelenting pleasure rips through me, my eyes shutting so tight I see blinding white, pinpoint stars against the inky black behind my lids, and the beauty of it astounds me.

Breathing hard, I feel myself floating away, my body wrung out and satisfied in a way, no surprise, I'd never felt before. Not until him.

Gentle kisses all over my mound, pussy and the inside of each of my thighs let me know JK is still downtown, and even though I'm limp in a way I know there is no way to avoid the double orgasm while drunk induced nap that's trying to claim me, I still feel him lightly lick my twitching clit, and declare on a whisper, "My spot."

Ugh, this guy.

Fucking witchcraft.

"Do you like me a lot?" I whisper, my eyes closed as I try to fight off sleep. "Because I want to know I'm not just a horse to you-pony? I want to spend the rest of my life with you. Is that what you want? Because-" and I don't finish before passing out.

* * *

The next morning, I wake up alone in my bed. Vaguely recalling JK putting me to bed and knocking my pussy out with his mouth and fingers. I also remember how drunk I got, but I remember everything I said. I hope JK knew what I meant was all true, how damn near obsessed I am with him. I'm not ashamed and I hope he's not creeped out, but knowing how relationships and couples are here, partner worship is completely acceptable and coveted. But at the end, just before sleep, shit, I shouldn't have brought that up then. I should've waited until I was sober and we were both at least dressed. Maybe I'll bring it up later. Just then my phone alerts me to a message and I roll over to search for my phone on the bedside table, glancing at the clock to see it's seven a.m.

THWS: Awake?

Me: Just now.

THWS: Coming?

Me: I'll be there in an hour.

THWS: You ok?

Me: Yes.

THWS: Ailment kitchen. Practice now.

Me: Thank you, see you soon xx.

THWS: Arrive safely.

Me: I will.

I smile to myself, ugh the amount of care he has for me just fucks me up. All in all, I do feel ok, not super hung over, but not 100% either if I'm being honest. I take a hot shower and decide to let my hair air dry into waves today, deciding to also go natural with light make up but a dark lip color so I don't look completely washed out and dead. I hum one of the groups songs before putting it on my phone and connecting it to my Bluetooth speaker in the kitchen and grab my clothes for the day. My black tee with GIRLS DO NOT DRESS FOR BOYS in red lettering, a black leather mini skirt, a long black cardigan and thigh highs along with eight-inch heel black ankle boots.

Sure enough, there's a small brown bottle of something on the counter with Korean writing, along with a pear and I scan the label on the bottle as if I can catch something I recognize in the words, but don't. Instead I crack open the top and chug it, the syrupy drink tastes bitter at first and then fruity wondering then if this is something I'm supposed to take a certain dosage of but have damn near chugged the whole thing. I shrug and swallow the rest, oh well, might be an interesting day if I'm med drunk. Grabbing the straps to one of the black purses JK gifted me, then the pear, I make my way downstairs.

Fred and an SUV are waiting for me in the garage and I bow at him as he waves at me and I smile at our role reversal in greetings. We make it to the Massive Smash building in no time and the thought of seeing JK has me walking a little faster. I've never had such anticipation to see someone as I do with him, everything with him feels like I'm an addict and he's my fix. Anyone before him, I'd worry I was more into the guy than he was into me, but not with JK. I hear the music from the rehearsal room before I even step off the elevator and it has me smiling and dancing down the hall with every step, passing by staff who smile and bow at me and my enjoyment of the music.

Entering the space, the music is playing but no one's dancing, and I remember today they are filming for their web show and the music must just be on for enjoyment. The guys are in various stages of being ready, Shoogi and Joon are sitting in the middle of the dance space in chairs on their phones, while Jinho and Hooni are near the tables while Jinho eats.

"Redbull!" my name's called from the back corner where the hair make-up stations are set up. Ye smiles at me as he's the one who called my name, his hair being blown over his eyes as he sits and gets his hair blow dried.

I smile at him but then I see JK sitting beside Jaimin as they get their make-up done and I walk up behind him, looking at JK through the mirror in front of him. He looks me over, I guess making sure I'm not on death's door before giving me a tilt of his lips.

"Rebel," Jaimin says as I notice he's holding up a cup of cold coffee, the contents half gone, and I reach over for it.

Taking a long pull of the delicious java before handing the cup back, JK gives me an annoyed glare in the mirror and I smile back at him.

"Morning," Hannah says as she appears from around the corner with sponges in hand.

"Hi," I smile, pulling up a chair from an empty station and sitting behind everyone as she works on JK's beautiful face.

I get why everyone in this industry wears make-up, they're selling perfection. But I love them all with bare faces. Their skin tan and freckly, little imperfections that make us human, stubble even, but that's not what the public wants.

"You look fresh this morning," Hannah comments and I look up at her, seeing she too looks like she fared well with the hangover gods.

"Yeah, I feel fine," I shrug and grab the pear JK left for me on the counter from my purse.

"Yes, Korean pears are like a hangover cure all! I had so much fun last night," she smiles, looking at her hands working.

We start talking about the events of last night, laughing quietly because she is working and the more we go on, I see JK becoming more and more solemn. Jaimin joking with him and trying to play with him doesn't even really conjure a reaction. I wonder if he's mad I went out or had fun. But that doesn't seem right, he was fine before I left and after I got back, maybe I read him wrong. It can't really be because I was drunk or something I said, or could it? He can't tell me here and I can't ask him, well aloud. Taking out my phone, I text him.

Me: What's wrong?

I look at Hannah talking as I watch him read his message from the corner of my eye and then begin typing.

THWS: Jealous.

Me: Of?

THWS: Can't go, us.

Oh my God.

Instantly I feel bad. He's upset that me and him can't go out, well alone at least and not without face masks. I look up at him in the mirror, but his eyes remain down on his phone. I feel guilty honestly and bad. It never occurred to me that he would, but hello I'd feel the same. The director calls the guys together and they all go to the center of the dance space and the cameras go on and they're told what they'll be doing today. I sit beside Hannah and watch as they play a round of games to win a prize and watch my bunny the whole time, seeing he's not his usual happy self. Fuck, I feel like shit about this. I begin to think of what I can do to make things better and slowly I hatch a plan. Before the filming is over, I whisper to Hannah that I'm leaving and I'll see her later. Trying not to disrupt or make a fuss, I grab my stuff and quietly exit.

Chapter Fifteen

(Yeol daseos)

THWS: Where you?

It's been two hours since I left the Massive Smash building and the text comes just as I'm finishing up in my apartment and I bite my lower lip as I respond.

Me: Home, can you come over?

THWS: I come now.

I smile and set my phone down on the counter and scan over the set up at the table and mentally check that I have everything set up in the bedroom. The tap at the door comes before I hear the keypad beeping as the codes entered and then the door opening. I move to the entryway and stand there with my hands behind my back.

"You leave?" he asks, looking concerned as he approaches after sliding his shoes off.

But his expression changes from worry to confusion and then a smile as he takes in my barely contained energy.

"I had to come and set up our date," I tell him, taking his hands and pressing a soft kiss on his full lips.

His eyes dart toward the table where I have his favorite food sitting, fast food and junk of course. He grunts and takes my hand as he moves toward it. I've literally gone ham on the goods; burgers, fries, desserts, soft drinks, and tons of snacks in packages to eat through the evening.

"Eat, eat," he states, and I smile as he grabs two burgers and we sit down next to each other, one of the burgers being handed to me.

We eat for a while in silence, since when he eats JK is focused on the food in front of him. I eat too, but not much because I am antsy for the date and what I've set up. Once he's on his second burger, he looks over at me as I'm really just sitting there watching him and it's then he takes in my attire. I've decided on a dress from the designer I like, one JK gifted me and probably didn't even see before buying it. It's black, skin tight, with long sleeves, a skirt that ends at my cooch and from the front looks like a plain dress.

"Look nice," he nods.

"Thank you, you bought it for me," I smile.

"I change?" he asks, looking down at his black shirt and jeans.

"Nope, you're perfect," I shake my head and lean in to kiss his pouty bottom lip.

"You eat?"

"Nah, I'm not really hungry," I shrug.

"Sick?"

"No, no" I shake my head, not wanting him to worry himself, because he would. "Just excited," I state, which sounds so stupid.

"For?"

"To be with you, spend the evening with you," I shrug and feel like a total stage four clinger.

His hand comes to my jaw, coaxing my chin up as he crinkles his nose and leans over to kiss me softly on the lips. "Kyoot," the Korean way of saying 'cute.' I'm then reminded of Korean dude and realize he likes when I get all cutesie over him.

"So," I let out with a long breath. "Can we talk about last night?" I ask and scrunch up my face.

His expression becomes one of worry, like he did something wrong.

"Nothing you did," I wave my hand, my eyes widening. "You did...amazing...great, great things last night," I swoon, as I remember back to his mouth on me.

"Because drunk?" he questions.

"No, of course I wanted to, you didn't take advantage of me or anything," I close my eyes and try to get the conversation back on track. "When I said how I felt about you. About not wanting to be just sex, that I want there to be an us."

He nods but says nothing, continuing to eat his burger. A nod is good, a nod means yes. Right? Ok, maybe he wasn't fully understanding. I sit there, watching him and try to think of another way to talk about this. I don't want to use the phone translator, but I just might have to.

He finishes another burger and then I can't wait anymore and don't want to think anymore, I grab his hand and some of the bags of snacks as we walk into the living room.

"Reb," he says, moving behind me and running his hand down the back of my dress, well rather, lack thereof. I said the front was plain, but the back, well that's nothing, aside from two pieces of fabric that crisscross from my neck to just above my ass. His hand stops right above that though and I move away, not wanting to get side tracked.

"Pick a movie," I state nodding over to the stand of blu ray disc's and DVD's I have in the shelving beneath the flat screen. JK opens the drawers and looks at all the titles I have, and honestly, I'm not sure what he'll pick. My collection is varied but mainly consists of horror and sci-fi.

"The Clockmaker?" he asks.

"Ugh yes, one of the best, ever see it?" I ask.

He looks at me with a suspicious grin, then shakes his head a little, returning his attention to the movies once more.

"What one you like?"

"Hmmm, well, my favorite is Hellraiser two, but if we watch that we need to watch one...but I don't know how you'll like it-" I trail off.

"We watch," he states, pulling the two cases out and then follows me down the hallway.

He nearly knocks into me as I stop by the spare bedroom and not further down to my bedroom.

"Open the door," I nod at the handle and bite the corner of my lip.

He does, not thinking anything to it and walks in. I've made a tent with spare sheets over the bed, strung Christmas lights all over the inside and moved the flat screen to the end of the bed.

"I made like a little theater," I shrug as he looks at the outside of what I made.

Lifting the one side he moves under the sheet and onto the bed, holding it open for me as I toss the snacks on the comforter and get in too. Before I get comfortable, I grab the movie cases and put the first film into the player. When I get the movie started I scoot back to the top of the bed where JK is laying, his head and torso propped up on the pillows. He outstretches an arm and I slide right between it and his body, curling up beside his hard body.

We watch the movie silently, and I don't know what I expected his reaction to be, but I expected something like 'ew this is fucked up, turn it off,' since that's what every one of my friends say when I get them to watch it. But he doesn't, he just watches, holds me and eats his snacks.

"Does it surprise you I'd like a movie like this?" I ask after a particularly gory part.

"No," he simply states. "Why?" he then asks.

I shrug, because I don't know why. "Everyone always thinks the movies I like are terrible, I wouldn't be surprised if you did too."

"You like, I like."

I roll my eyes and lean my head up to look at him, he's done snacking and just watching the movie. He just says things like that like they're no big deal, like there's no thought behind it or motive, just truth and I can't fucking handle it.

It begins with my fingers running along his jawline, that goddamned chiseled perfection, small pricks of stubble catch on the skin of my fingertips and I want to feel that on my mouth. Moving in with my lips, I graze his chin and his neck, before licking and placing soft sucking kisses there, paying particularly close attention to another freckle smack dab on the center side of his neck. What started as my fingers, now has me attacking his neck, one leg bent and hitched between his legs, the skirt of my dress pushed up to my hip as my other hand runs along his chest down to the top of his jeans.

I've been the one getting all the special treatment, and I think it's about time JK gets some of his own. His rigid cock is impatiently throbbing against my inner thigh as JK groans and eventually, moves the hand that was tickling the bare skin of my back into my hair as he dips his head and forces my neck to arch so he can kiss me. His other hand moves to my bare thigh, rubbing the expanse of naked skin there, back and forth, venturing up under the skirt to cup my bare ass. I moan and my breath quivers against his mouth as his fingers gently graze over my pussy lips. But it's not fair, he's had me there with his mouth and hand and I've yet to sample his goods. Before he can put a spell on me and distract me with his witchcraft, I move my body over him as I rise on all fours.

He watches me as I sit back and rest my ass on his thighs, my hands pushing the bottom of his shirt up just enough to expose the button and fly of his jeans. He wears them tight enough that I can see the shape and press of his cock against the soft denim and I bite my lower lip as my hands undo the bindings, noticing JK's body begin to move so he can sit up a little more, effectively helping me move the jeans down a bit. It's then his hands help me push down the front of his boxer briefs, and I barely see the huge dick come flying toward me as JK then is guiding my head down to it. Opening my mouth, I accept it. The moan that comes from him is like nothing I've ever heard. Satisfying, relieved, agony, passion, it's everything. It didn't surprise me he was so eager for me to blow him, but I am a little surprised at his straight forwardness.

"Oh Reb," he moans, his hands moving into my hair as I get his length wet with my mouth and use my closed fist to spread it down to the base. He's got very minimal hair down here and it's fucking hot as hell.

His dick is a good eight inches, not overly thick, but hard as granite with veins that feel like they have molten steel running through them. I slurp and suck, bobbing my head with short movements before taking him all the way to the back of my throat, my hand accompanying as I pull back and give his cock a hard pull with my fist.

His thighs and body are so tight beneath me, his hands clenching and releasing in fists as I suck the ever-living shit out of his cock. My hands covered in spit, it's dripping off my chin, it's coating his shaft and gathering at the base, and I'm reminded that his balls need to join the party. Looking up at him with a coy glance, I stroke his cock with one hand as I reach inside his jeans. He's breathing hard, mouth hanging open, sweat coating his neck, his hair looks mussed like he's run his hands through it over and over. When I free his balls, I lick the slit at the head of his cock before dipping my head and sucking his balls into my mouth one at a time.

JK begins chanting as I tease his sac and stroke him harder. He says one thing over and over and I take that as my cue he's about the come. Placing my lips on the head, I suck hard while still jacking his cock and he says my name in a long torturous groan and then fills my mouth with cum. He's sat up and pushed his fingers into my hair as he watches me, because let's face it, they always wanna watch. Once he's finished, I swallow his offering and lean up, wiping my bottom lip and breathing hard like him. Hands move from my hair to my cheeks as he runs his thumb under my lower lip and looks at me like I've just shown him nirvana.

Chapter Sixteen

(Yeol yeoseos)

Let me just say, that once JK and I crossed into the territory of oral, we were unstoppable. Anytime we were alone and there was a lock on the door, it was go time. I love to give just as much as I love to get and let me tell you, JK loved it all too. We even resorted to rock, paper, scissors once to see who would go first because we both wanted to, but space didn't allow the 69 position.

I felt like a teenager again, the feelings of having a crush and that crush being the bomb and also wanting to tongue fuck your clit constantly. It was almost like a competition between us, who could make who either moan the loudest, come the fastest or come the longest, it was always something we were doing. However, and maybe as crazy as this seemed, we never got completely naked. He usually never even took his pants off past his ass and I wore skirts a lot. I think we both knew that nakedness was being saved for sex. We still hadn't gone all the way. I didn't know his stance on it, and I didn't want to ask for some reason, like I didn't want him to be offended or put off by my eagerness to go all the way. I also wasn't sure about if premarital sex was a thing here since everyone acted so proper. Asking Hannah, she laughed and then assured me that yes, people took part in premarital sex and not to be fooled by the innocence portrayed by most.

"Remember when we first met and I told you to not go to a DVD bong for a date? Yeah, that's a place where you 'watch' movies in a private room, aka a place to have sex since he still lives with his parents. So trust me, South Korea is no different than other countries in that regard, they just hide it better."

I wanted to go there with JK, but I really was fine with the pace we were keeping and never once with him did I wish we were doing something different.

"Pack," JK simply says as he enters the apartment after knocking once.

"Pack? Like how much?" I ask, standing up from the dining room table.

"Two day," he nods, holding up two fingers.

132

"Wait-" he stops my words with his hand on my chin and a kiss on my lips, before he's retreating back down the hallway to his apartment.

"Two," he repeats, fingers still in the air as he looks back at me, giving me a bunny smile.

Confused, yet not wanting to overthink, I go into my bedroom and look for a small enough bag that's not luggage. I find my largest purse, which let's be honest is literally the size of a medium suitcase. Since I don't know what kind of weather to pack for, or what I'll be doing for these two days, I decide to just grab essentials I like and make it work when I get there. Tucking my toiletry bag in between my clothes, I zip it all up just as my phone buzzes with a message.

THWS: Parking garage.

I reply with the bunny icon I replaced the thumbs up emoji with in our messenger and grab my bag and purse. Heading to the elevator, I press the button for the basement and make the descent, when sudden realization that I'm clueless to what I'm actually doing kicks in. But more really, I'm excited, remembering JK's face when he told me to pack, the way he kissed me. I wonder if we're going somewhere where he won't be recognized as easily as he would be here in South Korea. Not that I mind going out with him wearing a mask, but I know my GNO with Hannah struck a nerve with him and I think he'd prefer being able to show his face while we spend time together.

The doors open, and I look around the garage before stepping out, and when I do, Fred gets out of the driver's side door to open the back door for me. As I walk closer, JK gets out from the backseat and reaches for my bag. I can't help but smile, but he doesn't look at me, well not at first, but when he does, he hits me with that grin I love so much. He says nothing but motions for me to get into the back, and I nearly trip over JK's oversized pack that's laying across the floor. I tuck my legs up on the seat and put my bag on the floor beside his as Jk sits down beside me, telling Fred something as he closes the door.

"Well?" I ask as we emerge and join the traffic of the street, even at midnight.

"You go to Japan?"

"No, I've never been to Japan," I shake my head, my smile threatening.

"We go," he says, pointing between us.

I squeal, like literally squeal. Then hold back my need to hug him and glance to the front at Fred.

"He say nothing, he know we like," JK tells me, again motioning between us.

With that, I wrap my arms around his neck and hug him.

"Really? I mean- is it ok for us to go rogue?" my question has me pulling back to look at his face. I know we have the next couple of days off work, but I still want to make sure I won't get JK busted for breaking some sort of rules.

His eyes look at me tenderly, his hand coming up to run a thumb across my cheek and then along my hair. He doesn't need to answer me, just the way he's looking at me is answer enough. The entire drive to the airport, my arms are wrapped around his arm, my head on his shoulder, my knees on his lap. I'm so excited I feel like my heart's going to burst. Like a kid the night before Christmas. Like a wish I've always wanted has come true. I want him to know how I feel and since I'm me and since this is us, I decide to tweet a song about it.

We're sitting in the airport at our terminal. The airport's dead and it's so odd to be somewhere in public with him, especially an airport and he's not being mobbed. I'm across from him, our feet tangling and tapping in some sort of foot game of tag. We're both on our phones, pretending like we're not paying attention as we play, and I find the song I think best fits how I feel at this moment. Olivia Noelle's - Fck Around & Fall in Luv. Posting it, I put my phone on my lap and watch him as he receives the notice that I've tweeted. He already has his wireless earbuds in and is looking down at his phone, while I imagine he's clicking the link and the song begins. Then, he's looking at me. I know his comprehension of the English language is better than his verbal skills, and I hope he understands enough to really get what I'm trying to say.

He must listen to the song again because it feels like an eternity later before he's smiling at me, low and almost shyly, and it causes me to kick his foot harder.

We board the plane, and he must've purchased all three seats in the row because it's just us two. Sitting side by side, he plays music for us on his phone, sharing earbuds as I spend nearly the entire two-hour flight comparing our hand sizes. I love his hands. Long and strong, they're much bigger than mine, and I love putting mine on top of his and tracing our fingers with my free hand. I think he likes it too, since he doesn't protest to my fidgeting and as we get closer to landing, he again plays the song I tweeted earlier. It makes my heart pound a little faster and my smile hurt my cheeks.

Despite my excitement, I start feeling tired, since this would be around the time I'd be going to sleep combined with sitting for a few hours. As the plane lands I can't stop yawning and clearing my eyes, but notice JK messing with his bag, eventually producing his camera. I don't think anything of it since he has that thing attached to him most times. I admit when we get off the plane and into a taxi, I'm literally dead on my feet and since I don't understand or speak Japanese, I have no idea where we're headed. All I know is we make it to a hotel and as soon as I see the king-size bed, it's lights out.

* * *

Calm. I feel so fucking calm when I wake up with him. I know he's with me before I even come to full consciousness, even with him nearly clear across the bed from me. We like to cuddle, but I find when we aren't confined to space, we both drift away through the night. With my eyes still closed, and my back to him, I squirm and slide all the way to him, my ass hitting the side of his body first. When there's no reaction, I roll over and half my body ends up on his arm and shoulder, even then no reaction. Turning my head, I see his black hoodie pulled up and covering his head, so I reach over and nudge the thick material away from his face. He sleeps with his mouth open, which I find endearing and cute for some reason. It's not like he's breathing t-rex breath on me, which helps. Rolling over to splay my arm and leg over his back and butt, I rub my nose against his and try to bring him slowly from the clutches of sleep.

But he simply mumbles and makes no attempt to wake up. The clock reads ten a.m. and I decide to get up. JK is a night owl and so am I, but I want to venture out sometime this trip. Getting up and entering the bathroom, I notice the soaps and towels are labeled with the Disney Resort logo and gather where we are. It excites me that he'd want to come somewhere like this, because I don't know many guys who willingly would, but I've understood that guys here aren't like the ones I'm used to. Tossing on some jeans and a mom sweater I jacked from Jinho, I leave my wet hair down after my shower and feel my body begin to call out for coffee.

I send a text to JK that I'll be back soon and head down to the lobby, where there are many shops, from Disney apparel to little cafes and themed restaurants. It's everything Disney brings to the table in regards to cute and sweet. After grabbing a coffee, I pop into one of the shops, searching for anything to do with my favorite Disney movie, Nightmare Before Christmas, and I'm in hog heaven with everything Jack, Sally and Halloween Town. But I hold off on buying anything until before we leave, however, some cute classic Mickey and Minnie Mouse garb catches my eye.

Since I'm no fool and know that couples love matching in Korean culture, this would be the most opportune time for us to match for real. We've both worn the same color on purpose before, but I want to take this trip to Disney to a whole other level. I find a black sweatshirt with Mickey on it for him and white one with Minnie on it for me. I know we both have blacked skinny pants and he wore his Timberland boots, while I packed the new ones I just bought last week to match his.

When I arrive back at the room, I hear the shower on in the bathroom and nearly rub my palms together with the excitement that I can get everything set out for him by the time he's done. I change into my sweatshirt, putting half my hair up into two messy pigtail buns that mimic Minnie, then my black pants and boots. Then I set his sweatshirt, and pants onto the bed. Just as I toss his boots onto the floor, the door to the bathroom clicks and I look up as he walks out, the white material of his shirt sticking to his still damp skin, his hair wet and messy, and a towel wrapped around his lower half.

"Reb," he says.

"Hi," I smile, standing straight and showing him my outfit.

His smile at me gives me the tingles and it's more that he's smiling at my presence and hasn't even noticed my outfit or his on the bed.

"I got us something," I say, extending a hand over to the bed.

He steps closer to look and his smile grows even wider, the bunny-smile I fucking love so much, and I notice he hasn't shaved this morning which makes me smile even more, I know this is part of him being himself and not Jung-keun from KT7. He doesn't mock the gift or look at me like I'm crazy or that I'm an asshole for thinking he'd wear a children's cartoon character. Instead, he looks up at me, noticing my shirt and makes the connection. He bows his head slightly, showing me that shy side of him that he gives me sometimes when I think the moments are too tender between us.

"Kyoot," he states, reaching out and pulling on the hem of my sweatshirt.

Nothing in me feels like I need to verify this, no *"Are you sure? We don't have to if you don't want to."* I know he does and that by us matching, it's cementing something between us.

He takes the clothes and changes in the bathroom, while I put on some makeup, mainly red lipstick to match the red of the character and a black choker to finish the look. By the time he's out, I'm ready and I can't stop smiling as I see him. We take selfies together, in front of the mirror and with our arms around each other as he takes a selfie above us. Before heading out to the park, he grabs his video camera and changes the battery for one he must've plugged in when we arrived this morning.

"I want eat," he states as we get on the elevator, and he takes my hand.

I nod, since yes, we should and smile at the giddiness his hand with mine causes. He's too much, I can't take it. The thought has the Warpaint song, So Good popping into my head and I decide to send it to him later. I begin to hum it and he gives my hand a little squeeze. Looking over, he gives me a grin and I know it's because of my voice. I'm no Adele, but that doesn't stop me.

When we get to the main floor, I point over to where I saw the cafes and eateries earlier and we head toward them. I think we both know at this point we are the least picky of eaters and I let him choose a place. As we stand in line, I see him take out his phone and watch as he looks up something.

"Do you speak Japanese?" I question.

"I know little," he answers, studying his phone.

I don't know why, but this surprises me. However, it makes me feel like we're on an even keel, *both* oblivious to our surroundings for once. He orders some dishes for us and we wait off to the side for them, filling our drinks and grabbing chopsticks along with napkins. The place isn't packed, but there's a lot of people, so when I notice a table for two by the entrance, I walk over and sit.

I send one of the pics of me and JK from the bathroom to my girls in our chat and wait for the inevitable 'awww' to come in reply. Putting my phone down, I set up the table and then look over as JK waits for the food. He's not looking at me, but rather at his phone and I wonder if he's being bombarded with work stuff, or even texts from his band mates. I wonder if he told them where we were going, if he even told them we were even going somewhere together. I assume they know we're together, sexually or a relationship, I'm not sure, hell, I'm still not even sure. But my affection for JK hasn't affected my work or the job I do for them. I haven't been showing him any favoritism or anything like that, so I don't think they would even care about us.

Then, JK looks at me and smiles and I know none of that matters.

When he finally joins me, he sits across from me, setting the multiple dishes between us and leans over to kiss me quickly before sitting. Fuck. Not only is he wearing something I picked out, he's got no problems with public displays of affection. It's then I realize, this is the first time we've been out in public that he hasn't covered his face. Yes, he's wearing a black baseball hat, but I can still see his face. I want to ask why he's so open here, but I don't want to ruin the moment.

"This hot maybe," he tells me, shoeing my hand away and deflecting my chopsticks as I attempt to grab some dark glazed meat. He takes a piece into his mouth and begins chewing, it's then I see the small flecks of peppers in the glaze.

He was making sure the food wasn't too spicy for me. FUCK. I *really* can't even.

I look at him expectantly and a few moments later he nods and points at it, and I take it as a sign that it's ok. We eat, and it takes me a while before I realize he's filming me, it doesn't stop me from pigging out or even trying to act decent in front of the camera. Whenever I do, he tells me to stop and part of me thinks he wants to see me as I am in these videos.

"We go..." he says and stops, thinking of the right word, "park?"

"Yeah, can we?"

He nods.

"Did you have anything you wanted to do here?" I ask, since hello, he planned the trip.

He shakes his head, pointing at me. "Trip for you."

My stomach does a flip. I've never had someone do anything for me, well, not like this. Plan a trip away from work, to do something for us to be alone that didn't consist of the backseat of a car or a cheap motel by the freeway. For the first time maybe, I feel like someone wants to spend time with *me*. Which *isn't* odd. But I find most people like me due to my quick wit, humor and outrageous antics at times. With JK, there really isn't any of that. Yes, I make stupid faces for photos and do happy dances randomly, but all the other stuff is lost on him. He's getting me, like the *real* me. Rebecca. Not Rebel, the quirky, weird haired chick. Rebecca, who loves holding hands, matching clothes and spending the day at a theme park.

"Eat," he tells me, and I realize I've just been lost in my head and not in the moment.

I'm hurtling, Lord am I plummeting into the sea of love with him. Can you blame me? I haven't been this lovesick since seeing Zac Efron in High School Musical. My fingers are clawing at the cliff, attempting to not fall, but the ground is crumbling beneath my palms as we walk through the park, riding the teacups and holding hands every chance we can. He films us the whole day, sharing ice cream, trying on themed hats, even when our kissing beneath one of the trees gets a little out of hand and we forget where we are for a few minutes. It's all perfect, and I mean really perfect. If this was before South Korea, before JK and this was a date with some dude back home, it would seem a scheme to try and fuck me, a fake date pretending to love what we're doing just so I would give ass at the end of the night in thanks. This is not that. The way his eyes light up when we see a cool roller coaster, or how he laughs at me when I scream about being splashed on a water ride. He's having just as much fun and in turn, I'm able to really let all my guards down and have a blast too.

When the sun sets, we find a spot to watch the electric light parade, off to the side and away from the crowd for the most part. His arm around my shoulder as I take pics of us some more and we mess with the filters as we wait. My feet hurt and I'm tired from being in the sun and out all day, but I wouldn't change anything. I haven't had this much fun in so long, maybe ever and I decide I want him to know that, but again, sending it in any other form than verbal seems so basic right now. So as JK does something on his phone, I type in my words and read over the translation, happy that I sort of already knew most the words as I reread it.

He knocks my knee with his as the parade starts and we both watch as the light covered floats pass down the street in front of us. I can't help but look over at him and smile, his eyes wide and mouth open like he does when he's totally immersed in something. Leaning over, he pulls me tighter with his arm as I place my lips by his ear and speak to him in Korean.

"Thank you for bringing me here and spending the day with me, I'll never forget it."

He looks at me, the neon lights flashing and coloring one side of his face as he takes in my words and the language. I feel shy, like maybe I said it all wrong or something. But then his hand is on my chin and his lips on mine, kissing me sweetly as I can't help but smile against his lips. Just then a loud pop startles me and I look away and up to the sky as fireworks begin to shoot off. Sigh, yup, that's pretty much what it feels like, fireworks. His hands still on my face, his eyes still on me as I look back. The way he looks at me, the way his fucking eyes say a million things to me, how they make me feel. I know I'm more than just a bed buddy to him. If he wanted that, wouldn't he have passed all this slow build and just fucked me the first chance he could.

But I want more. I want to give *him* more and everything I can.

"Can we go back to the hotel?"

Chapter Seventeen

(Sibchil)

My fingers run down the soft, pale skin of his cheek. Those beautiful brown spheres I've come to crave look down at me, so much of what he doesn't say and what we can't communicate shows there. As my fingers gently begin to fall from his jaw one by one, his hand snakes around my wrist, urging me back in contact and so I repeat my caress. His skin is beautiful, porcelain personified against the black of my nail polish.

Leaning in I inhale his skin as I press my nose to the column of his long neck, our bodies pressing together as he reacts to my closeness. His fingers brush against mine at our sides and they begin to stroke and move in tentative touches. My lips part as I breathe him in, my forehead following the cut of his chiseled jaw and my eyes close. I want to take in this moment, this time. He makes me understand that I never knew my true self before, that I never knew my feelings before. I've always used quick wit and words to express myself and not having that with him has opened something inside me. That by being around him I sense that everything is passing by and we can't stop it, but we can cherish it and make it real. I feel real with him. Destiny with him.

A low baritone sound hums in his throat against me and I gently press my lips to kiss the spot that vibrated his skin. Another sound emerges before a hand moves into my hair, his head pivoting as I hear him inhale my scent. I think about the songs we've posted to one another, the hidden messages and meanings that music can convey. I think about the long looks. The times I thought he was jealous and the times I knew he was. I think about everything between us that's been a thing since the moment we met.

Raising my head to look at him, my hand frees from his as I push my fingers beneath the heaviness of his sweatshirt. I know I'm taking a risk here. To show me his skin, is a big deal. Yes, we've been intimate, but never naked together. So, I slowly begin to glide my hands up, the material pushing higher with my movement and I watch his face for any sign of unease, but there is none. I can feel the ripples of muscle and tight skin as our eyes remain locked. When I reach his chest, he moves his arms, raising them to let me completely remove the hoodie. Even then, I can't look at him. I literally cannot look down. I know what's there, well, what I've imagined and seen small glimpses of while observing dance practice. Once I look, I know I'll fucking lose my mind and climb this man like a stripper pole. I can tell he's wondering why I'm not drinking him in, his eyes searching mine briefly, before a small smile curls the corner of his lips. I'm still gripping his sweatshirt in my hands in front of me and resisting the urge to bring it to my nose for a deep, embarrassing, eye crossing inhale. He gently tugs it from my grasp which leaves me feeling the unease of needing to grab something yet resisting the urge for that something to be him.

I inhale deeply as his hands make purchase on my hips and immediately my hands find his forearms. His eyes leave mine as he looks down at my body, dark hair falling across his forehead and I reach up to sweep my fingertips across the fringe before he's lowering his head and my lips press where his hair had covered moments ago. My eyes close as I smell him, feel his smooth skin, take in the firmness of his hands still anchored securely on me. He whispers something I can't make out, then again as he raises his head, trailing his nose along my cheek as I pull back and then...he's kissing me. The press of our lips soft, tentative, yet there's an underlying yearning that's so kinetic I feel it radiating off both of us. Again, the need, the *need* to just take him is so fucking there, but something in me is telling me not yet. This is perfect, this slow, languid, experimentation, I've never had this. Not even juvenile groping was this tentative for me. This is the kind of sex romance authors write about, artists sculpt, people in French movies act out. His lips brush over mine for a moment before returning for a longer, more firm press.

The lights from the bedside tables are on and illuminating one side of our bodies and I look at him, my hands moving down the side of his face to his neck and down to his pecs, Christ, his muscles. My fingers graze down the blocks of his abs, to the flat smooth skin below his navel and down to the material of his boxer briefs. His shaky breath stutters across my lips and as I lift my hands to repeat the motion, I feel the tug of his hands on the bottom of my sweatshirt, so I lift my arms and let him take it off me. I'm in a black sheer bra that leaves nothing to the imagination and my attention is on his face as he looks down at my chest. He shows no hesitation as he palms them, moaning as he leans in to kiss my neck and my arms fall around his shoulders. A soft moan escapes me as he plumps and squeezes my tits while his lips dance across the sensitive skin and my mouth falls open. In the same moment JK begins to pull the straps of my bra down, I reach to unclasp it and we both work to remove it from my arms.

Before I can get my bearings, JK is kissing down my body as he moves to his knees. My fingers dive into his hair as his long fingers grip the sides of my leopard print thong and he pushes it down my legs for me to step out of. His palms return up their path, this time inside my thighs and I try to push him away because I don't need oral or any other stimulation down there besides his dick. Looking up at me, he's confused, and I take his hands to signal for him to stand as I cup his face and kiss his lips, mumbling in between long laps of my tongue along his. "I don't need that, I need you to make love to me."

Next thing I know, I'm on the bed and he's crawling over me, totally naked. His body is as expected, ripped, muscular and strong and his ass used to be my obsession but I think it's now being taken over by his perfect dark nipples. I open my legs for him before my thighs are being pushed even wider by his hips. Lips attach to my neck again since he knows that's already my hot button, my hands grip his biceps as they strain and flex from holding his upper body off mine. My eyes close, neck kisses are the death of me, I practically shut down from the sensation and from his growling. Oh yes, he's fucking growling. Kissing, licking and growling...and then, biting.

"Fuck," I gasp, my nails sinking into his skin as my legs tighten around him.

His tongue laps over the spot he's just attacked with his teeth as I feel the blunt head of his dick pushing against me, searching for my entrance. JK's curled over me, arching his hips as he rests his forehead on my shoulder and looks down between us. I want to reach down and help, but as the thought comes, he's sliding inside. He groans long and loud as his head drops and his cheek now presses against my shoulder. I inhale and bite my lower lip, my eyes growing heavy with the feeling and knowing of what we're doing. He's so hard, *so* hard and his body's so tight and muscular, everything flexing as he steadily feeds my pussy his cock.

"Shit," I state damn near slurred and drunkenly, my legs falling open wider.

He pants something, then looks at me. His body pauses as he looks in my eyes, my heavy eyelids and trembling body having other ideas. He repeats his words as one palm slides up my cheek and his nose runs along mine, his other hand firmly cupping the side of my face and his upper body weight lays over me. I love this feeling, the heaviness and knowing I couldn't really get out of this embrace if I tried, but why would I want to. He's still not moving, and I place my hand over his, willing my eyes to stop being controlled by the feeling of his dick and open up. Our eyes connect, and I know this moment is something I won't ever forget. The looking, the feeling, the emotions, it's all right here and it's all I've dreamt about. JK's body is trembling slightly, and I sense some hesitation in his eyes, and I know why he's being like this, I've known for a while now or at least thought it was a possibility until this moment.

"Come on, it's ok," I coax him in a whisper, tilting my head up to run my lips over his and get him back in the moment.

He begins to kiss me back and I arch my back to push my hips up, grinding half his cock inside me. My moans are unchecked and the sound of my wetness as I slide up and down him has me needing more. JK growls with every push of my hips until he can't take it and his fingers grip my face and neck as he fully enters me. My mouth falls open in a silent 'o' and my breath stutters. His lips attack my neck once again as I grind my pussy greedily into his thrusts and his hands force mine above my head, my back arching as he lifts his upper body and looks down to watch my tits bouncing every time he bottoms out.

"Oh my God," I chant. "Yes, give me that cock," I plead. I say everything and anything I'm thinking, I can't help it. My words complimenting and demanding, telling him how good he is and how he's driving me crazy. Freeing my pinned arms, my hands touch every bit of his bare skin that I can reach, before finally my fingers slide into the notches between his ribs, cut with muscle and making my thighs quiver with the perfection of him.

Then, we roll and I'm on top. Sitting up, I reach back and place my hands on his hard, thick thighs. He grunts, reaching up and groping my tits as I begin to ride him.

"Reb," he moans, his cock throbbing inside me and I know he's close to coming.

I understand, I'm close too. We've been fucking teasing each other since day one and hello, I've had a hard on for the guy since before we met, of course I'm close. I milk his dick, riding him like I've *never* ridden anyone in my life. Like we're being filmed and it's about to go live. His thighs tense beneath my palms and since I don't want to be left behind, I take one hand and snake it in front of me. My fingers make fast work on my clit as he repeats my name and his fingertips dig into my hips. My ass bounces as I move faster, my orgasm beginning to fill my limbs with that chaotic euphoria. I moan loudly as I begin to come, my body doing I don't know what as my insides shoot off with sensation.

I'm only back to awareness when I'm brought down onto his sweaty chest and I happily lay on his slick holy water coated skin. We're both breathing hard and I hear his heart pounding beneath my ear. Looking up at him, he's smiling to himself, his face covered in sweat like it gets when he performs on stage. He looks rather pleased with this performance and I begin to make the comment when he tilts his cheek to look at me and says, "First time."

I smile, looking up at him, "I know."

He seems surprised, but I had a sneaking suspicion a while ago that he was a virgin. A sneaking suspicion that I realized was true when he had that moment of panic earlier. I don't know when the thought came to me, but his hesitation when we'd been intimate before, I thought was because he was trying to be respectful. Which he was, but it was also because he'd never done any of it before. I didn't know how to broach the subject or even if I should bring something like that up, for guy pride and all. What if I was wrong and made him feel self-conscious or like anything he had done with me up until this point wasn't mind blowing, because it fucking was. Knowing this was his first time and that it was with me, fuck, it instantly cemented and sealed something in me like he was mine. Shit, I can understand why dudes preferred virgins now.

"Well, it wasn't my first time," I smile.

"I know," he scrunches his nose and gives me his bunny smile.

With that, I move to smack his arm, but he grabs my wrist, rolling us as he pins it above my head on the pillow, his body moving over me and my legs instantly part around him.

"Again?" I tease, but in all honesty, I'm not surprised he could go again.

Nodding is his reply as he leans down and kisses me.

The virgin turnaround time is shocking, and I think of my FIT TO FUCK shirt and how a statement has never been more accurate. Who knew that once the seal was broken on that cock that it was like a homing beacon targeted at me, and I willingly accepted every time. The more we touched and kissed and got familiar with our naked flesh, the more confident he became in what we were doing and with his skills. He was open and experimenting, touching me in a way I've been touched before but with him it was so different. He made me feel so different. Maybe it was the way he looked at me as his fingers slid inside me, or how he ran his fingers up and down the back of my neck when his cock was in my mouth, how his hands linked with mine or how firm he held me, all I know is that this was a whole other level of fucking.

"You can kiss me," he smiles, mocking my words from the night on the rooftop patio as we lay in bed after another session.

The room's dark, the lights from the park shining in through the windows in a kaleidoscope of colors. We're facing each other talking and with that last comment, I smack his arm

"I didn't need you tell me," he adds.

"Well, I wasn't sure since you weren't making your move," I state.

"I was unsure...if I like you then," he tells me honestly.

Looking at him, I run my fingertips gently over his lips. "No?"

He shakes his head slightly, looking down as he takes my hand and begins to run our fingers along one another's. "I don't know, then roof, you sad hurt my heart...I thought you like Jaimin, not me."

He wasn't sure about me until that night we looked at the stars, the night I was upset about Chapman's suicide attempt. I was vulnerable that night and he clearly saw that.

"You have no nickname for me, just initials. Everyone else, not me. But they know I like you, that day you shop, Jinho hyung stop you. He know I want time with you, you with no one else but me."

He means our first meeting when I went down the line saying everyone's name and the then nicknames I'd assigned everyone. And now it makes sense to all the commotion Jinho caused that day. It wasn't that I was going out, but they knew JK wanted to spend time with me. The feeling his words give me, makes my heart soft and I can't hide my smile. All the worries I had about where he stood with me, how he felt about me are totally fucking gone.

"Oh, I *had* a nickname for you, but I didn't think saying that yours was 'my future boyfriend' was the best thing to say when we first met," I tease, but for real though.

"I like you, before you come here," he states.

"Huh?" thinking that my Korean translation and his broken English misheard his words.

"They say you come work, I look online, I see you," he says, mocking typing on a computer keyboard with our fingers.

"Ohhhh? And what did you think?" I smile, batting my eyelashes and stealing a hand to place on my chest.

His hand takes mine again, his other running along my cheek as he says, "I think you pretty...you fun...I like you on outside, not know inside."

Could this be? Was he looking forward to meeting me like I was him? I mean clearly there was no level of obsession like mine, I take the cake for that.

"You did?" my teasing turns to a tone I use for him, soft.

"I look at your Instagram and Facebook at night...every night. You say you feel like you need meet me...I feel too."

I don't know why, but emotion or something hits me, and I have to swallow hard. I don't know if it's his words reminding me how I felt before I came here, how he was a mission for me and now here we are. Here he is meaning so much more than a job or an assignment. He's naked in bed with me, touching me, telling me he also had the feeling he needed to meet me. It's in times like this, when the universe clicks and everything, EVERYTHING feels like it's meant to be and that strange sensation that all is right and harmonious comes over you for a split second. Of course, he notices my expression as the sensation takes over and I'm lost in it, his fingertip taps the tip of my nose gently and I'm back in it. His nose is crinkled at the bridge, looking all bunny-ish and cute, and I know he's about to say something.

"You say very dirty word when together, in bed."

I 'pfft' then begin to laugh, because he has no idea how dirty my mouth can really be.

"I can't help it, this cock is so good," I state, reaching down and taking said cock into my palm.

* * *

We spend the night in bed, in the bathroom, on the dresser, on a chair and well, you get the idea. We don't sleep and barely make time to eat, but of course we made a little time for that.

#Can'tKeepAHungryBunnyDown.

We didn't go back to the park, but eventually we ventured out into Tokyo. Shopping and eating, we walked all over, JK shooting video and me leading the way through the sometimes congested streets. With neither of us knowing Japanese made me feel like we were tourists, both winging it. It seemed like no one recognized JK as we walked, but we still, unconsciously I think, remained to appear as friends to anyone who would happen to notice us. Until we would be in the back of a shop, or once while we sat side by side at a little bar for dinner, kisses being snuck and hands occasionally making contact never failed to make me smile and fight the urge to grab him and haul his ass into the bathroom.

When we got back to the hotel that night, I tried on the clothes I bought that day and gave JK a little fashion show, to which he stripped everything off until I was naked.

"I like this best," he told me, pulling me on his lap before kissing me.

The two days fly and before I know it, we're heading to the airport and back to Seoul. This trip was amazing for as short as it was, and I feel like JK and me are cemented and solidified. There's an underlying knowing that we can't be open publicly about us. I've come to realize that the fans in this neck of the woods are overly and sometimes ridiculously critical of their idols. Think American boyband fans times a million in the possessive and opinionated. It's not a bad thing, but sometimes it blows my mind. They flat out tell idols during chats to change their hair, to stop making funny noises all the time, dafuq? They are territorial when it comes to idols and to think one is dating, I think South Korea would implode from the internal anger. I also know, it would end his career. I read once about a K-pop couple, both in the same group, when found out about, the fans refused to accept it and eventually the ridicule was so intense the group disbanded.

We have to take an earlier flight than when we arrived and this time at the airport, it's busy and we both wear masks and hoodies, more so because we're exhausted than anything else. We also remain in our personal spaces, sitting next to each other in our terminal, but not touching, hell we're barely even talking, my brains so fried. When it is time to board, I have to wake the sleeping bunny and as soon as we take our seats, my head rests on his shoulder and it's lights out.

"We go somewhere before home," he says to me in the back of the SUV being driven by Fred who picked us up from the airport.

The sun's begun to set now, and I've removed my hood and mask, although I feel like the bags under my eyes are big enough that they should've been checked as luggage on the plane. Regardless, JK looks at me as he says this in such a way I know he's planning to surprise me once more.

"I can't imagine anything being better than the last two days," I whisper in his ear and he gives me a semi-crinkled nose before putting his hand over my mouth.

Fred stops the vehicle and JK takes my hand as we exit. We're at an entrance to someplace and I look beyond to see a tower light up. There are crowds of people but it's not overly packed and I follow as he leads me towards a ticket booth. I look around as he buys tickets and then walks toward a line to take a gondola up to the tower. I bet the view is amazing up there and I turn to tell JK but pause as I notice he has his camera out and is filming me and our surroundings, so I just smile and look back at the tower.

We stand in line for only ten or so minutes and as we wait I notice all sorts of tourists speaking different languages, even some English, and I wonder why I've never heard of this tower before. JK's camera is trained on me during the ride up and out the window as we rise.

Before we get to the stop, JK takes my hand, the camera's back in his bag and he asks, "You heard Namsan Tower?" and I shake my head. The gondola stops, and people begin to shuffle off, it's then I notice that mostly the people who rode with us, look like couples, all holding hands and looking longingly into one another's eyes.

We step off and it's then I see, locks. There are padlocks of all different colors covering, and I mean COVERING, the rails and fences surrounding the base of the tower. I'm in awe of the amount and density, there's nothing but locks everywhere. Walking over to the railing, I see writing on each lock, and flip them with my fingers.

"Locks of love," he tells me, and I look over at him, consumed by this place and still processing the enormity of beauty in the meaning and visibly seeing all the love that's been here and still resides.

Reaching into his camera bag, he pulls out two padlocks and a black marker. Handing me one, I look down to see he's drawn a Korean flag and American flag on one side.

"You write," he tells me, handing me the marker, "Make wish."

My heart flutters and I can't help but smile, I don't know if this is as deep as I think it is, if it's more of a wish for a general love, or our love, but whatever his meaning, I fucking dig it. Taking the marker, I write our names and the date, then a heart and a bunny head. When I'm finished, I hand him the marker, but he waves his hand and I see he's already written on his. I want to read it but it's in Korean so there goes that.

"It wrote name and wish," he states, taking my lock and intertwining the loops before reaching over to the rail and connecting our linked locks to another, sealing it forever.

"Where's the key?" I ask out of curiosity.

"Trash. No need," he shakes his head.

Sliding my hands into the caves of his hoodie to cup his cheeks, I lean in and rub our noses together, before pecking his lips. "Take a picture with me," I state. We take photos of us and our locks, staying up at the tower for a bit as he also films with his camera. When we arrive back to the apartments, he comes to mine without even going to his and I don't know if it's because he thinks everyone's sleeping anyhow or what. We eat first thing and then shower, and maybe because we're both exhausted, curl into bed with pajama pants and hoodies on, ready to sleep. With my back to his front, his breath caressing over my ear as my lullaby, he softly and in that deep tone he uses, says, "Lock say I want us love forever."

Chapter Eighteen

(Sibpal)

It's been three weeks since our return from Japan and I feel like the time since has been like a dream. No, really, like how I used to imagine things would be like when I was a million miles away in California. Sometimes it feels like an alternate universe to even look at him face to face, but to hold him and kiss him, to feel him on me, shit that's a whole other level of surreal. I was a fiend for his touch, his look, his smell, the way the fabric of his clothes felt under my hands, the sound of his unlaced Timberland boots in the hallway, I needed it all and constantly.

The days I didn't see him much I felt damn near sad and wondered what life was even for. I was hooked, a ridiculous girl who let a boy take over her entire well, everything. The boy controlled my systems, nervous, respiratory, shit even my solar system. I hated myself on the days we weren't together, like haaaaated. I was pathetic and then beat myself up for having it so bad for him. But then he'd text, or tweet me a song, send me a photo, all showing me or telling me how much he missed me and couldn't wait to see me. This is why I was so hard up, because he was so hard up for me too, and had no problem telling or showing me.

I will say that this is something so opposite than any of my experiences in America. A guy acted like I didn't even exist until he knew he could get in my pants and I reflected the same behavior, acted like I didn't give a shit 99% of the time. I'd never had such an attentive partner and I too have never been so aware of someone's needs. I started carrying snacks in my purse because he was always hungry, I found out he had rhinitis, so I carried tissues, I was ready and prepared for anything he needed and one of the things he needed a lot, was me.

I felt desired and special, looked after and with him completed. I knew from before we met it was going to be like this, but as luck would have it, he felt the same. What I didn't expect was for it to happen so fast. We slow burned until he kissed me and since then, since Namsan Tower, it feels like we've been full steam ahead. We didn't say we loved each other, not out right, but shit what he wrote on the lock and the way we've been since, is all the knowing I need. I've turned into one of those chicks I used to gag over, the ones who were so in love they couldn't function without the guy. I mean I *can* function, just barely. But now I finally understand why, because the feeling of love, being loved and giving love is so fucking consuming. If my girls saw me now, they'd probably laugh their asses off at how whipped I've become. But again, I down myself when I'm alone and pissy over how I feel, then I see him, and he gives me the softest smile, his eyes looking into my body like x-ray vision and the low baritone of his voice when he says my name, I'd die a thousand deaths to live in those moments and it's in those moments I'm reminded of why I feel like I do.

JK and I don't get to go out much, not just us, and that's fine. The last thing I ever want is to come in between him and the guys. So often times when he tells me they're all going to eat or doing something and invites me, I decline. Again, I want to, but I don't want to be an eighth wheel.

But this time, I've done the planning. I found out Hannah's birthday was coming and arranged to take her to dinner at one of her favorite places. Somehow the guys got word of this and decided they too wanted to come and ok'ed it with Hannah. I made sure all the guys knew they needed to bring a gift for her to which I thought they'd ask for some help in choosing, but they didn't. Even JK told me he was all set on her gifts. So aside from the private room at the restaurant, ordering her a fabulously chic cake, I signed her up for her favorite cosmetic company's monthly box and for a spa retreat with me in Tokyo sometime this year.

It was a casual affair, but Hannah told me she wanted to dress up, so like any good friend I took my look to another level. Thanks to JK I had plenty of clothes to pick from and opted for a black almost trench coat looking dress that was loose and the tie around the middle cinched my waist. The material ended just below my ass and I opted for thick, black thigh high tights and black ankle boots that laced up the front. Sleeking my hair back with a center part, I gathered my hair into a low bun and left the hint of collarbone and top swell of breast when the dress was shifted just the right way. All I had on underneath was a matching lace bra and thong duo that I couldn't wait to show JK later. Red lipstick, bronzed cheeks, black smoky eyes and I'm ready to roll.

Gathering in the entryway to the apartment, JK's eyes scorch me when he sees me and the other guys all smile at my appearance since I don't think they've ever seen me so done up before. When we're all accounted for and I notice everyone has a gift in hand, Shoogi leads the way to the elevators as I walk between JK and Jaimin, who lately JK has constantly been referring to as Mister Jaimin, Jaimin-ssi. I don't know the reasoning behind it, but I'm obsessed with hearing JK say it, maybe because every time he does, it makes Jaimin giggle in that adorable way only Jaimin can get away with.

Glancing around to look at them, all make-up free, some in hats, Ye in a surgical mask, casually dressed, just looking for a night out, and all still looking so damn good. Sometimes I just stare at them, especially in these down moments and I'm offended with how handsome and good they look, so much so I often mock calling the police on my cell to report a crime, which they don't understand the joke, but that's not the point. I also can't ignore the fact that JK's glued himself to either my side or behind me, like he's shielding the others from checking me out. Oh, my protective bunny.

Down in the parking garage, we all pile into two SUV's, stopping to give Fred a bow while he gives me a wave and the swap in customary greetings still never fails to give me a smile. JK pulls my arm and I continue to smile since sometimes my bunny can be a little jealous and I let him help me into the vehicle. I'm sitting between JK and Jaimin when everything's settled, and we haven't even pulled out of the garage before Jaimin looks at me, puppy dog eyes on lock, accompanied with a little pout to his lips.

"Gansig?" (Snack.)

"We're going to eat, you'll ruin your dinner," I comment at the same time JK does.

"Jaimin-ssi!" he says loudly and the two begin to bicker in a dialect Joon finally explained to me called Satoori, the dialect makes them sound tougher or something but really it just makes me smile even more.

While they do this, I reach in my purse for the inquired snacks and pull out a small bag of spicy rice cake sticks, handing them to Jaimin who snatches them before JK can. Like any good girlfriend, I quickly push another one into JK's hand before he can steal the one I've given to his friend. They finish grumbling to one another before both thanking me and Joon turns around in his seat.

"Sorry, I don't have anymore," I tell him.

He waves his hand like he doesn't want snacks anyway. "Can we make time to talk soon?"

"Sure, now or..." I trail off.

"Maybe tonight, it's just personal stuff, not business."

"Oh, of course, whenever you want," I nod.

Not sure if this is about my personal business or his, like he wants to know about me and JK. But he seems chill and not like he's irritated so I take it for what it is and put it aside in order to have fun tonight.

Joon turns back around as Hooni tells a story that has everyone laughing while my man gently taps my ribs with his elbow. I lean over to JK who's quietly mumbling something about Joon to me, I assume asking what he said, his lips pushed out in that pouty way they all speak. But before he can finish and with a quick glance to make sure no one is looking, I stick my tongue out and run it up his protruding mouth, which effectively causes him to stop talking.

"You taste spicy," I say more to myself and look away smiling.

My move has JK silent beside me, then I see out of the corner of my eye as he leans over to check on Jaimin, who's looking out the window before he's taking my hand and placing it over the hardness of his dick. Shit.

"You can't do that to me," I mouth as I look back at him.

His brows raise, understanding he's telling me the same, touché. I can't help myself, I run my fingers up and down his length before he's taking my hand and placing it back on my lap and returning to his bag of chips at the same moment Jaimin turns to ask me something.

We arrive at the restaurant and are led back to the room, thankfully there's little fanfare over seeing the guys by any customers and I think they're able to sneak in undetected. The room, like the restaurant, is sleek and elegant but very softly lit and sexy. The room is a dark wood while the table is big and could seat more than just us nine, but it's set up with gorgeous flowers and candles all along the center like I requested.

"Where should I put these?" Shoogi asks me, holding up a bouquet I just noticed he brought with him. The flowers are blue and purple hydrangeas, and just as I'm about to suggest he set them by the plate at the head of the table, Hannah walks in.

She looks stunning in a fits like a glove soft pink dress that ends just above her knee, while the sleeves end at her forearms. A dress she showed me in a long line of options, I thought the pink suited her and I'm happy she went with it. Her hair's down and she looks all glowy and classy like always, just tonight a little more...happy. She exchanges bows with the guys and is all smiles, especially when Shoogi hands her the flowers. I swear I see her light up from the inside. I know chicks like getting flowers, but man, she was looking pretty happy to get them from him.

We take our seats as the food begins to arrive and drinks begin to flow. I sit between JK and Hooni, and I love all the little noises Hooni makes as he listens to the others talking or when he eats. Since I can understand a little more Korean now, I take part in the stories that are being told about when the group first formed and what they thought of each other than compared to now. We laugh a lot, eat a lot and drink a lot. No one's hammered but I think we're all nicely buzzed. By the time we're finished eating, I feel closer to Hooni and Ye who have been talking with me and JK most of dinner. Jinho and Joon have been talking with Jaimin while Shoogi and Hannah have been quietly conversing in between conversation with us all. I can tell by Hannah's smile she's enjoying herself and that makes me happy.

"You beautiful," JK says softly in my ear as the waitress walks in with the small chocolate cake decorated in little candles.

I give him a small smile as we all begin singing happy birthday in Korean and watch as Hannah blows out the candles.

I'm the first to give my gift, then JK hands her a large box that ends up being a new camera she can vlog with. Hooni's next with a bottle of Asian vodka and decadent looking box of chocolates. Jinho and Jaimin's is a combined gift of coffee and vitamins which are strangely expensive here. Then Ye blows everyone's mind with an entire outfit, from the clothes to the shoes to the purse that has me and Hannah both shocked. Then, Shoogi hands her a small wrapped box and says something to her that no one can hear. Delicately she unwraps the paper and reveals a bottle of perfume.

"This is my favorite, thank you! Thank you everyone for your generosity and celebrating my birthday," she smiles widely.

"Favorite perfume, huh?" I comment to myself and JK nudges my rib with his elbow. "What?" I whisper with wide eyes.

"Mind business," he mumbles.

I mock him childishly with a roll of my eyes and he pushes my shoulder with a playful smile. I smack his leg and we begin poking and picking at one another, while everyone around us starts talking about karaoke. Before I know it, I'm being whisked down some stairs to the lower level of the same building to a neon light paradise. It's a karaoke bar clearly and I'm near the back of the pack and don't hear Joon and Jinho talking to the woman at the counter.

I just follow as we're led to a private room bathed in black lights and a neon light disco ball thing with one wall completely taken up but a screen. Speakers are all around the room and I see props along another wall. My arms tugged and I turn to see everyone standing in a circle.

"Rock, paper, scissor," Joon says.

"Ah," I nod and make a fist, looking down at the other hands.

"Ani myun Jinhogo..Kai Bai Bo," Hooni sings out and we all shoot.

It takes a minute to see who's won the round and Shoogi and Ye step out of the game.

"Kai Bai Bo," he says again, and I shoot scissors, moments after JK taps my hand with his fist and I'm out.

The chant comes faster the fewer people now involved and when Hooni loses next, the game ends and I realize the teams have been divided. My sleeve is tugged away from JK's side and I face him, Jaimin, Jinho and Joon as they look at my team, me, Shoogi, V, Hannah and Hooni. I can tell JK is maybe slightly annoyed about the situation when I see his tongue bulging his cheek as Ye slides an arm around my shoulders and teases JK, who quickly pulls his tongue away and with those goddamn pouty lips and quips to Ye about something, probably how bad my singing is.

Jinho and Shoogi leave to go to the bar for us and the rest of us look through the song books and props. The guys come back with drinks and the games begin. Luckily, the professionals in my group take over for the first few rounds before the other team argues that we haven't had a turn. Fortunately, I think everyone's drank enough that don't sound like complete shit, it also helps that Hannah is good. We're all laughing and having a blast and Joon asks me if I'll come with him for the next round of drinks.

The invite is welcomed and I'm eager to get out of the room where the lights have been starting to fuck with my eyes. Even though still neon, not as harsh as the room and we walk down the hallway to the busy bar area near the front. Joon orders the drinks and pulls me up closer to the actual bar so I don't get swept away in the crowd as the bartender hands us waters while we wait.

"Joon. You're killing me, what did you want to talk about?"

He smiles and covers his mouth with his large hand as he's just taken a sip of his water.

"Sorry."

"Spill the beans man, what's up?"

Taking another drink of water, he leans forward onto the bar with his forearms resting on the top as he looks over toward the door, then at me.

"So, I met this girl."

Ok, I guess I was stressing because the weight that lifts off my chest causes me to sigh and my shoulders relax.

"She's well, not a girl-"

"A woman," I nod in understanding.

"Yes," he smiles, nodding back and I raise my brows for him to continue. "I met her online, actually, she's a fan."

"Tell me EVERYTHING!" I smile, exploding inside with how awesome.

"She's cute, short, funny-"

"Cute, short, funny, sounds like me," I tease with a wide grin.

"Blonde," he continues.

"Blonde?" I question with raised eyebrows.

"American."

"American!" I shriek, my voice getting higher with excitement at every letter.

"She lives in California."

"Wait, this isn't me, right?" I ask with furrowed brows.

"No," he laughs.

"Well, what's her name?" I smile, smacking his arm

"Jaz," he says with dimpled cheeks, a cute smile, and I can tell he's going soft just thinking of her.

"Oh my God, that's awesome, how exciting!"

He nods, looking down at his bottle of water.

"What's that face? What's the problem?"

"There's no problem, but...she's mentioned before that she doesn't think her parents would approve of us dating. She assures me it's fine, that she doesn't need them to determine her life, but...I feel bad about it. The last thing I'd ever want is to tear her family apart."

"Does she live with them?"

"Yes, she's finishing school so she's kind of dependent on them, she's working and paying for school."

"She can go live in my apartment if it's an issue," I shrug.

He gives me a long look before saying, "You'd do that?"

"Sure, why not?" I ask, sipping from my water.

"Because you don't even know her," he states.

"So? You know her, and you like her. I want to help with anything you guys need."

"Because it's your job," he nods in understanding.

"No." I shake my head, "I like you guys, I consider you friends, I'd do anything I could for you guys, work related or not."

"So, you would let someone move into your apartment, but what about when you go back to L.A.?"

"Well...I think I'm gonna stay here for a while," I answer, sipping my drink.

"Really?" he replies with raised brows. "Any reason?"

"I like it, like, a lot. I feel really good here, and besides I don't think my work with you guys is anywhere close to being done."

He gives me a thoughtful look, probably knowing that JK might have something to do with my statement. It's never been openly discussed that we're together, but it's not like we've been secretive. However, we are respectful and I refrain from humping him in front of everyone.

We spend hours singing and goofing around, but honestly the lights start making me not feel good, so I've stopped drinking and have been pounding the waters. Because we aren't sitting together, it takes longer than usual for JK to notice my decline and comes to sit beside me, instantly asking me what's wrong. I tell him and he's then suggesting to the others that we go. I feel like a shithead and tell him that I can just leave, but he brushes me off.

We get into the SUV, noticing Hannah and Shoogi are the last to come out of the bar. I watch them as Shoogi hails her a cab before he gets in the SUV. I wonder if this chemistry is something I'm now just noticing or has been going on the whole time and I never paid attention before. Could this be the mystery man she spoke of at out GNO? I make a note to ask her next time we're alone.

Me, JK and Jinho sit in the back, all the guys aside from JK talking about the night. JK's looking at me like he does when he's hungry and I reach my hand in my purse and retrieve something I know will make him happy. Picking the bag of banana kicks, which are corn snacks shaped and flavored like banana and covered in chocolate, JK's favorite treat and one I carry just for him. Looking over at me, he gives me a look that I can only describe as he wants to growl with frustration and then kiss the fuck out of me, and in return I smile while opening the bag and putting them into his palm.

Entering my apartment alone since JK's gone to his apartment to play video games for a while. I head into the kitchen and take some headache tabs and down a glass of water. Seeing my laptop sitting open on my dining room table, reminds me I need to check my work emails, which is the last thing I want to do with a headache, but I need to before I go to bed.

A while later, the keypad beeps and the door clicks open. I hear JK taking off his boots by the door, before he comes into view.

"I'll be there shortly," I tell him as I finish replying to an email.

Fifteen minutes later, my head feels better, and I feel good having taken care of work until tomorrow. Heading toward the bedroom, I turn off the lights along the way.

JK's sitting on the middle of the bed, legs bent and crossed under one another, remote in hand as he looks at the television on the wall by the door, but not me. He's lost in what he's doing, looking shook as he studies the options. Entering the bathroom, I remove my clothes but leave on my black lacey under things, the dainty lace barely containing my tits. Hearing the intro to Sponge Bob coming from the bedroom doesn't surprise me and I smile just before lathering face wash on my cheeks. One of the unexpected perks of coming to South Korea has been the skincare and all the shit Hannah suggested I get, Lord is it top notch and my skin's never looked so damn good. Putting the TAO cleansing brush into the cleaning station after giving my face a delightful wash, I'm still rubbing Vitamin C serum into my skin as I walk into the bedroom. JK is still sitting in the same spot and I walk over to turn the overhead light off and then to the side table by the bed and click on the low wattage of the lamp there.

Sliding down my panties, I move onto the bed and straddle his lap while also surprising him. Wrapping an arm around his shoulder, I reach down with my other hand and force it between his body and sweat pants. Gripping his hardening cock, I pull it out and lean up, kissing his lips as I feel the head of his dick at my already wet entrance, tucking him in. I moan and push both my hands into his hair as he kisses me back and his hands move to grip my hips, pulling me solidly onto him. He grows thicker inside me and my head falls back, allowing his lips to attack my neck. Back arching, my hands drop to his thighs, his thick, hard, fucking tight thighs and I dig my nails into them which barely even make a dent. JK growls and pushes me back and onto the bed, pulling the cups of my bra down before coming over me. He hooks one of my legs under the knee with his forearm and brings it up to my side, causing his dick to slide smooth and deep into me.

My eyes flutter, my mouth falls open as I feel the blunt head of his dick tease that spot at my core that only he knows how to reach. His smiling lips find my cock drunk ones and try to coax my senses back to control and return the kiss. When I can't manage to find that function doable he laughs deeply before kissing my neck and pushing my arms above my head. The shift has my back arching and my chest pushing upward and because he's so much larger than me, he's able to simply move his head and suck my nipple into his mouth while still pushing his magnificent cock inside me.

"I've been thinking about your cock all day," I sigh, his body jerking with my words. "That's all I feel like I do, think about us and the things we do. Sit down to work and I think about your cock in my hands, my mouth...check my emails and I think about you under the desk with your mouth on my pussy, your fingers, oh god your mouth all over me," I pant as he strokes me deep repeatedly and I grip his rock-hard ass with my palms.

"Rebel," he groans, his hands pinning my wrists as he thrusts harder.

I keep my voice low and quiet as he buries his head into my neck and my lips are right beside the shell of his ear.

"I knew it'd be like this, knew we'd be so amazing together, but I didn't know I'd love you so much."

The words find their way out before I can even gather my senses. But the moment they leave my mouth, as I say the words, I know it's true. He rolls us so I'm on top and before he can object I slide down his body and replace my pussy on his dick with my mouth and blow the life outta him.

"Go somewhere tomorrow," JK sighs after we've finished and are about to fall asleep.

I make a sound or something in agreement to which he adds, "Parents house, we go."

Chapter Nineteen

(Sibgu)

Let's just put this out there. I give good parent. Experience says that not too long after meeting me, they're generally eating me up with a spoon. I'm bright, funny, and respectfully polite. I think it's because I grew up mostly around adults, I can deal in parent land without being all awkward or inap-props. Well, you know, for me at least. So, no, I've had no complaints from the parental department.

Thing is, most of my 'rent taming over the past twenty-seven years has been almost exclusively those of my friends. Meeting the parents of your FWB buddy, or someone you're only dating casually isn't generally high on the list of things to do. More on the list of things to be avoided, am I right?

All of my experiences so far though aren't anywhere near enough to ade-quately prepare a girl for meeting the conservatively traditional Korean par-ents of the guy she's crazy about. As in, he is *the* one. Nowhere near enough.

I'd given up trying to get the butterflies in my belly to calm their shit less than a mile into the trip, and the closer we'd gotten to JK's parents place, the sweatier my palms had become. Even though JK was seemingly relaxed on the seat next to me, I'm sure I'd felt some tension from him in the way he held his body. Of course, that could also be my brain fucking with me.

I've noticed the guys keep strong links with their families, and even though they now live as a group, they all still made it a point to touch base or see their loved ones on the regular. And not like in the American way - where a phone call from mom meant flicking it to voicemail six times before guilt made you answer or trying to come up with an impenetrable reason not to attend Thanksgiving this year - but in a way that mattered. Their connections mattered.

When JK mumbled pre-sleep that we'd be visiting his parents and again in the morning, those magnetic chocolate pools of his had hypnotized me, and already under his spell, his full cheeks creasing with the tipped-up ends of his perfect mouth forming a shy smile, had finished me off. I'd agreed no questions asked.

Needless to say, I've definitely thought about it all day. Will they take one look at me and know what I've been doing to their son? Their talented, sweet, compassionate, loyal and let's not forget, pure as the driven snow before I came along, son? I've had visions of his dad coming at me with something sharp, while his mom cries quietly in the corner. Dramatic? Yeah, probably, but I have been getting right into K-Drama's since being here, so I'll blame that. At least I'm mentally prepared for the worst, right?

The basket in my hands at least gives me something to focus on while I'm standing a respectable distance from JK, as he presses the doorbell announcing our arrival. Yup, he pressed the doorbell. No barging in and yelling, *"I'm home but I can't stay for long, so feed me quick!"* for my guy. We're both wearing all black, me in my most respectable attire along with a pair of silver dangling earrings I stole from Jaimin.

"No need nerves, ok?" JK says to me, dropping the quickest of chaste kisses against my slightly open lips, before smiling so brightly all my nerves are stunned frozen. Even though I can hear footsteps coming towards us, my brain is telling me to drop the damn basket and get his mouth back. Which is probably why when the door opens, my mouth is opening and closing like a goldfish out of its bowl and I no doubt look guilty as hell.

"Neo yeogi issne! Deul-eowa, deul-eowa." The man who answers the door looks so happy as he bows his head slightly, while JK's in return is the more respectful and deeper bow reserved for elders. Mine is somewhere inbetween figuring to hedge my bets.

"Annyeong, Appa." JK says in return, walking into the man's open arms and hugging him with clear affection. JK's dad, Byung-woo, offers me a small smile, before holding his son's cheeks in an action I know without understanding the words spoken. He's giving him a parental once over. Clad in casual dress pants and a button-down shirt, JK's dad looks like an older version of him. Long, lean limbs, a mop of dark straight hair, and regardless of me guesstimating him being mid-forties, his barely lined face holds the same cheeky innocence.

Sweeter and much gentler spoken Korean words filter through to me, and I look past where the men are currently blocking the entry, seeing his mom, Sung-sook, coming towards us. A petite and colourful vision, she's wearing a cheerful green and white patterned blouse with an oversized collar and a matching green tailored knee length skirt. Her long hair is twisted ele-gantly behind her head and is so shiny I have instant hair goals envy. I watch as her already smiling face breaks into a laugh at something JK's dad says, her hand coming up to his bicep to gently push him away so she can get to her son. Her eyes, cheeks and mouth are all genetic gifts she's passed on to JK, and it strikes me that while he has his father's body type - albeit a much fitter and more defined version - he has his mother's features. Killer genetics.

"Nae yeolsimhi ilhaneun adeul. Dangsin-eun pigonhae boijiman haeng-boghabnida. Naneun haengboghada," (My hard-working son. You look tired, but happy. I am happy too) she tells him, drawing him into her arms for her own hug, one he graciously lets her have.

As if part of a perfectly choreographed move, all three of the Jeong's pick that moment to turn to me, and smile. Yup, killer damn genetics.

Initial introductions over, my lingering nerves have moved to the back-ground. Both of JK's parents have been friendly, if a little reserved, but I have no doubt they were likely just as nervous about meeting me as I was about meeting them. And just being courteous or not, JK's mom had seemed pleased with my bringing them a gift basket of Asian pears and oranges.

When JK had picked me up from my apartment and had seen me snag the tastefully presented basket from the hallstand on my way out the door, he'd looked at me with such affection I'd felt the warmth wrap around me like a caress. I could have asked JK what to bring them of course, but it was something I had wanted to do without his help.

The Jeong's home is impeccably clean and while the décor is modestly stylish, their pride in their children couldn't be more obvious. Where the parents of children who are outstanding athletes display their trophies and certificates, this apartment is adorned with mementos from JK's career. Stage performance photographs, back stage pass lanyards, framed magazine clip-pings, there's a myriad of reminders that I can't help but take my time to pe-ruse. I'm smiling at a photograph of JK on stage. Mid choreography, the look on his face is one of pure joy. There is no question that at the second this pic-ture was captured, there is nothing else in the world that he would've rather been doing.

"He's always been the show off. Good thing he can sing and dance, he's pretty but not very smart. Me, I'm both." In a predominantly Korean speaking household, the fluently spoken English can only be one person, JK's older brother, Jun-sang or JS for short. Looking to my side, I'm greeted by a mischievously smirking face, one that's a miniature version of his father as I look up at him.

"Hello, Jun-sang, I'm Rebel. It's nice to meet you," I tell him holding out my hand automatically, before remembering and withdrawing it to bow instead. I may have also muttered 'shit', which of course he heard and laughed.

"Oh, this is going to be fun," he tells me, and then gestures towards the top of a long table under a window. "This is where you'll find my achievements, if you decide you're more into intelligence than choreography."

"Dude, have you seen your brother dance? Yeah, for me, there's no coming back from that, sorry." I tell him with a shrug and he laughs.

"You know what they say about Korean men with large IQ's, don't you?"

His words have me laughing and even though smiling, I watch as JK pushes his tongue into his cheek. Automatically, and without conscious thought, I reach out and place my hand on the back of his head, dragging my hand down his soft hair to cup the back of his neck.

JK's eyes meet mine and there's the unspoken communication between us. I'm not sure if he understood the dialogue or the meaning of it, or if it was just because I was getting attention or giving attention. It doesn't take much for him to get jealous and I want him to know I'm here with him. Only when his brother says something in Korean, and JK's lips curl up at the ends while the fullness pouts out and responds, that I remember where we are.

As they banter back and forth in Korean, we make our way out of the living room and toward the dining room where JK's dad is sitting and his mom is placing bowls of food onto the white linen covered table.

"Ask your mom if she needs help?" I whisper, nudging his elbow slightly.

"She will answer no," he tells me.

Of course, she will, every mom says no. So, while JK and his brother take seats, I pass them and enter the kitchen. To the shock of his mom, she stares at me wide eyed as she gathers bowls onto her forearms. Without saying anything, I smile and bow my head slightly as I too take the rest of the bowls sitting on the counter into my hands. It's not a massive gesture I did, but when we walk back into the dining room, the smile JK gifts me with I'd do a million menial tasks to receive.

Dinner is incredible, and before we'd even started to eat, I'd told his mom that the meal didn't just look good but smelled fantastic. Because I knew how much it means to share a meal, it'd felt way too impersonal to use a translator app while sitting at the table. Instead, I'd made do telling her all of that using my version of Reb does Korean. Some words, lots of actions. His father, who I was learning was a naturally jovial sort of guy, especially for a doctor, had actually laughed along with me. At least based on JK's smiling at me, I'd assumed it was with me and not at me.

Sung-sook has remained friendly and polite, but in a way that only other women know, I also knew she was still very much on the fence about me. Honestly, I was cool with that, and I could even understand it. She wasn't mean or nasty, wasn't whispering things under her breath or anything. Or maybe it was just me, just me wanting to impress a guy I really like's parents. The having to learn to not use my main form of communication, words, that I did when I met JK and the guys, I'd forgotten until this moment how hard that was. Since, we've all learned to use a little of each language and again with the hand and facial gestures. But it made me feel awkward sitting there and not being able to communicate.

I wasn't sure if JK felt my internal struggle, but after the conversation between the four dies briefly, JK says something to his parents while looking at me, but I have no idea what he's saying until I hear the words that never fail to make a swell of excitement fill my chest. *The Clockmaker*. Instantly my eyes widen with elation, even with having no clue as to why JK's mentioning one of the best 80's slasher films ever made.

"You like this film?" Byung-woo asks, and my eyes dart to him, seeing he too looks excited and well, as fucking geeked as me.

"Like it? It's one of my favorite movies of all time!" I exclaim, then put my hand on JK's leg to brace myself as I ask his dad, "Do you?" then pause and wait with baited breath.

"Ah!" he says with wide eyes, "I was in this film!" he adds, patting his hand on his chest.

"No way!" my eyes dart to JK and he's giving me the bunny smile that crinkles the bridge of his nose and fuck if we weren't in front of his parents I'd be licking it.

"Victim number 4," his dad says, pointing at himself and knocking me out of the thoughts of violating his son in all manner of ways.

"I knew you looked familiar! Tell me everything, spare no detail!"

I find out that JK's pops was in medical school in Japan for a few terms and saw an ad for movie extras, he needed the cash and showed up, not knowing he'd go down in history as not only being in a cult classic, but one of the bloodiest and goriest murder scenes ever put on film.

"It was banned that year? I didn't know that, but I can see why."

We're now sitting in the living room, his dad showing me some behind the scenes photos and other memorabilia. It's just the two of us and we've been talking other horror movies since he too is a fan of the genre. I tell him about my old neighbor and some of the special effects from some of the movies he likes that I know first-hand about, you know, before computers and shit.

"Yeobo, will you help me?" JK's mom says from the kitchen.

"Excuse me," he states with a small bow while standing.

"No worries, where's the washroom?" I ask.

"End of the hall," he points.

I bow my head before we part ways and head down the hall. There are photos lining one wall and I stop to look at them. JK's parents wedding, him and his brother's baby photos and as toddlers, up until what look to be recent. One catches my eye of a two or three-year-old JK with his bunny grin and a half-eaten corn dog in hand. Hands slide around my hips as his firm chest pushes up behind me.

"I see nothing changes," I smile, pointing at the photo in regards to his smile but mainly the always eating.

"I'll eat you," he says in Korean, or something to that effect.

I begin to giggle as he presses his lips against my neck.

"What were you up to while I was with your dad?"

"Talk to brother," he answers in English.

"What were you talking about?"

"You," his brother says as he walks passed us in the hall and we both look at him. "He's got it bad for you," he adds, and I smile even wider as JK tells him to "Shut up."

"Dijeoteu," his moms soft voice comes from where we can't see, and I know this word very well due to her son, dessert.

We eat dessert and share some bottles of Soju. The alcohol level in the beverage isn't high, but I've witnessed many people slowly get bombed off the stuff since I've been here, and this is no exception. The laughs become a little longer and louder, the stories more animated. And even though I can't tell what a lot of it's being said, I laugh too. JK is getting buzzed, which I haven't seen before, actually I've never seen him drunk before. For a moment I think it's because we're with his family and the other times he didn't drink because we were with men that could potentially hit on me or something. But I like seeing him like this, carefree almost, bunny smiling and talking a lot. By the time we're leaving, his brother also decides it's his time to go, both parents are hugging me, and mom is sending us back to the apartment with containers of left overs and homemade kimchi.

His brother gets into the SUV with us since he lives on the way and JK sits between us, a protective hand on my thigh as his brother talks to me in English drunk speak.

"It was nice to meet you Rebel...I'm shocked my bro fell for an American, but not you. You're really beautiful, but it's not that."

I smile at him as both me and JK watch him. JS's voice is beginning to rasp as the talking got loud at his parents and the alcohol has made him de-hydrated. He shakes his head and it's silent for a moment before he looks at me and says, "He'd risk his career to be with you, that's what he told me."

Those words leave me feeling a pit in my stomach. Not even once did I think about what us being together could and would do to his career if the fans found out. He would go from God-like status, to nothing worthy of their devotion. It may be harsh, but I saw in my research how critical fans can be, I don't mean the fans we know, but fans in this country mainly. If any of them act in a way they don't like, they let them know. The reminder is sober-ing and leaves my stomach solid with guilt. The last thing I'd ever want is for the guys hard work to come crashing down because of me.

JK notices my change in vibe, of course he does and looks at his brother, speaking like he does to Jaimin when he's bothered. His brother keeps shak-ing his head while saying 'nothing.' I think because maybe he doesn't want to confess that he's broken his brother's confidentiality by telling me, which would make JK mad for that reason and for him making me feel this way. But it's no one's fault, actually I'm happy he told me, I needed to hear it.

The SUV stops and his brothers shaking my hand as he smacks his brother's leg while getting out and then it's silent. JK still sits in the center right beside me, but he shifts to put his arm across my shoulders and pull me into his side. My head falls back onto his rock-hard bicep as I look up at him. His eyes are warm and slightly glazed from the liquor. Our eyes holding one another's has my fears abating slightly, because I forget pretty much everything when he looks at me, and the part of my heart that convinces my brain a little that it's all worth it for him. But am I worth it for him? I don't want to think about this right now, I'm buzzed, and this could literally go south quick as hell if I give any more thought to it tonight.

"Why look this way? Parents like you," he assures me, running the fingers from one hand down my cheek and then over my hair on a return pass.

I give him a small smile and nod slightly, the alcohol also influencing me. The kind where I wanna cry but also wanna make out. I blink slowly and bring my hand up to his neck, fingering the freckle there. JK's hand slides up my thigh, *very* high up my thigh to rest on my apex, causing me to give him a smile.

"Feeling some kinda way, Jung-keun-ssi?" I smile while raising my eyebrows.

With my words he's smiling and leaning in to run his lips over mine, so soft, so light it has me gripping his jean clad thigh with my other hand and my body leaning up to make contact, but he retreats.

"You tease," I sneer and turn my head to look out the car window, crossing my arms beneath my chest.

But my playful nature dies when I feel the first press of those glorious lips of his on the column of my neck, it has me deeply sighing. Thank fuck we pull into the underground parking when we do, because I'm about to attack him, Fred or not. We both nearly fall out of the vehicle and I put my arm around JK's slim waist to brace myself and him as we walk toward the elevator, but he has me screeching when he unexpectedly picks me up like he's carrying me over the threshold. Fred gives us a look but then smiles as he waves goodbye to us.

"I can't believe you did that in front of Fred," I chastise with a smile as we board the elevator.

"I want do this," he states, before putting my legs down, pushing me into the wall and kissing me.

The kiss is hot and wet, hands groping and stroking, breaths panting and chests pushing together. His fingers grip under my thighs as I bring them up around his hips and feel his dick between my legs. I moan and rock into it, stroking the hard denim covered ridge with the lips of my pussy, causing him to also moan. Moments pass, and I realize the elevators stopped and the door keeps dinging as it remains open for us to get the fuck out.

"You better get to my apartment before we desecrate this innocent elevator," I comment between kisses.

We begin to move, my back knocking into the sides of the hallway as we continue to kiss and are lost in one another. I don't know how the door gets opened, but we're in my apartment when I stop and finally take notice. Shirts and my bra are removed roughly, hands moving over bare skin as we still kiss, and my feet hit the floor for us to push down our own pants. When we're both naked, my pants still connected to my ankles when I'm turned around and lips kiss the back of my shoulder and neck, hands grip my hips as I feel the blunt head of JK's dick poking my ass cheek, then just above my entrance, before finally sliding inside. We both moan and my forehead presses into the wall as I bite my lip. His hands move to my wrists as he stretches our arms up high on the wall, arching my back and popping my butt out as he executes a flawless dance with our bodies. His naked chest on my back, his big hands on my small wrists, the rhythmic tempo of his hips against my ass, his lips on my skin, his breath in my hair, his smell, it's everything to me.

Leaning back, his hands bring mine down as we grope my chest, coaxing my nipples, like they could get any harder, before his hands leave mine and he grabs my hips. His chest leaves my skin and I know he's looking down at his work. Pivoting my head, I glance back to see that yes, he's watching his wonderfully giving cock slaughter my all too eager cat.

"Your dick looks so good when you fuck me," I pant.

He grunts and grips me harder, his cock swelling and surging into me with not so much finesse. Tightening my walls around him every time he glides out, I know he's close.

"Touch," he demands breathily through his teeth.

My hand instantly reaches down between my legs and I begin to circle my fingertips over my clit, my body instantly jerking and hips rocking. It doesn't take more than three or four strokes before I feel my orgasm hit my core and my hands move to grip the sides of his thighs as I come on his dick. JK whimpers almost and his rhythm breaks as he drives harder, deeper, and my hands slide back to my ass, gripping the globes as I hold myself open for him and he begins coming.

"Sarang haeyo," he chants, and I feel my heart begin to pound even harder with his words.

"I love you too," I smile.

Chapter Twenty

(Seumul)

It's been six months since I've been here and working for the group. So far, the job has been amazing and I feel like together, we've seriously done some awesome shit. The cartoon line the guys wanted is in production, each character representing and designed by a member. All of them are adorable in their own way and to me fit the guys perfectly. It's a no brainer that JK's is a bunny, a ripped with muscle bunny, pretty accurate. We're heading to America near the end of the year and the world tour is starting, where more American dates than they've had before, have been sold out. Even though the radio play still isn't there, I don't think it's necessary, obviously. Their music has been added to a popular online music engine that has increased downloads and sales since. The guys have upped their game on their social media accounts and have seen an increase in followers. We also got the word from Cola-Cola that they want to use the guys as ambassadors for their next campaign, we're talking personal collectible cans, along with print ads and television commercials.

We still had a lot of things we wanted, but we were making progress I was happy with and so were they. And needless to say, Min-ssi of the label didn't say one thing at our most recent meeting to check my progress. He just avoided eye contact, looked at papers and nodded. Regardless, I haven't received a plane ticket or any paperwork terminating me so I'd say we're on the right track.

The guys were practicing for the tour, usually anywhere from 14-16 hours a day, along with working on a new album. While they worked their asses off, we were all there with them, doing everything we could too to make this tour the best yet.

Even though we were in the same room, at the end of the day, when JK and I fell asleep together, I felt like I hadn't seen him all day. He'd asked me to come on tour with them, and yes, I wanted to, but I wasn't sure if I could justify it professionally. Sure, I could do the same work here or there, but clearly, he asked me to tour as his girlfriend and I wasn't sure if Sawyer would be down with me going. I know my telling him I'd have to find out over and over was making him frustrated, but I really didn't know if it would be best for us.

Photos of us at the airport on the way back from our trip to Japan had hit the internet. As soon as I got the first alert it was even a thing, I quickly called Massive Smash management to get the OK for me to release a press statement in regards to it. They agreed and I was able to shoot out a generic yet effective, "she works for the group." It was squashed so quickly, none of the guys even said anything to me about it, or even acknowledged it had happened. JK did finally when we had dinner at my place that night. I asked him how he felt about it, to which he shrugged like it was no big deal, and the reminder of what his brother had said to me, that JK would throw away his career for me, finally gave me the courage to tell him what I thought.

"I love you JK. You can say it's fine, and like, you don't care if F.A.M.L.Y knows and that in turn ruins your career...but I don't want that for you JK. You work too hard and are too talented to throw away what you guys have worked for. It's not worth it-"

"You worth it," he states.

I sigh, "We can be together...but it doesn't have to be different than this. Being a secret isn't a bad thing," I offer.

Instead of actually having a discussion, he shakes his head and ends the dialogue. I knew he was scared, deep down he was, who wouldn't be. I was all over the board most days. Sometimes I was fine and didn't give a damn who knew, he was my man and I loved him. Other days, I was sick to my stomach to the point where I'd worry so much I'd end up puking. I hid my inner turmoil from JK and the others the best I could, always putting on a smile and encouraging them as we rode back to the apartments together. Reminding them how good they did and how as they sat there dog tired, I knew they were gonna put on an amazing show.

"I want eat," JK states and looks between me and my purse expectantly, as we sit in the Fred driven SUV parked outside the Massive Smash building and wait for the others, so we can go home after a long day of work.

"Okay, just send me the paperwork and I'll have a look at it," I tell my client, Daisy, as I hold my cell between my shoulder and cheek, reaching in my purse for snacks.

Before I can even get the package fully out, he's taking it from me and ripping open the top. I finish my call a few moments later and look over at JK as I put my cell in my purse, both cheeks bulging with food as he chews with his lips parted and gazes out the window beside me. There's something in me, maybe like a weird mother instinct, that makes me feel good to provide food for him, or maybe it's my time in South Korea, knowing the guys feed each other because it makes them feel good. JK's eyes meet my fond ones looking at him and he gives me a questioning look, like I've said something aloud he didn't catch.

"You do get you're the only guy on the planet I'd carry dried squid legs in my purse for, right?" I ask.

He smiles, THE smile. The fucking smile that makes me soft and hard all at the same time, if you get my drift. He nods in understanding, leaning in to give me a too quick of a kiss.

"And it's *that* smile that makes it ok for you to kiss me after you eat them."

Just then the rest of the guys come out of the elevator and come toward the SUV, Jaimin scooting in on the other side of me as we all try to fit into one car. I don't know why we're only using one vehicle but whatever, and we manage to squeeze in, Hooni taking up the other side of Jaimin and some-how, I end up with one cheek on JK's lap and the other on Jaimin. With a low growl that I can only hear from my guy, his arm moves around my waist to pull me more onto his lap.

"Hey!" Jaimin says in Satoori and takes my arm to playfully pull me back onto his lap.

They begin to play tug of war and I just laugh as clearly Jaimin is fucking with JK, JK isn't finding it funny. My phone begins to chime with an incom-ing call and before I realize it, I'm turning on FaceTime to see Cassie, Ryver and Allyson all looking back at me.

"Rebel!" they greet, and I can tell they're drunk.

"Hi!" Jaimin says in English, with a wave as his face takes up half the screen.

The girls smile and practically melt in front of me over not only how cute Jaimin is but his English, see it's not just me that finds that shit adorable.

"Oh shit, they're cute!" Cassie smiles brightly.

"What's going on?" I ask.

"Is that the one who you said smelled awesome?" Ryver asks, referring to Jaimin.

I widen my eyes and give them a stern look.

"Who?" JK says low in his chest as he nudges my back.

"What are you guys up to?" I repeat.

"Just got done getting drinks, Clemmie said you puked when she talked to you the other day-"

"Puke?" JK asks.

"I didn't-well, I did, but-"

"Were you drunk?" Allyson asks.

JK and Jaimin ask Joon loudly over my shoulders what puke means.

"No-I don't know what happened," I shake my head, wanting to change the subject.

"You were sick?" JK asks me once Joon's translated.

"You're stressed, I can tell," Cassie nods.

"You're doing that thing with your brows like you do when something's bothering you," Allyson adds.

"I'm not doing anything with my brows," I state with a shake of my head.

"You were sick?" JK repeats.

"You should do some Anusara yoga. Do you remember what I taught you?"

Everyone's speaking at once and I find my annoyance causing my voice to raise as I announce, "I'm not sick, I'm not stressed, goodbye," and end the call.

Putting my phone in my purse, the SUV is quiet and I know it's because of my little outburst.

"Puck," Jaimin says all of a sudden.

"No, no, pook," JK corrects.

"Puke," Joon corrects them and everyone in the car tries to say it correctly.

By the time we exit the get to the apartments, I feel like I want to do the very word they've all been practicing.

"You watch movie?" JK asks me, as we ride up the elevator with the other guys.

Normally it makes me laugh to myself when he thinks the guys don't know we're together and hang out in my apartment at night, but whatever makes you feel like you're slick JK. But I don't feel like laughing and I don't know why, but I nod and we both stop at my door as we walk down the hallway.

"You didn't tell me you were sick," he states as soon as we get our shoes off and settle on the couch.

JK and I now speak a mix of Korean and English, but I understand more of what he says and he understands more of what I say, and honestly, I don't really pay attention anymore as to what language it is.

"It happens sometimes when I have a lot going on."

I say this but I don't think it's ever happened to me before. He looks at me as I turn on the television and flip through the channels.

"You have stress?"

"I guess," I shrug.

A few minutes pass and he's still looking at me.

"Want to play game?" he finally asks.

"A game? Aren't you tired? You've been working all day and you have to get up early tomorrow-"

"I want play game," he states.

"Sure. What kind of game?" I finally relent.

His eyes light up at my answer and then thinks for a moment, "You first, or me?"

"Rock, paper, scissors," I smile, shifting my position to face him.

We shoot one time and I win, knocking his scissors with my rock.

"Go to room, take off clothes," he smiles.

I give him a raise of my brows and he play taps my face and I dodge him and get off the couch. Not sure what game this is, however I like being naked and me being naked means either he's also gonna get naked or we're having sex, then it's win-win for me.

Deciding that maybe naked isn't what I want, I open my closet and look through my lingerie, digging for something I haven't worn for him before. My last online shopping spree I did make some purchases from Dita von Teese's line. I ordered a specific pair of black panties because the name *Sheer Witchery Satin* reminded me of the witchcraft JK always tosses on me. I'd also gotten a matching garter belt and bra, where if it wasn't lace it was sheer and when I put the panties on, there's lace at the top but the sheer, shows all my cat, including the slit of my lips from the front.

A knock at the bedroom door has me hurrying to get everything on as I tell him to hold on.

"You ask me question," he states.

"What kind of question?"

"Any...you get right, I come closer," he adds.

Hmmm, I think I'm gonna like this. Chucking the pillows off the bed, I climb on and move to the center before sitting.

"When's my birthday?"

"Fifth, October."

I then decide the way I'm sitting isn't flattering, so I prop the pillows up behind me and lean back.

"Where did I grow up?"

"L.A."

I hear his hand on the handle outside the door.

"What color are my eyes?"

"Green."

The handle turns and the door opens but he barely steps in, his smile falling as he gives me a shook look at seeing me there.

"Reb," he breathes out and I shift my legs, bending them and teasing him with a peep.

"How long have I worked at ESM?"

"Six years."

Another step closer.

"How many sugars do I take in my coffee?"

"No sugar."

Another step closer.

"What's my favorite horror film?"

"Hellraiser..."

And I raise my brows as he fades off.

"2!" He hurries out, putting up two fingers.

Nodding, he steps forward.

"What's my favorite perfume?"

"Alien," he answers after thinking for a moment.

He's at the end of the bed now, and I can see the imprint of his hardening cock straining against his gray sweat pants. Even in workout clothes he's a vision. His wide brown eyes wait for my next question while my insides twist with anticipation of his touch.

"What's my favorite position?"

He moves one knee onto the bed as he answers, "Behind."

I swallow thickly as I feel his body heat near my feet, and he puts a hand down onto the bed by my ankle to brace his body weight. I bend my legs, pulling them toward me before spreading my legs and showing him the goods through the material. His mouth pops open as his eyes focus there.

"What do I love about you?"

His eyes move to mine and they go soft, "I don't know," he smiles and shakes his head.

"You have to move back then," I sing-song.

His smile falls and he leans back.

"What makes me come?"

"Touch your thigh," his voice low and gravely as his hand makes contact with my inner thigh. "When touch here," he adds, his fingers sliding up to cup between my legs as he cups me over my panties. "Here," his fingers moving up along my torso. "Kiss, here," his mouth kissing over both nipples, then licking up to my neck and mumbling "here."

He works me up, kissing along my jaw and causing my fingers to plunge into his hair, my head tilting back as I attempt to bring his body down onto mine.

Pulling away, he looks down at me, breathing hard.

"What do you love about me?" he asks, equally as breathless.

Smiling, I lean up and peck the tip of his nose, my fingers curling around the neck of his hoodie and pulling him closer, my mouth to his ear. "Everything," I whisper.

A low growl rumbles against my chest from JK and I plan to roll him over, but he pulls me up as he lays down, pointing to the door as he tells me, "Your turn."

Chapter Twenty-One

(Isib il)

I'm used to working in chaos, I thrive on it most times. It pushes me and sparks something in me that reminds me really why I love my job and why I got into it in the first place. The ability to fix something, to know how and what to do and getting it done. To see the relief on a client's face when I single handedly lift the weight off their shoulders, it's sometimes better than sex. Well, sex before JK.

However, not so much when you are blindsided by the chaos. When it hits you like a bullet, that bullet tearing down the curtain to a world you've created and gotten comfortable with. A world that shielded you from why you were there in the first place, from what your job really is.

This morning I'm alerted before dawn that a video's been leaked, I don't really understand at first. Is this something to do with the group? But as I read further, I wake up more with every word, and realize it's focused on JK...and me. Frozen, that's what I am. Confused and almost in a daze. Maybe it's the fact I was woken from a dead sleep, something had urged me to not wait to check the alert. When I sit up in bed, I confusingly look over to see the side JK normally occupies empty, not recalling him leaving at some point. It's too early for practice, maybe he's just in the bathroom.

Whatever, I look back at my phone and reread the article that says;

Video leaked today of K-pop idol, KT7's singer and dancer Jung-keun, and a female foreigner. Photos of this same female were leaked of her and Jung-keun at the airport where it was disclosed she was a member of their staff. Further investigating found her name is Rebecca West and she works for ESM, the largest marketing firm in the world. Worldwide clients from all careers, A-list celebrities to independent business owners. We were unsure what role Ms. West was playing for the group, but now since this video's been released, we're quite sure we know. The video seems to be a compilation of not only candid footage of JK and Rebecca walking around Tokyo Disney, but also more intimate times between the couple. Needless to say, fans reaction has been, as expected, less than pleased with not only being lied to initially, but also that the proof is undeniable that these two are indeed a couple.

Video leaked, how? I close my eyes and yesterday at the studio pops into my head. JK was using the computers there to edit, since he doesn't have video editing on his shit. We stayed late, he geeked out, and simply kissed me quiet when I asked what it was, while I spent time on the phone making international calls and hashing out details with several interested companies for brand endorsements with the guys and product placements at their tour venues.

Eventually, I'd dragged my heavy limbs into the production booth, bent over his back to rest my head on his shoulder and exhaustedly breathed into his neck, "Can we go home?"

All I cared about was that he'd kissed the top of my head while he clicked about 700 buttons, then stood up and took my hand, "Ok," and we'd left the studio.

I don't know how but I feel like this pertains to what's happened this morning.

Between you and me, I think it was always going to happen, and more importantly if we had a future it needed to happen, but I would have controlled it more. *We* would have controlled it more. For all my worrying, and fuck, I should've planned a go-to since the photos of us were leaked, but I didn't.

At the very least, we would have been prepared.

I really needed to get my shit together so I could deal and deal quickly with what I know I'm bound to walk into as soon as I get my ass out of this bed and go to the guys apartment.

Fuck getting presentable, I throw on one of JK's black hoodies he left there, sans bra and shoes, I tightened the knot on my pj pants as I gripped my phone and prepared myself for the onslaught.

I recognize that none of the bazillion alerts waiting for me were from JK. Not a one.

But I didn't have time to process the hurt that had started to creep in and knew I needed my professional mind right now, not my personal one. The news JK was dating me and that we were together in a romantic capacity has broken overnight and is now common knowledge. And when I say common knowledge, I mean that F.A.M.L.Y know. A lot if not most of the alerts on my YouTube, Twitter, Instagram, and Facebook are from those offended fans that were dealing with the news.

I only read the headlines, not the meat and decide I can't right this second, because I'm currently on my way toward my front door, when it opens and JK enters, stopping me in my tracks.

"What happened?" I ask when we make eye contact.

"Mistake," he states.

"Who's mistake?"

"I left the program open. The guy who checks my edits thought this video for public, he uploaded it. Not realize private, for you and me, mistake."

His words have my anxiety ratcheting up with how relaxed he seems.

"Why are you so calm?" I growl through clenched teeth.

"I don't know what you want me to do?"

I literally want to yank my hair out, "Are you serious? There goes your career! Everything you've worked for, it's gone!"

Just then a wave of nausea hits me, and one hand covers my mouth as the other covers my stomach and I take off for the bathroom by the front door. I barely get the seat lifted as I start vomiting. Lord do I vomit and even when that's done, the dry heaves come until I'm shaking as I drop to my ass beside the toilet. JK's there, water in one hand and a towel in the other. He wipes the cool damp cloth across my face as I close my eyes and feel them burn, along with my throat.

"You have to make a statement, we both do. That we're not together. I'll have to fly back to L.A.-"

"No!" JK says firmly, and it's only now do I realize we've been arguing in 100% Korean.

I inhale deeply, feeling what I've been thinking ever since the photos from the airport leaked.

"I," I begin and pause, my eyes watering to the point I can't see him, "don't want you to lose everything because of me."

My voice breaking as I speak. His hands take my jaw in his hands, but I can't look at him.

"I would give up everything for you. What is what I do? Sing? Dance? What we have is something some people never have."

Blinking I look up at him, his eyes overflowing with tears also as he continues.

"I would give up so much more to keep you. Career is nothing. I won't let you go."

"What if..." I pause and swallow down the emotion so I can talk. "What if I'm not worth it in the end?"

The words barely leave my mouth before JK is kissing me, never mind I just threw up, neither of us give a shit. Because this kiss is everything. It's reminding me of past, present and future. It's conveying every single word he could say but wouldn't reach me like this kiss does. Pulling back, his hands grip harder as he leans his forehead against mine.

"You say your destiny was to meet us, to work with the band and meet me. Maybe my destiny was to become famous just so I could meet you."

* * *

The day the bomb dropped, JK hung around me, just observing me. I was in talks with Massive Smash who forbade, fucking FORBADE me from making a press release. I felt not myself, foggy and out of it, was this a nervous breakdown? I couldn't think like normal Rebel in go-mode, no, no, I was in hazy-mode.

JK's words resonated with me. Hitting me deeper than anything had before. Something clicked in me in that moment that I needed to get my shit together and we needed to figure out what we were going to do.

I started looking into how I could open my own label and sign the guys and we could be entrepreneurs together. But then I wondered if Massive Smash would be dicks, not dissolve their contracts, keep them signed to the ten-year contract but not use them for anything, not allow them to continue to make music, which also wouldn't allow them to sign with anyone else.

I still felt like we could win over the F.A.M.L.Y somehow. I just wasn't sure how. I needed to look at what they were saying online, but fuck, I was scared. I also felt like shit.

That hazy, foggy feeling, oh and the nausea was hitting me hard. My head's pounding, and I finally relent since I'm not making any headway in my thoughts, let alone every time I try to look something up on my phone I want to yack. Taking some meds for the headache, I lay down and fall asleep.

"She's clammy," Hannah's voice cuts into my sleep, then a soft and a not so soft hand touch my forehead and cheeks.

"I'll call my dad," JK states.

With those words I fully wake up to see Hannah sitting on the side of the bed. She's looking at me sympathetically and I'm about to ask her what's wrong when she says, "I was worried, so I came over. Why haven't you released a statement?"

I'm then reminded of the shit storm and my phone ringing beside me, on cue, it's Sawyer.

"Take it, I'll be right here," Hannah says, handing me the phone.

"Hi," I sigh.

"Rebecca?" Sawyer questions.

"Yeah," I sigh again.

"This doesn't sound like you," Cassie chimes in.

"Not at all, what the fuck are you doing? No press releases?" Piper adds.

Not only am I on speaker, but also a conference call since Piper is in England.

"The label doesn't want me to, I'm trying to think of what to do," I state, rubbing my hands over my face as I put it on speaker because why not, I can add Hannah to this conversation.

"Is Hannah with you?" Sawyer asks.

"Yes."

"Thank you for heading over," Sawyer adds.

I then realize Sawyer must've called her to see if she'd heard from me.

"Oh my God, did I just turn into a Chapman suicide call?" I gape, in reference to my client.

"We're worried," Hannah says, putting her hand on my thigh.

"This isn't like you Rebel," Ryver states.

"What am I supposed to do? The label won't approve anything I send them, JK doesn't want to acknowledge that his career just took a dump, I'm alone in my panic here," I pause and swallow thickly, feeling the pre-vomit symptoms remind me that there's that too. "Besides, I can't fucking think,"

I growl, pressing my palms against my eyes. Then, a fragrance hits me like a wave.

"You have new perfume?" I question Hannah, pinching my nostrils closed as the smell makes my stomach roll. It has to be new, she always wears the same perfume and I never remember it smelling like shit.

"Are you going to be sick?" Hannah asks as she gives me an odd look.

Just then there's a knock at the door and I see JK's sweet face, then his dad's face.

"My dad's going to make sure you're not ill," JK states. "I will be in the living room if you need anything," he then adds, and I give him a small smile, when what I really want is to hug him and kiss him and fall apart a little.

God, what is wrong with me? This *isn't* me, but I feel defeated and weak, and that pisses me off. But I can't get a hold of myself, maybe something *is* wrong with me. When JK closes the door and his dad heads toward me with his medical bag, Hannah hops off the bed and speaks to him quietly. I can't hear the words or the tone, but his dad looks at her with question, before setting his bag on the dresser and retrieving an empty urine cup.

"I gotta go ladies," I state, ending the call.

Chapter Twenty-Two

(Seumel dul)

After JK's dad left, I felt even more lost. Hannah went home shortly after and eventually, I swallowed my pride and went out to JK who was still leaving me alone. I found him in the kitchen making ramen, and by the look of the other bowl, he was making it for both of us. His back is to me as he faces the stove, and I feel my resolve waver as I approach, my arms wrapping around his waist as I press my cheek against the back of his shoulder. His strong body is literally my touchstone in this moment.

I never thought when I imagined coming here almost a year ago that this is what JK and I would create. That he'd be my everything and I'd be his. We had our careers and friends but also a relationship I never imagined I could have with as much as I love my work. But I did with him.

We were stupid to think this wouldn't eventually happen. Stupid to think we could just lie and people would always believe we just worked together. All these thoughts don't change what's happened and I need to understand where JK's at, because I can't believe he's just fine with everything he's worked for imploding. His hands slide over mine as he brings one up to kiss the skin of my wrist, and that's all we need between us. No words.

My stomach feels settled enough that I tell JK to eat the noodles and I drink some of the warm broth slowly. He's not asking me about his dad's visit, which is all the better because I don't want to talk right now.

After dinner and some television watching on the couch, he takes me to my bed and cuddles me.

I can't sleep however, because I feel a burst of energy. Getting out of bed, I finally get online to check out what's being said so I can get some ideas on what to do.

I remember the comments I received from co-workers before I left for South Korea, the clear racism and ridiculous bullshit people said to me, and evidently, they weren't the only ones. Bottom line, in the year 2018, if my generation and those behind mine weren't open to mixed race relationships, then the enlightenment of the *"love is love"* messages sprouted ad nauseam all over social media - the newspaper of my generation - was all a fucking lie.

Because if the haters were currently proving anything, it was that my generation didn't believe in *"love is love"* at all. In fact, when it comes to love, there were still unseen, unspoken lines when it came to not just race, but culture. Something I'm not very proud to admit I had had very little understanding of. Until now.

Now it was happening to me and now it was pissing me the fuck off.

Any loving, committed, consensual relationship deserved no one's judgment or scrutiny...well, except that lady who wanted to "marry" an oak tree or something, that sister needed her meds upped.

But a happy, consenting American girl being in a relationship with a happy, consenting Korean boy - why the fuck should this be a problem?

Answer, it damn well shouldn't.

Again, I knew the world of fandom was not your usual level of scrutiny, and the possessiveness with which some fans vehemently stalked, defended & coveted their bias was next level shit.

But the hate, oh my God, the hate coming our way was something else. Nope, scratch that, it was mostly coming *my* way. And when I say hate, I mean vitriol rolled in revulsion with a side of choking rage and set on fire. The things being said, the graphics being drawn, the clips being made...I can't even begin to process. Don't even start me on the trending hashtags with my name attached. And so being me, I'm choosing to not even try.

Why the fuck should I? Their problem, not mine.

And when I say this, I mean the dealing with the shit about me; I'm not cool with the potential damage being done to the band, the label, or to my man.

JK, it seemed in the eyes of most, was heartbreakingly under the spell of an evil witch from the heathen-filled western world. One who'd apparently done everything from sacrificing live chickens to using the magic of her slutty vagina to lure him to his emotional downfall. But this was good, this meant if I was out of the picture, JK's career wouldn't be down the toilet. Because yes, I was considering 'pretending' to be broken up with him.

The haters were currently an unruly horde, their sites and links the first to pop up if you searched my name, but theirs was not the only voice out there.

Smaller in number but no less vocal, there was a positive and supportive voice amongst the loyal fans. Again, while not as prevalent as the haters, more Stan's and 'Ships for us as a couple were popping up every hour. These F.A.M.L.Y, true fans of the band, their talent and their music, only cared that JK was happy. And in their view, based on the leaked pictures of the two of us, together and smiling and clearly loved up, he was.

Well, he was worried about me. Me, not his career, but me. Even with the positive, it wasn't enough.

Then something caught my eye, a trending tag that kept popping up and led me to a twitter account of a F.A.M.L.Y who was threatening suicide if me and JK didn't break up. My gut dropped, my stomach rolling and there I went again, hurtling toward the bathroom. I toss my cookies and sit there in the dark. To think someone felt so strongly about two people they didn't know, so much that they'd threaten to kill themselves over it. I watched the video she posted, this was no Chapman bullshit, this was for real. Remembering how bat shit crazy I was over JK before we met, I would've been a little devastated to find out he had a girlfriend, suicidal, no, but still. Unlike with Chapman, and like I do with anything that makes me uncomfortable, putting up a wall, I need to face this.

"I'm going to fix this," I vow out loud, and decide that I need to fight for me and JK, because I can't give up on us, not now.

* * *

Looking out the tinted rear window of the Fred driven SUV as it moves through streets I'm not overly familiar with, I don't take any of it in. Not the scenery, not the hustle and bustle, and certainly not the people, their activity proof that life around me has continued as if my world hasn't shifted off its axis.

Staring without seeing, listening without hearing, touching without feeling, this has been my existence since my world was rocked, in more ways than one.

I know and represent a few tortured artist types who would use what I'm currently feeling and channel it into their next masterpiece or whatever.

Those fuckers can have it.

Yesterday was a first for me, feeling broken and a little hopeless, and I already know that this shit is *not* for me.

I don't wallow, I don't lie down and not get back up, and I don't give up easily. I'm not the kind of girl who walks away without fighting for what she wants. Fights for what she believes in but most importantly, what she knows is meant to be.

My soul has it's dukes up, ready to fight, I need to do this, I need to prove to JK that I can do this.

Fight for the both of us.

Don't misunderstand me, I'm saying JK is not weak; I think he's completely the opposite. He's stronger than any man I've ever met. The pressure he is under is immense, and there are not many people I know who could handle the scrutiny, the expectation, and the intrinsic value of being respectful that he lives under.

Things need to change, with perception and the idea that stars and celebrities are perfect and, in this case, never look at another woman other than F.A.M.L.Y., that somehow they aren't worth anything anymore when they have a personal relationship. What is that? Jealousy? A wicked bitch who stands in the corner with her arms crossed shouting *"If I can't have you then no one can!"*

I understand why some celebs go off their rocker, to break, and in some cases, curb stomp the public opinion of their perfection and squeaky-clean reputations.

But here, in South Korea, from what I've seen idols are so fucking terrified to break that mold. Maybe it's because their culture is ingrained in them to not let older generations look down on them, there's less, *"Fuck you, I'm gonna do what I want,"* here. Especially with famous people. We all know how the masses can ruin a career. Doesn't matter the facts or the feelings, it's black and white and however the press spins it is usually the case served in the court of public opinion.

I've seen first-hand, the guys wear masks of normalcy to hide their emotions, but I know sometimes their miserable.

Fans and F.A.M.L.Y, whether it's welcomed or not, need to realize these guys, these 'famous people,' are still people. Yes, they serve a purpose to entertain, but is that their entire life? No. They still have wants and needs, desires and goals. Jinho graduated college while taking on all the groups duties and no one praised him publicly. That's a huge thing he did and yet, it wasn't important to mention in the media.

The more I think about everything I've witness while being here, being around this industry. I want that to change. For them and for us. I might be one person, but shit. Sometimes, one voice is all it takes. I might fail, but I'll try.

I look across the seat to the man sitting next to me and suck in a slow, deep breath. They have the same jawline, the same shape to their profile, so he hints to what his son will look like when he's older. Calling JK's dad for help was a no brainer. Yes, he's a skilled and respected doctor, but he was also a father, and therefore uniquely positioned to understand more than just one side of the situation.

I first texted him, since after we met yesterday, he told me to contact him at any time if I needed. The text assured him I was fine but that I needed to get some advice about a situation that I wasn't sure how to handle 100%. He called me back and stated he was on call at the hospital and never slept well those nights. He also said he would help me with whatever I needed and so I explained the situation.

I already felt like the man was like a second father to me, especially after yesterday, when I had some sort of moment and dished to the Doc about JK.

How I felt about his son, how long I'd felt this way, why I felt that I needed to be the one to fight for us, how much I respected his son's integrity and loved the purity of his goodness for always putting others first, and lastly, what I believed was our future together.

I also put out there that I understood that I was likely not the image of who he and his wife had had in mind when doing what parents do, visualizing their child's future happiness, including who they would marry.

Neither of us spoke for a few seconds after that, him because I think I shocked him with my directness, and me because I wanted to let my words settle between us before I finished by making my point.

Which was that while I may not be who they imagined for his future, they wouldn't find anyone better than me to give him what I also imagined they hoped for him to find.

Real love.

All encompassing, the kind of love that took his breath away at the same time gave him life, love that grew and changed as he did, but only in that it became stronger and would remain unconditional until the day he died.

For JK to have that I'd told his father straight up, they would find no one better on the entire planet than me to give that to him, and, for him to be able to give that back to me knowing it would be cherished.

Korean men, I have come to learn are not of the bullshit *"hide any emotion that isn't considered butch philosophy,"* which is why when JK's dads eyes filled with watery emotion and his head nodded deeply in acknowledgement, I wasn't shocked.

I was honored.

So, having talked everything through with him, during our call, the only indication he gave that he was surprised by my planned approach to the situation was when I added, "And I would like for you to come with me."

Having arrived, we're standing quietly together, both of us holding satchel-sized bags, I listen to the last of the doorbell's tinny notes as we wait for the door to be answered.

Our visit has been prearranged, and while the key reasons for the visit have been discussed over the phone, there is a lot that is yet unsaid. It's nearly seven a.m. and although I was worried to have contacted all parties too early, I was assured it was more than fine and seemed desperate.

Sawyer, naturally, fully supported this strategy, my strategy, although her counsel and advice during our numerous and lengthy calls through the night had been greatly appreciated.

The girls have weighed in too, as sisters who have my back and as colleagues with advice to share.

This is not going to be easy, my plan, but for whatever reason, I am quietly confident.

The middle-aged man that opens the door looks tired, like he's not had a good night sleep in a while, and I would imagine that it's likely he hasn't. His shirt and pants are clean but deeply creased as though he's spent a lot of time sitting, however based on the finger mussed look of his dark hair, I wouldn't say he's been sitting to relax. His face is open and friendly, but when I look closer and take in the creases by his mouth, coupled with the slight defensiveness in his posture, I can see he's wary too.

All of this is entirely understandable considering the reason we were currently standing on the doorstep to his home.

"Hello, Rebecca?" he asks, his Korean made more attractive by the deep timbre of his voice.

"Yes, I'm Rebecca from Massive Smash, and as I said on the phone, this is Dr. Jeong Jun-sang. Thank you for agreeing to this, you have my word that you may ask us to leave at any time and we will."

A quick flash of sadness passes across his face, making my gut clench with sadness of my own, before he bows his head slightly.

"Of course. Please, come inside."

JK's dad puts a ghost of hand at my back and ushers me through the door before him. So much like the way his son handles me, gentlemanly and considerate, my heart lurches before I remind myself to get a grip. If this strategy works like I hope it will, like everyone involved needs it to, when I go to bed tonight there won't be a ghost of a fatherly hand at my back, but instead the warm, hard, solid body of his son.

We all enter the living area of the house of the man who let us in, and meet his equally tired looking wife, a small, modestly dressed woman whose face is puffy from recently dried tears.

Greetings over, I politely decline their invitation to sit, instead sharing that I would leave them in the experienced hands of Jun-sang to talk.

He was more than prepared for the conversation ahead; the satchel bag around his body filled with information that he hoped would help them out.

Having known them personally for only minutes now, I already hoped the same thing.

While I wasn't staying, I wasn't leaving either, because I had come to talk to their sixteen-year-old daughter, Min-jun, the KT7 F.A.M.L.Y mega Stan that had publicly claimed she would kill herself unless JK broke up with me.

Min-jun and I were about to have a talk, just us girls.

Following behind Min-jun's mom as she walks us towards her daughter's bedroom, I go over in my head the main things Jun-sang told me I could expect.

There are so many ways I could handle this conversation but dealing with any sixteen-year-old girl is already a crapshoot, let alone one like Min-jun, so I figure I'm just going to stick with my plan and see what shakes out.

It does give me comfort that JK's dad is here with me, along with her parents being in the loop, but again, for whatever reason, I'm confident.

The small woman in front of me stops and for the first time since we entered the hallway, she turns back to look up at me. Her eyes are filled with sadness, and love, and the tired yet resilient look of any parent that has been through the wringer with their kid.

I should know, I've seen it directed at me. While not in the same way as Min-jun of course, but I know I gave my own parents a grey hair or two well before they were probably due.

"Please, Rebecca, she's a good girl, she's just..." her soft voice breaks with emotion as she stops talking, a few tears escaping to run over her pale cheeks before she swipes them away.

I take a step towards her, lifting my hand slowly so she knows I'm going to touch her shoulder, giving her time to retreat if she doesn't want my comfort.

She doesn't retreat, if anything I end up hugging her more, because as my hand meets her body she crumples into my touch, making tears prick the backs of my own eyes as I speak. "I know, and again as I assured you over the phone, I'm not here to make things worse, for any of you. I promise."

She cries softly for a few seconds, and suspecting she needs the release, I don't rush her. Sometimes it's good to unload on a stranger, it's like crying in the shower, you can just let shit out.

Feeling her posture firm up, I let her go and she gives me a watery smile and a nod, while I lick my lips and swallow, getting my own game face on.

Min-jun's mom is too sweet, and the woman is fucking with my mojo.

We'd agreed that Min-jun should know someone from the label was coming to see her, as to what reason her parents gave I left up to them, but I did ask that the fact it was going to be me, be kept from her.

Everyone hesitated on that requests for a while, but over several phone calls I didn't back down and just kept talking through my reasoning. Somewhere along the way I must have gained her parents trust, convinced them my motives were to help not harm, because here I am.

Min-jun's mom knocks gently on her daughter's bedroom door but doesn't wait for a reply before opening it and taking one step inside, meaning I'm standing in the doorframe, looking in.

My first impression is that her bedroom is like that of most teenage girls. Double bed, dressed in bright linens and loaded with contrasting pillows of all shapes and sizes, as well as clearly loved plushies front and center. Dresser and closet, the first of which is so loaded with beauty products you can't see the top. Walls & shelves decorated in chosen fandoms with images and swag, a music docking station, phone, desk, chair and laptop.

Everything about her bedroom says normal, happy but likely moody and hormonal teenage girl, everything that is except the girl sitting at her desk, her head down with her back to us.

Dressed head to toe in oversized black clothing, her dark, shoulder length hair looks lank and in need of a wash, followed by a vigorous brush. Her legs are tucked up under her on her chair, her eyes unmoving from her computer screen as her fingers fly across the keys and she couldn't be less interested in what her mother is saying.

That is until Min-jun finally looks over her shoulder and the disinterest on her otherwise pretty face instantly changes to open shock at finding me standing in her doorway.

I think she unconsciously lets her shock sit on her face, not quick enough to get it together to hide it, and I feel her mom tense beside me. The mood in the room ramps up further when Min-jun's look does change and it morphs into disdain.

"Min––" her mom starts, but I step into the room, effectively cutting her off by moving in front of her and introducing myself.

"Hello Min-jun, I'm Rebel, but I think you know who I am, right?"

I've intentionally spoken to her in English, and again intentionally, kept my voice calm and a little meek.

I know she's fluent in four languages, English being one of them, but I doubt she knows I'm aware of this, so I pause to see if she's going to passive-aggressively play the *I don't understand what you're saying* card.

She doesn't, which is the first sign I get that I'm right thinking this will turn out ok.

"I know who you are," she states coldly, and for a girl with such a sweet voice, she just gave those few words a whole heap of attitude.

Again, I go gently, "I'd like to talk, if that's ok with you?"

"Whatever," she dismisses and moves to look back at her computer screen, but I catch a glimpse of worry or something like it in her eyes.

Not to be a bitch, but I'm happy to see that, it's actually another good sign.

"Would you like your mom to stay or are you comfortable if we chat alone?" I ask, and while I don't mind because I have an approach planned for either scenario, I'm hoping she says alone.

"Mom can go," she says without looking at either of us, so I offer a small smile of reassurance to the older woman as she hesitates in the doorway, then closes the door behind her as she leaves a moment later.

I move to the middle of the decent sized room, not speaking, my satchel still around my body and stop. No huffing, no puffing, just waiting for Min-jun to make the first move, and I'll wait as long as it takes. But, the rebel in me wants to jerk her by the hoodie and scream in her face to grow up and knock it off. Instead, I'll wait. Like with Min-ssi at Massive Smash and like a hundred assholes who think that ignoring me would make me go away, Min-jun will soon realize it's a lost cause.

I know she's feeling my stare when her fingers on the keyboard slow down, eventually stopping all together.

"Well?" she asks, her back still to me, her voice going for impatience but she doesn't quite pull it off.

"Well what?"

"You said you wanted to talk to me, so talk," she says, and I watch as she closes the lid on her laptop.

"I came to talk to you, not the back of your head, so when you're ready to face me, then we can start."

All the meek gone from my voice, I drop my bag from my shoulder to the floor with a soft thud and plop my ass on the end of her bed, crossing one leg over the other.

"Excuse me?" she gasps, dropping her legs from the seat of her chair so she can spin to face me.

"Are you ready to talk?" I ask.

"What is wrong with you? You can't say that to me," she scoffs, her face flushing with anger and embarrassment.

"I just did."

I didn't lie to her parents, I wasn't here to hurt her, but I wasn't going to coddle her either. Way I saw it; Min-jun needed a dose of reality, but in a way that opened her eyes, not tore her down.

"I knew you'd be a bitch! Who the hell do you think you are, talking to me like that?" she sneers at me, riding her anger, which I'm ok with for a minute.

"I can talk to you anyway I want," I shrug.

She opens her mouth to fire something back at me, but I don't give her the chance.

"Never had someone talk to you like this to your face? Or is that something saved for behind the safety of a keyboard?"

Min-jun drops her chin, her bottom lip wobbling as her eyes fill with tears.

Her tears and flash of emotion cause my throat to get tight, but at least I know I'm chipping away at something. "I'm actually not a bitch, but I'm hoping after we've spoken you'll make up your own mind, this time doing it actually knowing me a little."

Min-jun is struggling to hold my eyes now, so before I lose them all together, I continue.

"We haven't commented publicly, which I'm sure you know, but we're not going to."

I don't conceal any of the pain I'm feeling in that statement, and I see by the way she rocks back in her chair I've surprised her.

"Why?" she asks, her chin joining her bottom lip in wobbling as she tries to control her tears.

"There's nothing to say, nothing to defend. Me and Jung-keun are together. We're going to be together." I state firmly, but I feel my own eyes fill, and swallow down the hurt on her face is causing me so I can stay on track.

Min–Jun doesn't speak, but the tears she's been holding back run down her cheeks. I don't know what her tears mean exactly, I hope I know, but I could be wrong, so I ask her to be sure.

"I'm sorry if this makes you upset. But," I pause. "We don't want to hide anymore and we shouldn't have to. There was something bigger that brought me and him together and I've never been happier in my life. which is why it hurts me to see you like this, over us."

"I don't want him to be with anyone, it-" she pauses and her chest heaves as she begins to sob, "hurts so bad to see him with you."

She tugs the sleeves of her ratty old hoodie down to completely cover her hands as she covers her face. I feel helpless in this moment, because I don't know what to fucking say to that.

"Min-jun," I say, then shift forward and let my ass drop off the end of the bed, so I'm now sitting on the carpet next to my bag, my legs crossed with my back resting against her bed. "He's willing to give up his career to be with me," I say but then wonder if it's the wrong thing.

"What?!" she shrieks.

"I was the one who wanted to lie about us, hell, I even considering flying back to L.A. without telling him just to save his career. But he doesn't want to live a lie, and after...well, I now feel the same way."

She continues to cry and I feel like it's time to level and for shit to get real.

"It comes down to, us being together or him ending his career...what's that worth? You hurting yourself? No way."

Min-jun is crying softer now than before, looking down at her sleeve covered hands, her posture so slumped it's a wonder she's still sitting in the chair.

"I don't know how to make it better for you, how to change the way you feel. But, isn't there part of you that wants him to be happy? I guess misery loves company, but I can't stand the see Jung-keun sad. And when I saw him sad last night, crying when I told him my fears over all this, confessing I didn't feel worthy of his love and the loss of what he's worked his life for...fuck, it gutted me and I never want to know that I ever made him feel that way from something I said."

She looks at me then, so I keep talking.

"I personally think what really hurts all of us, me and JK the most is that one of the KT7 F.A.M.L.Y feels so deeply for them, that she would consider irreversibly harming herself because of something one of them had absolutely no control over doing."

Min-jun's eyebrows knit together in confusion, but there's no anger, so I pat the carpet next to me. Without thought, Min-jun drops off her chair to join me on the carpet, not next to me, but still closer than she's been since I came into the room, both of us now on the same level.

"No control over what?" she sniffles.

We're just two girls, talking about boys, in her bedroom.

"I mean falling in love, Min-jun. JK fell in love. He didn't plan it, he didn't set out to fall in love, it just...happened."

Her feet are pressed to the floor and her bent legs are being held against her chest by her arms, holding herself secure, so I decide to add a bit of levity to check where she's at in her head.

"And for the record, I didn't put a glamor, or whatever that one blogger called it, on him either. I mean I know my styling is killer, just look at the cuteness of these boots, but there's no magic here girl, just me."

I get the smallest and shortest, fraction of a smile I've ever seen, but I'll take it.

"And I fell in love with him, too. I fell, I've fallen, I am. In love. With him."

Chewing on her bottom lip, she just looks at me, but she releases her knees and shifts to mirror my cross-legged pose.

"I will do anything for him, for his happiness, including coming to see the girl who wants to end her life if we don't deny our hearts and ruin ours," I state.

Her head jerks in response; wide eyes glued to mine.

"I didn't think about it that way," she sniffles, dropping her face to look at her lap.

It's then I look around her room to see posters and photos of all the guys, but my man's face takes the cake in amount. Seeing his face gives me confidence as to why I'm here and what I'm doing is the right thing. I give her a moment to compose herself and process what I've said.

All of a sudden, Min-Jun bursts into tears, full on, wet, messy, flooding tears, joined by heaving snuffles, heavy snot and wailing. She sags into herself, but as she's crying she starts talking, one big, long confession that has a beginning and an ending, barely pausing in between. And it's only because I'm fluent in crying girl that I understand a word she's saying.

"I'm so sorry, I didn't mean it, not really, I'd never hurt him like that, not any of them, but I said it and then everybody jumped on it and I couldn't take it back and everyone was talking about it, and then the hate against you got worse and I worried and tried to take it all back and I couldn't. I couldn't stop it and I hate myself for it, I hate myself for saying it, because I didn't mean it, the killing myself part, but I did mean what I said about you being all wrong for him, because I believed that, what everyone was saying that you were using him and that you were a bitch and you were going to break his heart and ruin the band, but you're not, you're really nice and you love him and he loves you and I'm the stupid one who can't do anything right and I've made the whole thing worse and now they'll all hate me and I can't fix it. What I said has disappeared offline, so someone took it down, but people still talk about it, I'm suicide girl and I don't want to be because I wish it didn't happen, I wish I could take it back, I'm so sorry Rebel, please don't hate me, please, don't hate me, please... please..."

Fuck. About half way through all of this I'd removed the distance between us and held her while she let it all out, rocked with her as she spilled her guts and because she just kept going, I just kept holding her.

I know from her parents that since this all went down, Min-jun had said maybe five words a day to them, she'd almost completely closed down, withdrawn into herself and they didn't know how to break through. Then I'd called, and they suddenly had a few more pieces to the puzzle, but she still wouldn't let them in. She wouldn't leave her room, she stopped bathing, she hardly ate, and she would only get out of bed to sit for hours to stare at her computer.

Yes, Min-jun was F.A.M.L.Y, she loved the guys passionately, my guy in particular, but the sad reality was this breakdown wasn't actually about JK falling in love with me, but more that our relationship going public, albeit accidentally, had become the fixation she held onto as her depression had slowly pulled her under.

My heart broke for her.

Being so wrapped up in Min-jun's unrestrained meltdown I missed her bedroom door opening, until I hear my name being called.

I look over to the door and see Dr. Jun-sang and Min-jun's mom watching us, both of them seem relieved Min-jun's wall had come down, because now they could start the process of helping her.

"Min-jun," I say her name and wait while she collects herself, the sleeves of her hoodie taking the brunt of her cleanup efforts. "Sister, you have got to go easy on that sweatshirt, I don't think it can take anymore."

I don't know why, probably just the ridiculousness of my observation after the heaviness of the reason behind it, but that makes both of us giggle and then our giggles turn into laughter.

"Rebecca, do you need me now?" Jun-sang asks, so I stand up, hauling Min-jun off the floor with me, and shifting us so we both plonk back down on the end of her bed.

"No, thank you, if it's ok Min-jun and I will be out in a minute" I answer, and I can feel her eyes drilling into the side of my head.

"All right, see you soon," Jun-sang says, his smile warm and it makes me feel as though he's maybe proud of me or something, whatever it is, I like it.

The second the door closes again, Min-jun pounces.

"No way! You speak Korean?" she says, switching to her native tongue.

"Of course, the guy I love is Korean, and if I'm going to nag him for the rest of his life to pick his towel up off the floor, put his toothbrush back in the holder, and take the trash out before the bag gets too full to tie off, I want to be able to do that in Korean. No way then he can smile at me, give me that look of his that makes me soft and pretend he didn't understand me, so I end up letting him get away with it. I'm already whipped when it comes to him, I don't need another chink in my armor."

While she started out smiling during my sassy rant, the reality of the situation caught up with her again, and I see her face fall once more.

"How do I make the pain go away, the sadness of knowing I'll never be with him?"

I inhale deeply, giving her a sympathetic look.

"I don't know, honestly. But I came with someone today, the man who was with your mom a minute ago, he's a doctor. I'd like for you to hear him out about a new treatment for depression, your mom told me over the phone that you've had struggles in the past––"

"Ok," she says, cutting me off and shocking the shit out of me.

"Really? Just like that?"

"Rebel, I feel awful about today, about everything I've done to you and JK, and the group, and my parents, but honestly, I just *feel* awful. All the time. I know my depression is back, worse than before, and even if I didn't, I'd agree anyway, because you asked me to."

Jesus.

Part of me wants to start crying again, that hopefully the beginning to the end of all of this drama is coming.

For all of us.

Bringing the happy up instead, I clap my hands together. "Well, all right, let's do this...but...just between us girls? Dude, you have got to change out of that hoodie, that thing is done. Like, D-O-N-E, done."

Min-jun looks down at her clothing, looks back at me, smiles and nods her head.

Reaching for my bag where it's still sitting on the floor, I open it up and pull out a couple of band tees, a pair of sweats and two hoodies, one with the band's logo and one with JK's name on the back and the year he was born.

"Here, just so happens I brought you replacements," I say, passing them over to her and watching as her face lights up with glee.

"No way! I can't accept all of these, I don't deserve it, you've already done so much, oh my God, I can't believe it..." and I lose her attention to the magical allure of brand new swag.

As she looks through it all, we talk about how she's the first, well other than me, JK's dad and Hannah to know I'm pregnant so I'd appreciate her not saying anything. I'm using this moment to show her I'm putting faith in her to keep the secret and that I hold her to that high of a regard. I then tell her I hope to marry JK one day and that I hoped fans would be ok with that. I could tell she felt happy to know my secret and that I was asking a favor of her.

Swinging my now much emptier bag across my body, I make sure to pull my hair out from under the leather strap and move toward the door so Min-jun can change.

"Wait!" she yells, "No way I'm putting these on without showering first, do you think I've got time? I'll be quick."

"Sure, I'll let my future father-in-law know you'll be out in a minute," I say breezily.

"Your father-in-law?" she squeaks, voice high with excited surprise. "That man, the doctor you came with, is JK's father?"

"Mhmm, but the longer it takes you to get ready and get out there, the longer it's going to take me to start making that a reality. So, pull your finger out and move!"

I open the door and am almost through it when Min-jun calls my name, "Reb?"

"Yeah?" I answer, turning my head back into her room.

"You really do love him, don't you?" she asks.

"I love him so much," I sigh.

"I really am sorry Rebel, for everything..."

"We're all good, girl," I nod.

"I just wanted you to know I've already made up my mind, and you were right, you're not a bitch. You're actually the shit Rebecca, and I couldn't think of anyone I'd rather JK love, than you."

Chapter Twenty Three

(Isib sam)

I feel dead on my feet by the time I'm headed back to the apartment, from not sleeping the night before, the stress from yesterday and the crying of today, I'm ready to crash.

It's silent for the most part as Fred drives us to JK's parents so we can drop JK's dad off, but at one point he looks at me and says, "You did well today."

It feels so good to hear that from him, and it's exactly what I *needed* to hear. I'm nervous to talk to JK and to the guys. I feel like I cocked-up all the work we'd done together, how far we'd come since our personal life has now overshadowed our marketing agenda.

Like I said, worse-case scenario is Massive Smash stops letting KT7 record, tour, be anything while not dissolving the contract and keeping them locked out of signing to another label. Other god-awful scenario is JK gets kicked out of the group and the guys hate him. As much as I didn't think the latter was possible, I had no clue how the guys were reacting to the bomb dropping. They hadn't seemed to care either way when the photos of us originally leaked, but that was dismissed publicly. This however was bound to ruin their careers too, and fuck, I literally prayed Massive Smashed let them go and we could all move forward, in that case I'd work my ass off to make sure KT7 wasn't going down.

After dropping the Dr. off, I got an alert on my phone, then another, then another. My girl Min-jun went viral...again. This time, her video was quite different. She was nearly busting with the excitement from my visit, telling the whole story and showing off the swag I gifted.

I felt...relieved. Not just for the nice shit she was saying, but that she wasn't threatening suicide and had agreed to seek help. I was proud of her. I was proud that she heard me out and listened and took the first step to begin a healthy life.

Next thing I know, Fred's parked down in the garage and I eject myself from the backseat and into the elevator. The ride up has me nervously fiddling the ends of my sweater between my fingertips, repeatedly blowing lungful's of air from my puffed-out cheeks and telling myself it was all gonna be ok. It *has* to be.

The door dings and I exit, walking slowly out to the hallway and I think I hear loud voices and commotion coming from my apartment. Oh great, there's a lynch mob waiting for me. With my hand on the knob, the other shakily hovering over the keypad, I steel myself and prepare for what awaits me on the other side.

"Oh my God, I can't fucking believe it!"

"This is crazy!"

"We did it you guys!"

Say what? Standing in the entryway, I can see from here the seven members of KT7 are all jumping around my living room like lunatics.

"Redbull!" Ye shouts as he sees me coming slowly down the hallway.

Were they all on drugs or something? He hurries to me, grabbing my arm and bringing me into the melee.

"Redbull!" They all repeat and try to coax me to also jump, but I'm either sleep deprived or missing some huge information as I stand there confused.

"What's happening?" I finally spit out.

"We've been nominated for a Billboard award," JK pants as he comes toward me, taking my hands and giving me the largest bunny grin.

"What?"

"Yes, we've been nominated! In America!" Jinho tells me.

"But..." I trail off. Happy, but still confused. "What about-"

"F.A.M.L.Y being upset? They will be fine," Hooni tells me.

"No, the other shit-"

"With Massive Smash? Min-ssi was on his way to talk to us, then we got word from billboard, they can't touch us," Joon shrugs.

They all begin to jump around again, smiling and laughing.

"So, that's it?" I question, *still* confused.

JK's hands cup my cheeks, standing still with me while the others go crazy around us. "Everything is fine. I just saw the video about you going to see F.A.M.L.Y. girl. You saved her, you helped her. Just like when the rest get to know you, they'll love you, too," he reassures, running his nose along mine.

My eyes close as his words and the news about Billboard sinks in, there's no way it can be this easy, or can it? Again, destiny?

"I'm pregnant," I state, swallowing thickly and pulling my face back slightly to look up at him.

His smile doesn't waver but grows wider as his eyes do too. And just like after our first time, he replies like I had, "I know."

Jung-keun

I dreamt about Rebel, many times actually. Ever since I was younger, I had dreams of a blonde girl. I never saw her face completely, or even her sometimes, but I always saw a hint of blonde hair no matter the dream. The day we were sat down and told a woman from America was coming to work for us, to help us, we were all receptive to the idea. We knew we were destined to be big and then we got really ahead of ourselves, too big for our company to handle. There has to be some form of hopes in a group, even if they seem too big and too unobtainable. We still held onto those larger than life goals, and when we heard she was coming, we thought maybe our goals weren't that out of the realm.

Getting back to the apartment that night, I went into my room and Googled her. The woman's face struck me at first. She had light eyes, one nostril contained a ring, she liked to wear crazy eye makeup, her nails painted and shaped like talons, sometimes her hair was blue, or pink, or purple, or silver, but most of the time it was a shade of blonde. Was she the one? The one I'd always seen in my dreams? I felt connected to her, instantly. Dreams in my culture are taken very seriously and aren't something to dismiss easily. I found myself texting my mom who knew about my dreams of a blonde, and then I told her this. About seeing Rebel on the computer.

The time came sooner for her to come and I felt my nerves churning like I haven't felt in a long time. Like I used to feel when the group first started, and I was a young teenager. I wasn't confident, yes with singing and dancing I was, but suffered from those common teenage feelings of insecurity about looks and things like that. Girls made me nervous, even when Rebel first came. I was afraid she wouldn't like me, wouldn't be attracted to me. She's older than me, but so is my mom to my dad. I know I'm young but sometimes I act younger, immature and that she might think I'm childish. So many thoughts came into my mind, so many negative things that she would find about me that had me convincing myself that she wouldn't like me.

I thought maybe when she came I should ignore her, it would hurt less than if she rejected me. Then, she arrived. Her hair was a dark blonde, she was shorter than I thought she'd be, but was she stunning. My eyes were as locked on hers as hers were on mine. The sensation that came over me when this happened was a euphoria that had me imagining flashes of life with her in my mind. I never thought about the future aside from my career. I signed a ten-year contract and then it's entering the military when I reach that age, just like the rest of my generation. But beyond that, I never thought that far ahead. Never thought about a wife or children often, but knew eventually, I guess, I'd have that. But here she was. Everything clicked into place, the dreams, the knowing that she'd been with me all along in my head, but there she was in front of me.

I couldn't take my eyes off her as we all looked at her and she said our name along with a nickname she'd given us, well, them. She didn't have a nickname for me. I found out later she did, *her future boyfriend*, but it did hurt me a little at the time. Jaimin knew I was interested in her, I think they all did, especially when it was decided she would stay in his room. Remember when I said I could be immature? I gloated and then they started teasing me that I was jealous. I denied it, but why else would I be mad about her staying in someone else's room.

I think we all fell under her spell. She was open and receptive to the way we are and our culture, without question she trusted us to show her. Not only was she smart, a hard worker, and driven, she was so cute. Her photos didn't do her justice, because that was just the physical. You needed the whole package to really appreciate her. She talked fast most the time, using dirty words a lot, her voice was husky and sometimes she sing-songed, that always makes me smile, and when I'd hear her humming our songs, I was done for. She moved around a lot, was always on the go, you could tell that's how her brain was, too, always thinking. But she was cool, too.

Any chance I could be next to her or sit by her, do anything near her, I would. Of course, the guys made fun of me, teased me a lot and I just ignored it. I thought she liked Jaimin-ssi until the night on the patio. I'd wanted her so bad, desired her every look and wanted to be the one who made her laugh. I understood little of what she said, but I think she told me she'd thought about me before she arrived. Me. She told me I could kiss her. Kiss her. I felt like an idol had granted all my wishes true in that moment. I knew my dreams were real and for a purpose.

Eventually I began to see she treated Jaimin-ssi like she did the others, but it was me she treated differently. She looked at me longer, smiled at me like it was only for me. At practice I felt like I was the only one she looked at and I often caught her, which she'd smile but not look away. It was hard to make a move when we lived with the guys, but it was always on my mind. Then my chance came. She returned to the practice studio with dinner, alone. She wanted me to show her the dance I'd been working on and I felt like it was her way of again giving me permission to make a move.

Her body moved like she'd always been dancing, and boy could she move. She listened to me, watched me, and even let me touch her a few times to further provide assistance. I felt like my dick was going to explode seeing her there all sweaty and dancing, and I immediately thought about how she'd looked naked and sweaty. When she changed the song and began thrashing around, she was perfect in that moment and in that moment, I made my move.

I'd never kissed anyone other than a peck on the lips, but with Rebel, I let instinct and desire take over. I must've done an ok job because she melted in my arms, her lips molding with mine. Not understanding a lot of English, I understood however when she told me she was wet from our kissing and the words echoed in my ears. I thought about that, the way she sounded when she said it, the way that wetness would feel on my fingers, on my cock. As if I wasn't jerking off enough, that memory had me putting my bottle of lotion to work.

When I did get another chance with her, I knew I needed to touch her wetness. I wanted to taste it, but I knew that was too fast, we were going to be together for a lifetime, we had time. However, there was something about her that had me barely restraining my urges, barely able to control myself. I felt like I could do anything with her and like she wanted me to. Again, I didn't know what I was doing, but I let my instinct guide me in pleasuring her. Because I know she'd probably done this all before, I didn't think badly of her when she dropped her skirt and got up on the desk. I liked she knew what she was doing, she could teach me to please her how she liked, and I was a very fast learner. Seeing her there, smelling her, I felt like I couldn't contain myself.

I asked her if she was wet as my fingers moved around her, mainly because I wanted to hear her say it again, but she didn't understand what I was asking. My fingers slid in her, the sounds she made, the way I made her body react, the way *my* body reacted, exhilarated. Rebel was it for me. But I didn't know how I was going to keep her mine. I couldn't just take her out, not as me, because if the fans found out, that would be it and I wasn't sure if she was ready for that. I love our F.A.M.L.Y, they're the reason we're even here and are experiencing what we have and will. They mean the world to me, but so does Rebel. Still, I couldn't chance a relationship, an open relationship with someone at this time. Not until I knew Rebel was in this with me and also wanted the same.

I didn't want to feel jealous that she freely went out with Hannah and could go have fun with someone else. But I was jealous. And by then Rebel knew me well enough to understand that. The date night she planned alerted me that she might be feeling toward me the way I did to her, but it wasn't until our trip to Japan that I knew. I'd spoken with Ye-hyung, confessed how I felt for Rebel and that I wanted to do something special for us. He thought about it, threw out ridiculous and absurd ideas, which led me to asking Jaimin-ssi. After he laughed at me and told me knew it and teased me over having a crush, he finally suggested Disneyland.

That trip changed everything. Not only did we make love, but I knew then that she loved me like I love her.

The fans seeing the photos of us at the airport, Rebel instantly released a statement, but part of me wished she hadn't. I felt kind of relieved that it was out there, a freedom almost. Like I was in control of my personal life, I wasn't as perfect as everyone wanted us to be. I knew Rebel wouldn't understand this, since her job is to extinguish the rumor fires and resurrect the ashes.

Taking her to meet my parents was the next step I felt was needed in our relationship. I'd already told my mother that I knew Rebel was the one I dreamt about and she was eager to meet her, so was my father. When my mother told me she was inviting my older brother, this meant she was just as excited as me for Rebel to be accepted by the family as I was. I don't know how other families would react to knowing their son was dating and planning on marrying a foreigner, but I think my mom knew before I did that my dreams as a young boy were hinting toward that route for me.

Rebel was nervous but didn't show it once we arrived at my childhood home. She fit in the way I knew she would, the way she always did since I've seen her here in South Korea. Slowly she was learning Korean and same with me with English, but language was no match for Rebel. She has a way of communicating that I think only she can get away with, her hand gestures are top notch when it comes to that. That dinner, she really bonded with my dad and I knew my mom liked her even though they exchanged little words.

My brother liked her and told me that mom had told him everything. He teased me like my group brothers did, but he approved of her. I don't know why in that moment and why with him but I confessed that I'd risk everything for her, meaning my career, and he just looked at me stunned. But it was true. Maybe I knew what was coming, it was inevitable.

My dreams recently had been of something huge coming, my mom had had the same dreams, but we both interpreted it as Rebel being pregnant. Like I said, dreams are heavily analyzed in my culture and at first, I thought I might be wrong, maybe it was the video being released that I was dreaming about. It was no planned, but I also felt the video being released was destiny. Again, I was relieved in a way that it was out there, that people could see how big our love was. When Rebel started to be sick, I thought once more my true dream was correct.

Unexpectedly, Rebel seemed not herself. I thought she would click into work gear and come up with a statement, but she didn't. Even though Massive Smash told her not to, it wasn't like her to follow the rules. I'd been talking with Massive Smash all morning, after talking with my brothers, telling them I didn't want a statement made, I wanted nothing done. The label was pissed and wanted to meet with us, but I told them not yet, which was unlike me. I'd never spoke out before, especially about something like this. I'd wanted to be with Rebel, and I would've done anything in order for that to happen, even stepping away from the group if needed.

When I sat down with the guys and we talked, they already knew I was in deep with her, but I explained my dreams, explained my feelings, which I also never do with them, close or not. They listened, and I prepared to be lectured by my hyung's about why they needed to step away from me and the drama. But instead, they agreed that it was time we change the rules of being an idol and that maybe it should start now.

To know I had my family, blood and not blood, backing me, I knew in that moment we would make it.

Hearing Rebel voice her fears, fears that I would sacrifice and, in the end, find her not worth my love, sucker punched me. I hoped my words, and if not, my kiss expressed the love I knew was unwavering to her.

Hannah came over worried and I decided to call my dad since Rebel looked ill. I waited, trying to take my mind off what my dad would find out with his exam, how Rebel would react, and I barely could keep my excitement in.

Eventually she came to me and I felt joy in her touch. She didn't talk, but just her closeness was perfect.

Waking up alone, I wasn't alarmed that she wasn't there. I'd woken to her on the phone through the morning, one of which I heard her using my dad's name. I didn't know exactly what was going on, but when I got out of bed I called my mom and found out what she was up to. My girl was a fighter and knowing that she was going to visit s F.A.M.L.Y in distress, during a time when she should be worrying about herself, reaffirmed that she was in it for the long haul.

Waiting in the group apartment for Min-ssi to come over, we'd anticipated he would fire me, since the group could still go on without me, now that I wouldn't be an object of F.A.M.L.Y affection. The last thing we expected was the news we received. A Billboard nomination. We all freaked out, knowing our label couldn't disband us now. I didn't know really, but when the news broke about my relationship with Rebel, I felt that no matter the backlash that everything would be fine. But no way did I imagine it would be something as huge as a nomination from America.

We all ran down the hall to Rebel's apartment to share the good news, knowing that her hard work, just as much as ours, had something to do with the nomination. She wasn't back yet, so we just continued to celebrate. Shocked over the news is an understatement, we couldn't believe it. Ye was the first to notice my Rebel standing there. She looked stunned and confused, a lot confused. I stood there frozen looking at her, a smile plastered on my face as I just watched her.

Even after the news was told to her, she didn't comprehend. My feet moved as my heart wanted me to be near her and I took her face in my hands, telling her it was all ok.

"I'm pregnant," she blurted out, her eyes searching mine for the reaction I think she'd assumed I'd have, but all she was met with was my smile.

Epilogue

(Balmun)

"Come on," Hooni coos.

"What a good girl, over here," Shoogi says in his deep voice.

"Peek-a-boo!" Jaimin chimes as he covers his eyes and lays on his stomach.

"Min-seo," Joon waves his hands as he repeats the name over and over with a huge smile.

"Woohoo, Min Min, wooooo!" Jinho sing-songs as he snaps his fingers repeatedly in between blowing her kisses.

"Look, look, baby, Min-seo, look," Ye chants as he waves her favorite plushy around, which happens to be her dad's alter-ego bunny cartoon character.

JK is saying something that I can't hear as he's got his face behind his Nikon camera as he crouches in front of our almost one-year-old daughter, Min-seo, but she was my Star. The guys stand behind JK trying to get her to look at them so JK can get a shot of her face, but she's being stubborn and thinks the white fluffy rug she's sitting on is more interesting.

I stand near the entryway to the living room and of course take my phone out to video the fucking adorable scene. JK insisted he take her first-year photos, piece of cake he said, and I wondered how long it would be before he recruited his brothers to help.

But it was like this for everything, even before she arrived. My whole pregnancy it was like I had seven boyfriends. I was always being brought food, water, vitamins, pillows were propped under my back anytime I sat down, as my belly grew bigger, I was gifted with the coolest pregnancy clothes. They were vocal in planning the nursery and providing things for her because they wanted to, and were just as excited as me and JK were for her to arrive. But they've also been there to help our little bunny, from feeding to learning to crawl, reading her books, singing to her, getting her to walk, they've been there with us the whole way.

Other than the life changing event her birth would bring, she also was the piece de resistance to the nine months leading up to her birth. The Billboard nomination was only the beginning. The tour kicked off and I tagged along to each sold out venue, traveling all over with the guys and getting to experience it all with them and with my man. I don't know how it became a thing, but at one stop, Ye gifted me with a painting of a baby bunny he suggested I put in the nursery. The idea kick started all of us to buy anything bunny related we saw in our travels as they called Min-seo, baby bunny (agi tokki), when she was in my tummy.

Midtour, the guys released a new album and new videos, bringing new success, and new F.A.M.L.Y members. They were doing it, they were doing it their way and fucking owning it, and me and the rest of F.A.M.L.Y were alongside them for the ride. Massive Smash let them do their thing and that was unheard of in their industry.

Then the Billboard's came and we flew to L.A. and I treated the guys to a tour of my old stomping grounds. Although that wasn't much more than me pointing things out on the car rides since their schedule was packed with interviews, meetings with other artists, photoshoots and preparing for the show.

However, I had time to go get fitted for a dress to attend the show. The guys wore all black suits in that way that screamed sexy, expensive, cool, yet casual, like only they could. So, I decided on black clearly and because we were in America, why not wear something 'American Rebel' would wear? Yes, pregnant, but who says you can't be pregnant and sexy? One of my clients designs and runs a small boutique, where she wrapped me in decadent black fabric. A short-fitted dress with a low dip V that accompanied my now ample titties, in a tasteful way of course, exposing the cusp of each shoulder before becoming long sleeved. Sheer material took over where the end of the dress was and traveled down to the floor, I also grabbed a pair of strappy black platform heels and knew my outfit was done. You could see the slight swell to my stomach at that stage and that to me was the focal point.

After my fitting, I swung by the ESM offices where they threw me an impromptu baby shower, even though I wasn't far along. They'd already been sending goodies to the apartment unbeknownst to me, but we all went soft for the baby clothes they just had to show me. I found myself at the shower having a hard time eating the food, I thought maybe it was pregnancy, but something had me thinking it was otherwise. Because when you're pregnant you google everything, I found out I wasn't alone. Most Americans have to adjust back to the flavor and taste of a lot of food, everything seemed salty AF to me, but whatever.

The girls took me to lunch, where I ordered noodles. Lunch ended up being more like a lunch that led into a dinner that led to me taking them back to the hotel to meet the guys. We hung out in our suite and they had some drinks while me and JK sipped water and he finally got to meet the girls I consider my sisters.

Another addition to the party was Joon's girl, Jaz. The one who we talked about at Hannah's birthday, the one who I offered to allow stay in my apartment and when we found ourselves sitting together on the couch, I extended the offer personally. She was so sweet and thankful but still had hope her parents would warm up to Joon. I was excited to find out that she would be sitting next to me during the Billboard show and we definitely bonded that night. Not only were we surrounded by celebs, but our men looked amazing. Hannah was my guest but was working, so in between hanging with us at the seats, she periodically had to pop backstage or over to the guys to freshen them up.

The buzz around them was amazing, as was the fan turn out for them on the red carpet and when they were announced as the winners of their category, the noise was incredible. It all brought tears to my eyes as they walked up to receive their award and I knew it was just the beginning for them in America. It reaffirmed that we'd done the right thing coming out as a couple, because even though some people didn't agree and stopped being fans, the group was gaining them constantly.

The BBMA's were the springboard to a whole other level of success that opened up for the guys. It seemed like everything that had happened, did happen for a reason. Since the guys were untouchable, their label really didn't tell them shit. They were definitely breaking boundaries within their industry and I was happy for that, too.

After the awards, touring was back on and I got more and more pregnant along the way. My OBGYN advised me to keep off my feet as much as possible toward the end of my pregnancy, but yeah, ok. Regardless the guys were always finding ways to make me sit and chill. Jinho was always supplying me with ramen, Jaimin with snapchat fun, and Ye with Musically app amusement. Shoogi would just randomly gift me with flowers while we took turns playing against one another in a game app, while Joon and I read the same books and talked about them, and Hooni entertained me with dancing and just being himself. As for my boy JK, he never ceased to amaze me with his love and attention. Sometimes I could watch the shows but sometimes I stayed at the hotel. On those nights, he'd order me room service to come after he'd left or set me up with my favorite horror movies and snacks. On the nights I did go to the show, he would signal he loved me with a little code we came up with, and no, I'm not telling what it is. One night he grabbed an American flag someone had in the crowd and carried it around like a cape, winking at me as he proudly represented me.

If I hadn't respected the hell out of the guys before the tour, I certainly would've after all I witnessed. They were like machines. Performing day in and day out. Not only did they invite F.A.M.L.Y to come to soundchecks every show, they also ran through the entire show every day. EVERY DAY. Do you know how insane that is? They performed sick, tired, injured, emotionally exhausted, never complaining and never stopping, and their fans never knew about any of it. Because the guys are so close, they often took out frustrations on each other and it shocked me to see them like that, even if I knew they always made up before they went on stage, it still didn't make it easier. But I felt myself also kicking into mom mode during those times, always there for a shoulder to lean on and always there to hear out whatever someone had to say. I was like Switzerland, I never broke confidence and never tried to get in the middle, just was there.

We made it back home just before our daughter was born and thank God because as much as I acted like I was ok potentially giving birth on the road, I really wasn't. Jaz was now living in South Korea with Joon in the apartment and we grew very close. I know she was happy being with Joon, but there had been some rift in her family due to it and I wasn't at all sure she was incredibly happy living here. Hannah and Jaz both helped me design the nursery, and although we'd all had dreams the baby was a girl, I still wasn't so sure and kind of didn't want to know. So, the room was cream with a light gray for accent tones like the crib, bunny artwork, blankets and curtains, gender neutral.

Everything was ready, so all we had to do was wait. JK put a bouquet of white, long stem roses on the bedside table every week with a note attached. Sometimes it was one word, something like LOVE or CHERISHED. Other times it was notes about how he couldn't wait to see our baby, to see me holding her, things that always made my eyes water and thank the stars that I was led to this man.

The best thing JK gave me, other than our baby, was when I was in labor. We were alone in a room at the hospital, it was the early stages and all was calm and quiet. Opening the box, I saw a beaded bracelet nestled inside.

"These," JK told me, sitting on the bed beside me as he plucked the jewelry from the box, "blue sandstones represent the universe, the gold stars between are the stars." His fingers fondled the circular stones as he said, "Neptune, Uranus, Saturn, Jupiter, Mars, Earth, Moon, Venus, Mercury." Pausing, he lifted my wrist, kissed me there as he added, "And this is the Sun," referring to my arm as he slid it on.

The beauty of the gift, the thought of it, as well as the nerves of becoming a mom had a few tears escaping my eyes as I rest my forehead on his and took in this moment.

"I love you," I whispered and was gifted with a bunny grin in response.

Labor wasn't easy, but I had my girls and JK, along with his mom there with me, and in the end, our little girl arrived. JK chose the name Min-seo, and I thought the way it sounded was cute. But like I said, she was my Star. Social media blew up with F.A.M.L.Y celebrating her birth as her name became a trending hashtag.

Instinctively, I wanted to shield her from the public. But then I realized how hard a life that would be for her and us. Feeling the motherly and marketing instinct merge into one, I released a statement the night she was born.

I asked for respect from not only F.A.M.L.Y, but also the media in the fact that this was our baby and she didn't ask to be in this life. JK and I agreed we didn't mind showing her as long as everyone was chill and not greedy. I knew I was asking for a lot, but somehow my plea didn't go unheard. F.A.M.L.Y had been outside chanting and singing, waiting for us to leave and to get their first glance of our baby. I tweeted that morning as we were being discharged from the hospital that Min-seo was sleeping and I didn't want her to wake up, so for everyone to please be quiet, pretty much as a joke because yeah right like anyone would. Surprisingly, they did. Exiting the hospital, JK held our newborn to an awaiting crowd and because they'd heard us out and weren't screaming, JK revealed the face of our daughter.

This behavior became a thing and any time Star was with us, the fans acknowledged that. For whatever reason and not because of fans, Star disliked the airport. She would cry from the moment we got out of the car until we boarded the plane, and then as soon as we got off until we got into a car. F.A.M.L.Y caught onto this and tried everything as they lined the inside of the airport to see the guys, singing as one, waving toys and trying their hardest to get her to be happy. Even the guys would try to distract her as I held her and they stood behind me, playing peek-a-boo or trying to pretend to get us. Eventually she grew accustomed to the traveling but still had her moments.

Even though we lived in a separate apartment to the guys, which JK purchased from the firm for us, they were always over. Again, my seven boyfriends not only took care of me now, but also Star. Talk about swooning over the guys when they performed, but to witness them putting on a show for a baby, someone call 911 because I was a goner. Just like with me, they all had their little things they did with her. Jinho liked to create baby food, Shoogi often napped with her on his chest, Joon read to her, Hooni danced with her, Jaimin made her laugh, Ye took photos with her and my babe JK did anything she needed. She had become like an eighth member, being out of the shot in her baby rolling activity thing while filming dance practice, to actually being able to walk and coming into frame and dancing as best she could along with them. F.A.M.L.Y loved it every time she popped up in something and the guys never got mad or annoyed with her. But out of us, JK was the disciplinarian.

Yes, JK was young, but he snapped into fatherhood instantly. There was never any discussion pre-baby about regrets or worrying this wasn't the right thing, we knew she was just as meant to be as me and JK meeting was.

I hadn't planned on getting pregnant again, but here I am, Min-seo is about to be one and I'm six-months pregnant with baby number two. This time, well, this time we think I'm carrying a boy. The gender doesn't matter to me, because I'll have one-hundred babies with JK if I have any say over it.

"Min-Min," JK says, pulling his face away from the camera. "Look at Daddy," he adds and she turns her head quickly as he pulls the camera back.

The guys make hopeful sounds and then Shoogi sounds disappointed in JK's skills as he comments that there's no way he got the shot. Star's chin begins to quiver as her lower lip pulls down and we all know the tears are coming. Seven men rush toward her, but JK is the first to pick her up and they all tell her it's ok as she cries out, before moving around animatedly which turns into them doing the choreo for a new song they've been working on. Min-seo is wearing a little bunny romper with hood adorned with floppy ears and it takes Hooni taking the ends and gently popping her on the nose to make her tears stop.

Ending the video and walking into the kitchen, I post the video on social media with the hashtags, FirstBirthdayPics and NailedIt. When it's finished, I call Hannah to invite her to lunch this Saturday with me and Jaz, but after a few rings it just goes to voicemail. I leave another voice message and a text, since I feel like that's all I've been doing lately. I don't know what's going on with her, she says she's busy and she probably is, but she hasn't been work lately and I want to make sure she's ok.

"Was that Hannah?" Shoogi asks.

"Voicemail, have you talked to her recently?"

"No, why would I?"

"Haven't you two known each other for like a hundred years?" I shrug.

"What's wrong?" he questions, bypassing my statement.

"She's been aloof, when we do actually talk it's through text, she's just short and not like herself."

"Why don't you go see her?"

"I went to her apartment with Star and when I buzzed the door she told me she didn't want visitors."

He gives me a look, more like he realizes now the reason for my concern.

"Would you go over there soon and see if she'll let you in, or at least talk to you?"

In Shoogi style, he just makes a low approving sound and nods slightly.

"I think I got a good shot," JK announces as he enters the kitchen and immediately Shoogi is taking Star from her dad's arms. "Can we go through them now? I don't think I'll have time before her birthday party," JK says.

I nod and he turns to walk to his studio in the extra bedroom of the apartment. While I turn to ask Shoogi if he would mind laying Star down for her nap but he's already walking into the living room and to the Airsack. The Airsack, a gift from Sawyer, is like a new version of an oversized beanbag chair, totally comfortable and was thought to be where I could breastfeed Star. However, Shoogi got one lay down on the thing and it became where they napped. Whatever, I can't blame him it's so comfortable, I told JK we should invent a mattress sized one.

Grabbing the small package I left sitting on the hallway table, I make my way to the room and see JK at his computer desk already tapping away and blowing up the photos of our daughter.

"Look what Jaz found," I say walking up beside him, pulling the baby Timberland boots from the box to show him.

"Ohhh, cute," he smiles, and reaches out to rub my back while one hand continues on the mouse.

He moves the chair back and guides me to sit on his lap as we both look at the pics, his hand comfortably resting on my small baby belly. I adjust my belt, since my pregnancy attire as of late has been, a long sleeve shirt, jean overalls that were JK's but are now mine, and a belt cinching the denim just above my baby bump, the end of the pants rolled up to show off my high-top black converse since my combat boots don't accommodate my growing ankles. Between pregnancies, I'd had my hair chopped to my shoulders and bleached platinum. It's now growing out and new baby means no bleach, so I've been rocking an ombre.

We go through them and laugh, aw, and just look at how stunning our baby is. She's a mix of both of us, her eyes are my color but shaped like his. Her nose and cheeks resemble his, and her hair is a dark reddish brown. As of late, she seems to be taking on my disposition, which I'm not sure is a good or bad thing. Her two front teeth resemble his and one of my favorite things about her physically is the freckle below her full bottom lip, just like her dad. My Star, such a sweet girl, always excited to do things and laugh. She's so love-able and kind, and I know that not only me and JK had something to do with that, but so did her six uncles.

"We should frame that and give it to your parents," I suggest, pointing at one of the shots.

"Mhmm," he agrees.

"I want one for the front entryway, or I could move the one from the bedroom to the entryway and put a new one in our room," I state.

"Speaking of, I have something for the bedroom you can put up," JK tells me and I look over at him with raised brows.

"Do you now?"

"I do," he grins and kisses the tip of my nose. "It's outside."

With that he stands and takes my hand as I give him a questioning look. As he leads me through the house, I smile at Shoogi and Min-seo passed out and notice the setting sun shining in on them to cast the perfect lighting for a picture. I turn my head to look at JK once again, his pale-yellow dress shirt tucked into his faded jeans, tight enough to see the definition of his thigh muscles and that ass. His thin waist is accentuated by a belt and causes his shoulders to look to even more broad.

"Damn, you're a sexy as fuck dad, do you know that?" I growl as I smack his ass and he pulls my arm to bring me beside him, grinning at me as we walk through the sliding glass door and out to the patio.

There's a dinner set out on a table in the middle of the grass, along with candlelit lanterns around the gardens. No wonder he had such urgency to get me to look at the pics and I assume this is what the other guys were up to when they disappeared after photos. But then it hits me.

"Did I forget something?" I ask in a panic.

"No," he smiles and gives a little laugh as I take a seat at the table.

"Is this a proposal?" I whisper.

Giving me a sweet look, he shakes his head and it only makes my face contort to an even more confused expression.

"We haven't really had a date since Min-seo was born, like remember our first date when we watched Hellraiser? I wanted to do that again," he tells me.

Sigh.

"Thank you," I gush, and I feel my pupils morph into hearts.

We'd discussed marriage, but agreed we didn't need to be married just because we were starting a family. And honestly, touring didn't leave time for shit, I didn't need anymore stress at that time. But secretly, I plan on proposing to JK after this baby is born.

"Who cooked?" I ask, looking down at the food between us.

"Jinho-hyung."

Hearing that makes me excited, yes, he still cooked for us a lot, but I also had mastered Korean cuisine, well, Rebel style Korean cuisine, so I did a lot of cooking for us too. However, I still preferred Jinho's over mine.

JK and I sit and eat, and it was nice to not have to stop every five seconds to feed Star or the hundreds of other things a one-year-old requires during eating one meal. The sun sets and when we finish eating, which let me tell you, we did it in no time being that we could just sit and eat. I see the stars appearing and ask JK to sit with me over by the rose of Sharon garden I planted last summer. JK gifted me with one of the plants when he officially moved in, then another when Star was born, and another when I found out I was pregnant with baby number two.

Curling into him, we look into the sky and know our time is limited, that Star will wake up shortly and parent duty will take over.

"Didn't you say you had to show me something?"

"Oh, right."

He moves aside and pics something up, handing me a frame. The frame's white, the border is white and in the center is a circle with what looks like a star map.

"This is from the night we first looked at the stars together."

Sure enough, I see at the bottom corner the date and time of that moment we sat on the roof and I told him my story about how I knew I was meant to meet him. I didn't think he understood me then, but now I know he did. I literally can't with this guy. I don't know what I did to deserve this man, who's ass I kissed in a past life, but he's mine. He brought me to this country I love, made me prouder of my job by the job I've done for a group of guys who welcomed me into their lives and became my family, created a beautiful daughter with me, loves me unconditionally, and all because I believed it would happen.

"Fuck," I sigh, "I love you."

I kiss his lips, his hand moving to cup my cheek as I pull back to look into his eyes.

"I love you," he tells me, his eyes looking fondly back at me.

"Oh-ma!" the sweetest voice I've ever heard comes from behind us as a now awake Star comes out to the patio.

We both smile at her and I reach out as she gets closer, bringing her on my lap as she snuggles with us and sucks on the end of one of the bunny ears on her hood.

"Eat," she says in English and I kiss her cheek.

We've been teaching her English and Korean, so far, she knows both very well for the amount of words at this age. Not surprisingly, since the apple doesn't fall far from the tree, her first word naturally was 'eat.'

Picking her up, we all get up and JK moves to the table.

"I'll clean up," he says to me and I thank him before we make our way back into the apartment.

"Rice or noodles?" Shoogi is steadily talking away, to no one, and I stand there holding my daughter with a smile.

"Hey," he finally notices and stops, turning his attention to us and not the contents of the refrigerator. "I thought you were in here the whole time, you little sneak," he says walking to us and poking Min-seo gently in the tummy and causing her to laugh.

"It's ok, I got it," I comment, moving toward the fridge to get some dinner ready.

"See you later," he says, just after opening the door to help JK enter with the plates in his hands.

"Say goodbye," I prompt Star.

"Bye," she says in both languages and gives a little wave.

"Ok," I sigh, bending down to look in the fridge as JK begins washing the dishes. Taking out containers of steamed broccoli, and steak I cooked a few days ago and setting them on the counter, I also grab a box of instant rice.

"I'll do that, she's getting restless," I say to JK and he wipes his hands before taking her from my arms.

Min-seo begins to fuss and before a crying fit, I hear JK tell her "Go hide," before little feet go pattering through the living room and I know a game of hide and seek will distract her for a little while.

Heating up the food and making the rice, I get a phone call from Sawyer and talk to her as I do dishes. KT7 has been my only new client since I came here, until recently. Me coming here for ESM was to be the beginning of a possible new area for us and within the last several months, I have been working with other artists. A few actors and actresses, two painters and one author have hired me to work for them and I of course accepted the challenge. Things have been going well, and I feel like I'm juggling everything just fine, but sometimes I do feel spread a little thin. I wish my job turned off at five p.m. and I could just be a wife and mom, but it doesn't. I love my job but I also love my family and I'm working out a way to juggle both. Yes, JK makes boatloads, but I want to make my own money and not lose the desire and drive I have just because I'm now a mom, I can do it, I just need a little help sometimes.

"I think two, the more of us the more we can take on. I have no problem with what I have, but you know Min-seo is my main priority now. It would be nice to have someone else here to help with the load when mom duty calls and when I have this baby," I say, stirring the rice.

"Two definitely makes more sense, eventually I'd love to be able to tackle the market and make ESM Asia another stronghold for the company," Sawyer remarks.

I plate Stars food and blow on it to cool down as JK puts her in her high-chair. He's talking to her in a low voice as I set some of the food in front of her and she slams her hands down as she wants the steak, but it's still too hot.

"Min-seo!" JK says over her crying and tells her it's hot and she needs to eat the rice now.

"Sounds like a handful, I'll speak with you later this week," Sawyer tells me and we both hang up.

JK and I lean on the counter as Star eats and we talk about work, our daughter, the baby coming, KT7's alter ego characters, KTToons, first stores opening in Japan and L.A. this weekend, first birthday parties and KT7's new album coming, or as they say in K-pop, their comeback.

"They want daddy to color his hair, what color should he have?" I ask Star.

I know exactly what she's going to say, because she only knows how to say one color, her favorite. JK knocks my knuckles with his hand before she answers and I smile at him.

"Pink!" she says loud and proud and we both laugh, me and her I mean, not JK.

"How about brown?" he asks her and we both make a displeased face.

"Pink!" I say this time, putting my hand in the air and Min-seo screams with glee and a mouthful of food.

"No, no," JK shakes his head with a smile and I reach over across the breakfast bar and push the tip of my index finger into his cheek. If I know anything about my man and my daughters request, it won't be denied for very long.

After dinner, I take Min-seo for a bath and remember my star picture was left outside. JK says he'll get it and I decide to get in the bath with our daughter. We sing songs and splash around, and I love how caring she already is of my belly and what's cooking inside. We get out of the bath and JK's playing video games in his office, but after I get her into her jammies he comes to get her so I can get my pajamas on. After blow drying my hair, I come out of the bathroom to see both sitting in bed, curled up together as they eat dried squid legs and watch cartoons.

Standing there, I watch them, both wide eyed and stuffing their faces. My hands rest on my belly and I can only imagine how this little boy will fit into our family, but after him, we might want to look into some birth control for a while.

"Mama," Star says, seeing me and reaching out.

Walking over to my side of the bed, I lift the comforter and slide in beside them. Star yawns and rubs her eyes before crawling over to me. Opening the top to my pajama's, she lays down in my arms as she latches on and closing her eyes. Even though she doesn't understand, JK doesn't let her watch SpongeBob, so when her attention isn't on the T.V. anymore, he puts it on. Star reaches one hand up to twist my hair in her fingers like she's been doing since she was a newborn and I feel the baby in my tummy moving underneath the weight of his sister laying over him.

"Jung-keun," I whisper and it takes him a few moments to look at me, when he does he smiles and I reach out for his hand to join mine and slowly slide them under an almost asleep Star to feel him.

When I used to think about JK being shook over things, it makes me laugh, but nothing ever compares to the expression he makes when he feels our children inside me. He rests his hand there until I get up and put Min-seo into her room in her crib. When I come back into the room JK's taking off his shirt and smiles when he sees me, and courteously waits for me to get to the bed before turning the television off. I slip off my pajamas and smile at him being lazy and trying to get his sweat pants off under the covers instead of just getting up and taking them off.

Sliding into bed, I move over him and begin kissing his neck, but he rolls me over and lays on his side as he kisses my neck and gropes my tit with his hand. My eyes flutter, but I notice he's hung up the star framed photo by the door. I remember back to that night, how badly I wanted him to kiss me, to touch me, and it still feels that way.

As much as I wanted to deny that maybe my destiny was just to come here and work with KT7, I knew deep down JK was meant to be mine, but I didn't know if he'd feel the same.

His hands are warm on my skin and I feel the hard metal of the ring he wears in his left ring finger that I gave him for our most recent anniversary. Sometimes he wears it and sometimes he doesn't. Either way, I know he's mine. We're each other's.

It was our destiny.

Bonus Epilogue : Shoogi

Making my way to Hannah's apartment, I ask Fred to pull up in front of her place and wait for me on the corner and I'll call him when I'm ready. Knowing she wouldn't let Rebel in, made me feel a bit better. I was beginning to think it was just me Hannah was avoiding, because she did have reasons to not talk to me. She knows me better than anyone in my life, she knows how I am, she knows my moods. But she's never flat out not answered my calls. I've been a dick to her in the past and as of late, but she always gets over it, so I was letting her get over it. Now I know it's more than that.

Punching the keycode into the elevator of the building she lives in, the man at the desk waving to me as I pass by. I've been here many times, enough for him to recognize me and not stop my entry, even if it has been a while since I've dropped by. Heading up in the elevator, I don't know how I feel. I want to get to the bottom of what's been going on with her. I should have before now, but again, I shrugged it off that it had something to do with me, and in that case, I didn't want to talk about it. Rebels words however kicked something in me that I needed to see Hannah.

Hannah lives in a luxury apartment in Seoul, just like she always said she would. She's made herself a success, and when I think back to when we first met, I always knew she would. I also always knew I'd be right beside her the whole way. She has a way about her, a quiet thunder rumbling beneath the surface. I thought she was a bony, American girl who never worked a day in her life when I met her. And yes, my assumption was right, but she was driven. She worked hard, never quit and now here she is.

Getting off on her floor, I walk down the hall. The gray walls are home to expensive looking lights and art, simple and elegant, like the woman who I'm here to see. Mail is piled up outside her door in neat bundles, and I look at them in question as I pick them up. Why is this all here? I can't imagine her leaving this out here every day. When was the last time I saw her around work? Shit, two weeks? It's hard to say since we're working in the studio at the moment and not needing her department. I leaf through the mail and see enough here for about that amount of time and with a trembling hand I begin punching in the code to the door.

The code goes through and I push the door open, only to be stopped by the second lock on the inside.

"Hannah?" I call out and the sound of my voice sounds foreign to me.

My heart is racing, and I call out for her again. I can see through the crack in the door that something is cooking on the electric cooker, but I don't see Hannah. A flood of relief comes over me, and I didn't want to acknowledge it but the fear she was dead lifts off my chest.

"Hannah...it's Rebel," I rush out, and I don't know why but a story comes into my head and out my mouth. "She's in labor, there's something wrong with the baby," I quickly announce.

"What?" Hannah's voice comes from behind the door before she's pushing the door closed on me to undo the lock, the metal sounding its freedom before the door opens and there she is.

Her hair is hanging down and looks unwashed, she looks thinner than normal beneath the white robe she's in. she pulls me in by my arm and quickly slams the door closed, locking it before turning to me.

"The baby-it's too early," she pleads, looking at me and I'm startled by her appearance.

"I was lying, Rebel's fine," I state and watch as her expression shifts, slowly concern melts to confusion, then sadness.

"That was-"

"I'm sorry...she said you wouldn't let her in, you won't answer calls, I wanted to see if you were fine," I tell her.

She crosses her arms over her chest and hangs her head.

"I'm fine, you can go," she replies, glancing at the door behind her.

"What's all this?" I ask, holding up the mail.

"Thank you," she rushes out, grabbing the mail from my hand and walking into the kitchen.

She drops the mail into the garbage and stands in front of the cooker on the counter. The apartment looks clean, but I see the plants wilting in the windows, the fruit in a bowl on the dining table is beginning to go bad.

"Is this because of what happened between us?" I ask.

She's always had this effect on me. The power to speak freely with her, something I've always been able to do with her and only her.

Walking to the kitchen and closer, but before I can get to her she moves away, tightening the material at her neck with her hand. The sleeve of her robe slides down to reveal bruises on her wrist beneath her grandfather's watch she never takes off.

"I'm going to go to bed now, can you please leave?" her voice warbles as she says this and her eyes train on the floor by my feet, she looks frightened.

"Hannah."

My hands move out in front of me to show her my palms, but I don't think she'd be scared of me, would she?

She shakes her head repeatedly, her breathing picking up as her eyes begin to well-up.

"Hannah," I repeat. "I won't hurt you-"

"You did," she nods. "You did hurt me," she sniffles, looking up at me.

"I'm..." I trail off, gathering my words to talk since I feel like this time I might actually lose her in my life if we don't discuss this. But before I can, she does.

"After my last birthday party, I thought- I thought things between us were finally going somewhere...I knew you'd reject it all," she pauses, her brows furrowing. "But I didn't expect to overhear you tell BW to ask me out," she states with clenched teeth, tears streaming down her cheeks.

Ever since Rebel arrived on the scene, we've been celebrating birthdays. On Hannah's last birthday, which was celebrated with dinner and karaoke again, she invited me over here afterward. I let her convince me that night that I deserved her and love, the very things I've been wanting for years but always denied in the past. I knew it was stupid to make love to her, because I knew once I let it happen that we'd be something different, something I couldn't be. I couldn't let her love me, not completely. We agreed to take things slow however, and I know I did that just to make her happy. But she was so hopeful, her smiles and excitement when she woke up next to me in her bed, was too much. So, I did what I always do, ignored, denied, deflected. When BW came to Massive Smash to visit and told me that he wanted to date Hannah, I urged him to. I don't know why I said it, him of all people, but she needed someone better than me.

"Hannah, I-"

"That broke me, Shoogi," she states, and the urge to comfort her has me clenching my fists. "I said yes, just to make you mad...to show you I didn't care, that I was just as over you as you were over me."

Her voice lifts as she raises her brows at her reasoning. Instantly, knowing this, that she did go out with him, makes me angry.

"So, it *is* because of something you did," she nods with confirmation as her face falls and the tears come again.

Her whole body begins to tremble and her robe loosens, causing my eyes to widen with what I see. Moving toward her, I bring my hand up to her chest and push aside the fabric, briefly seeing bruises all over her skin, before my hands are pushed away. But she's crying so hard she doesn't attempt to cover up again. I feel my heart cracking at seeing her this way. I've only ever seen her like this when her mother died, but even then, it was nothing like this. My hands take her face as I stand closer, trying to get her to look at me and focus. Not to hurt, but to get her to calm down.

"What happened, Hannah?" I ask, my voice loud as I nearly shake her to get her eyes on me and for her to hear my voice.

Her hands move to my wrists, wet eyes meet mine as she hiccups. "He raped me."

Printed in Great Britain
by Amazon

72795012R00139